ONE

HAVE YOU EVER MET SOMEONE WHO IMMEDIATELY made you feel like you've known them your entire life? You might use the word charming to describe them, but that doesn't quite fit the immediate connection you feel. There seems to be something inside them that goes beyond any sort of verbal descriptions you could use to explain the interaction.

That's how I found Walter Morris the first time I met him. The warmth in his smile, that particular glint in his eyes. Even the handshake had just enough squeeze to imply somewhat of a familiarity without going over the top. The expression on his face when he first introduced himself reminded me of someone conveying, *Hey, pal, how's life been treating you since the last time I saw you?* It felt almost as if he already knew each and every day of my existence, and asking the question was just a formality.

When the man walked into my office behind my assistant, Grace introduced him as Mr. Morris. I could tell the man had class, and his suit alone perhaps cost more than some people's monthly mortgage. When I threw in the manicured nails and the neatly trimmed beard, I could tell that he was a man who took care of himself. He wasn't exactly ripped, but for a man in his early fifties, he certainly did look to be in great shape, someone who obviously worked out regularly and avoided the dessert bar as best he could.

"Please call me Walter," the man said with that same smile when I asked him to sit after thanking Grace. He set his briefcase down beside the chair.

"Can I offer you a coffee or some water?" I asked, and when he waved a hand to decline the offer, I went back to my seat.

"I'm sorry for dropping in unannounced like this, Mr. Carter, but the matter I need your help with is somewhat time-sensitive."

"Call me Ben, please, and why don't you tell me how I can help you?"

I don't know whether it was confidence, perhaps arrogance, or maybe even a mixture of both, but the way the man held his emotions in perfect balance was how I believed he projected a kind of calmness. At the time, I wouldn't have been surprised to learn that he had a good number of grandchildren with whom he enjoyed quality time most weekends. Hell, he probably would have made for the perfect Santa Claus, given his demeanor.

"Have you heard of a man named Dale Rich, by any chance?" Morris asked, and the name immediately raised a recent memory without bringing forth a face.

"The name sounds familiar, yes," I said.

"But you're not quite sure why?" He smiled, adding a slight nod. "Understandable. From what I understand, Mr.

THE
HITMAN'S
LAWYER

David
ARCHER

Oliver
BLACK

THE

One takes life.

HITMAN'S

One defends it.

LAWYER

Fate is about to make the switch.

A **Ben Carter** LEGAL THRILLER

RIGHTHOUSE

Rich wasn't the kind of man who enjoyed the spotlight too much. He was an antiques dealer, for the most part trading in exotic pieces which he peddled to collectors across the country."

"Was?"

"Yes, unfortunately, Dale Rich was murdered two nights ago out behind the Kimpton Hotel Monaco."

That was when the penny dropped, my brain finally catching up and reminding me of the newspaper headline.

"From what I read in the paper, he was also quite connected within City Hall, if I'm not mistaken."

"I believe he went to school with the mayor's wife, yes," Morris said.

"OK, but I'm not understanding my purpose, though, unless you're under suspicion for the murder."

Morris chuckled somewhat. "The police arrested a woman named Corinne Lucas last night and are currently holding her down at Zone 1. I believe that it is the connection Dale had with Corinne within the antiques business that is the reason she's been arrested. I'd like to hire you to defend Ms. Lucas, if I may. I will be paying all necessary costs, as well as expenses incurred, for you to clear her name. If need be, I could deposit an upfront fee into a trust fund for you to draw upon as needed."

"Who is she to you?"

I don't think he expected the question. For the briefest of moments, I could see his focus break just enough for his eyes to narrow as he considered me. The moment, however, didn't last long.

"A friend, you might say. Someone who I consider dear to me."

"A murder defense can be expensive," I said. "We're not talking small change here. Weeks, perhaps even months of ongoing work, a trial, a full-time investigator."

"Like I said, I'll cover all necessary expenses," Morris said as he doubled down on his request.

While I normally would have jumped at the chance of such an offer, something held me back, stopping me from jumping in head first. It wasn't that I didn't find the man's offer appealing. On the contrary, in fact, it sounded like one of the best offers I'd received in a very long time. I imagined Dwight pushing me aside to shake the man's hand, ensuring a significant case with the potential to keep the lights on in the building for close to a year. And yet, something held me back, something that didn't go unnoticed by my prospective client.

"I sense your hesitation," Morris said. "Not entirely surprising, given the case."

"It's just that your proposal sounds a little too good to be true," I said and immediately heard the lie from my own lips. That wasn't the reason at all.

What I found unable to believe wasn't the proposal at all; it was the man himself. He just came across as a little *too* perfect, a little *too* sincere. I couldn't work out whether that was just how he was or if this was some kind of elaborate ruse to...to what? That was the thing I couldn't figure out. If he *was* being disingenuous, for what purpose?

"How do you know Ms. Lucas?" I asked, posing the same question with a different approach.

"We were neighbors for a long time. Her ex-husband ran off with my ex-wife, and you might say that I feel a certain sense of responsibility for their betrayal."

"So you are kind of like her protector, figuratively speaking."

"Yes, I guess that's one way of putting it. Corinne is a good woman. She didn't deserve what happened to her, and she certainly doesn't deserve this."

"So you don't think she did it? The murder, I mean?"

"Most definitely not," Morris said. "Not only do I know her to be one very courageous woman, but she wouldn't have it in her. She's a very gentle woman, if you know what I mean."

I'm not sure at what point I finally managed to push aside my apprehension, but before I knew it, I half stood out of my chair and reached out a hand toward my new client.

"All right, Mr. Morris…Walter…you have yourself a defense attorney. I'll get my assistant to put together the necessary paperwork and have it emailed through to you this afternoon."

"One other thing," Morris said when he reached the door and turned back around to face me.

"Yes?"

"I know this might sound a little left field, but I'm wondering if you might keep our agreement between us?"

"You mean from the press?"

"I mean from your defendant," Morris said, surprising me yet again.

"You want me to keep you hiring me away from Ms. Lucas? Why on earth would I need to do that?"

"Corinne isn't the kind of woman to accept help. Or should I say *my* help?"

That's when a vision came into my head, one that painted Morris as the kind of man who couldn't take no for an answer. Either through guilt or obsession, I imagined him to be the kind of person who needed more than a simple no to quit. Maybe that was the moment when I should have changed my mind and recanted my acceptance of the job. Looking back now, it was probably at that very moment when I could have still backed out of the entire case and let it continue without me, having never gotten involved. Instead, I went against every instinct telling me not to continue.

"I'll make sure it remains between us" was what I said, and after giving me a final nod of approval, Walter Morris left my office.

What followed was a very long fifteen minutes dragging by as I stood at my window, staring out across the parking lot long after my new client's Maserati had pulled out onto the road and disappeared into the day. It was his ghost that I couldn't take my eyes off, the last place where he'd stood before climbing into his car and vanishing from my view. It was also his words rolling around my head, the ones about not letting the defendant know of his involvement, the woman just a neighbor whose suffering he took responsibility for.

"Grace, would you please start collecting everything you can find on the Dale Rich murder?" I asked my assistant once I managed to get back to my desk.

While there were an extensive number of articles on the Internet I found for myself, they didn't delve anywhere close to the level I needed them to. Information was key in any murder investigation, and details mattered almost as much as time itself. When I read through one of the first news articles I came across, what I found was a story I'd heard many times before.

The details mirrored too many others in our state, perhaps throughout the country. A lone businessman, cutting through an alley for some reason, was attacked and left for dead. His wallet, cell phone, and watch were found to be missing by authorities, the only suspect being the one person nearby that security footage picked up as having entered said alley minutes before. A bellboy working at the hotel who went out for a cigarette discovered a fifty-two-year-old man lying in a pool of his own blood. He'd been stabbed fourteen times in both the back and the chest, twice directly through the heart.

It took law enforcement officers less than twenty-four hours to locate and arrest their prime suspect, a woman witnesses described as being highly agitated in the moments before the killing. She'd been talking on a cell phone at the time and appeared to be engaged in an aggressive conversation when seen entering the same alley. The one piece of evidence still missing, however, was the murder weapon.

The one thing I knew for sure was that the investigation would need the best person on the case. Thankfully, I already had that person on my payroll, and I sent Linda a text after reading that first article a couple of times, asking if she had time to drop into the office later that afternoon. There was something I needed to do first.

Be there with bells on was her reply just a few seconds later, and I smiled at the image in my head. My investigator certainly had a way with words, and I responded with a simple thumbs-up emoji. With Linda coming to see me later in the day and Grace out at her desk accumulating what I needed to get a better understanding of the case, there was just one more thing to do to get myself into a prime position for taking on a new case.

Before getting up, I first leaned back in my chair and gazed up at the ceiling, closed my eyes, and tried to envision the scene for myself to get myself into the moment, if you will. A woman arguing on a cell phone entering an alley, a man following her but maybe a minute or two behind, perhaps taking a shortcut to whatever destination he had. She attacks him, robs him of his belongings, and then simply vanishes.

I opened my eyes again when the scene didn't play out the way the news reports described it. It just didn't flow right.

Usually, mainly when the accused is eventually found guilty, each moment seems to slip effortlessly into the next, the minutes passing as if floating along a river. Not so with the one I was trying to envision, and that was why I pushed myself out of the chair, grabbed my briefcase, and headed for the door. It was time to go ask the kind of questions that built a defense.

TWO

THE MIDDAY SUN FELT ALMOST UNBEARABLE DURING the brief walk from the building to my car, and once I slipped behind the wheel of my Mustang, I didn't hesitate to fire up the engine so I could max out the A/C. I'd only had the car a little over a month after that whole debacle with the SUV. Oh, that's right. I haven't brought you up to date on that part.

After losing my previous ride to a failed bombing attempt the previous year, I somehow talked myself into getting an SUV instead of another Mustang. It was because of the comments from some of my colleagues, most of whom drove the usual range of expensive and classy German-made automobiles. Several preferred the prestige of riding higher than the average vehicle, giving them a somewhat superior position in traffic. Personally, I didn't think I cared either way, but after a couple of test drives, I opted for this BMW that set me back a pretty penny. Fast forward six months, and I absolutely hated it.

It certainly felt like being force-fed a giant piece of humble pie when I eventually walked into the Ford dealership, but the feeling of betrayal quickly fell away when I saw my new ride for the first time. I didn't even need to wait; the floor model suited me perfectly. And when the salesman threw in a few optional extras plus a couple of the services for free, I knew I couldn't say no.

There's just something comforting about returning to an old favorite. I just couldn't get used to driving above the majority of traffic, the sensation feeling almost snobbish, in a way. I'm not someone to look down on people, either proverbially or physically, and appearance isn't something I've ever taken seriously. Yes, I know that lawyers like to drive all manner of fancy cars to convey success, but to me, it's just another form of deception. A person's character isn't determined by how flashy their vehicle is or what label their clothing is. Give me a good soul any day.

It took just a minute or two for the temperature to drop to a more comfortable level, and once on the road, I turned the car into traffic on my way across town. I settled in behind a cab that, surprisingly, nearly followed my exact same route. It ended up leading me almost all the way to my destination, only turning off a street before the police station. I found a spot to the right-hand side, and either through fate or just perfect timing, someone pulled out of one of the few spots shaded by trees.

"Thank you very much," I muttered under my breath when shooting the departing vehicle a wave and quickly slipped into the space.

When I climbed out, the heat immediately slapped me in the face, and the difference in temperature felt like a wall. I recalled the weatherman forecasting a high of ninety-three during the news broadcast the previous evening, but I swear it easily felt above a hundred. Given the speed with which the sweat on my brow began to build, I made getting inside the building a priority.

Thankfully, the A/C in the station was doing its job with some efficiency, the transition from the outside temperature to the inside one again feeling like slipping between two different planes of existence. The sweat immediately reversed course, and by the time I reached the counter and asked to meet with my new client, all hint of the uncomfortable stickiness had vanished.

"One moment," the woman manning the reception area said once she confirmed my client's location and asked me to take a seat.

I didn't bother with sitting, per se, and just kind of hovered near the back of the waiting area with the rest of those in limbo. For the next ten minutes or so, the number of people waiting see-sawed up and down. Every now and then, someone new would be called up while someone else walked in to join the rest of us. I ended up being one of the longest-waiting people, not being called up until all of the original people in waiting had gone.

"Mr. Carter, come on through," the same woman called out to me and led me through to the back of the station, where a couple of interview rooms were located. She pointed me into one, and I took a seat while my escort disappeared again.

This time, I didn't have to wait nearly as long, footsteps almost immediately clapping down the hall before slowing right outside my door. A cop walked in first, rounding the corner ahead of a woman whom I immediately recognized from the only photo I'd seen of her on the website I'd used.

From first impressions, I had to agree with the man who had hired me for the job. Corinne Lucas didn't look like the kind of woman capable of murder. She didn't even look like the kind of person able to raise her voice enough to offend anybody, let alone hurt someone. She was tiny, barely five feet tall, with arms the size of twigs. Aged in her late thirties, she hadn't yet given in to the course of time that wears us all down, still hanging on to her youthful looks in every way possible. She'd tied her long dark hair back into a ponytail that exposed her face in all its beauty. Even without makeup, I saw barely a hint of wrinkles or any blemishes, her skin almost perfect.

If someone had asked me if I thought the woman was attractive, I would have agreed wholeheartedly. Even under pressure and with the weight of the world on her shoulders, it was impossible to deny her beauty. It wasn't until she looked over at me with her dazzling blue eyes that her real beauty hit me.

The cops left the handcuffs on her, but unlike some of the more dangerous criminals I'd spoken with in the room, they didn't tie them to the bench. I waited until the escort had left the room and locked the door before greeting my new client.

"I'm Ben Carter," I began. "How have they been treating you?"

"All right, I suppose," she said, her voice low and lacking confidence. "Why are you here? I can't afford a lawyer."

"My firm tends to keep an eye on the forums, and every now and then, my boss gives the go-ahead for one of us to offer free representation."

It wasn't *exactly* a lie, aside from a couple of subtle facts, but I didn't think they would matter in the long run.

"I need to get out of here," she said, not entirely unexpectedly.

"That's what I hope to make happen, but first, I'm going to need information from you."

"I don't know what I can tell you. I didn't kill Dale Rich."

I could sense that she was close to tears and understood the trauma she must have been going through. Facing a murder charge is no easy thing, the prospect of life behind bars one of the scariest prospects a person can deal with.

"Did you know him at all?"

"Not quite in the sense that these people seem to think. The first time I met him was during a fundraising ball, but that conversation lasted all of about a minute."

"Any reason why?"

"He hit on me, and the wedding band on his finger was enough to convince me not to take things any further."

"What about after that? Ever run into him again?"

"A couple of times. It's hard not to see a familiar face within an industry as tight as ours."

"Did he ever hit on you again?"

"Yes, he did, about a year later."

I sensed something and dug further. "Another rejection?"

She pursed her lips and looked down at her hands. The color in her cheeks gave her answer away her long before the words revealed the truth.

"Unfortunately, that time Dale managed to time it just right. I'd had a little too much champagne during a fundraiser, and one thing led to another."

"The wedding ring didn't turn you away that time?"

"He wasn't wearing one, and when I asked him about it, he told me he'd been separated for quite some time."

"When was the last time you saw Rich?"

"About a month ago. We ran into each other at a gas station and ended up in an argument."

"May I ask what you argued over?"

"Me not returning his calls after the last time we got

together. I told him I wasn't interested, and I think he took it personally."

"How do you think you both ended up in the same place at nearly the same time? The police seem to think it might have been planned."

"I had a dinner reservation with a friend at the Jade Dragon. You can check. The place has a back door on Garland Way that's open to anybody. I was on the phone with my ex at the time and wasn't exactly in a great mood. I didn't want to make a scene out on the street, so I took the conversation down the alley."

"You didn't hear anything unusual out there? Nothing to indicate a fight of some sort?"

"No, not at all, although I wasn't exactly listening for anything. I was too focused on the phone call. My friend Donna texted me at some point during the call I was having, saying she couldn't make it, and I didn't even bother taking a seat. Wasn't about to sit there alone."

"One thing I noticed when you reached the street again. You headed north *away* from your car. Why didn't you go back the way you had come?"

"I was angry about the call and just needed to clear my head. There's a coffee shop a little further up Sixth, and I went there for a bit of solitude. I also remembered a creepy guy begging for money and didn't want to run into him again. I ended up hailing a cab a while later."

Her story made sense, and if I could prove all the minor details, then I figured I could use them in such a way as to strengthen our case. I still wasn't sure about the police evidence—hadn't had enough time to access it—but I didn't think it would have been anything physical. If all the evidence the authorities had on my client was circumstantial, then my bid for winning her parole should have been a slam dunk.

"I need to ask. Have you ever been in trouble with the police before?"

She shook her head without hesitation. "Got a speeding ticket once, but that's about it."

"What about anybody you associate with? Boyfriends, colleagues, exes?"

"No, not that I know of. My latest ex is a Marine and about as clean as you can get. I doubt he'd let a shoelace hang too long, if you know what I mean."

"How long were you together?"

"Four months. Not exactly award-winning, but it was good while it lasted."

"Corinne, I need to warn you. This isn't going to be an easy case to win, not by a long shot. If there is anything, and I mean *anything*, in your life the prosecutor can use, believe me, they will. Now is the time to tell me."

For a minute, she just stared back at me with those frightened eyes of hers, the iridescent blue almost intensified by the stress. It also highlighted the distinctive black ring running around the edge of her irises, only adding to the beauty of them. In another time and place, I might have considered them hypnotic and found myself caught in their power.

"I'm not one to have secrets, Mr. Carter. I lead a very simple life. I work, I pay a mortgage, I have a dog. This kind of thing doesn't happen to people like me."

"Actually, you'd be surprised how many times this happens to people like yourself. More than you could imagine."

"And are they guilty?" she asked, shifting her weight uncomfortably.

"Sometimes," I said, not bothering to hide the truth.

We spoke for a few more minutes before the detectives investigating the case joined us, and not long after, Corinne Lucas was formally charged with first-degree murder. The process didn't take long but did offer me a chance to request access to the evidence they had against my client. Once we had gone through all of the formalities, I spent around another ten minutes or so with Corinne alone, but that was just to take her through a few things planned for the immediate future.

When the time came for me to finally leave my client again, I did note a slight change in her demeanor. She no longer looked quite as vulnerable and confused as she had when I'd first seen her. I think with a bit more understanding of the process and perhaps sensing some hope that she might actually have a chance at freedom again, Corinne walked out of the room with her head held up a little higher. She walked with a sense of purpose, and that gave me hope that she might actually have the strength to spend time in lock-up.

Once back in my car, I first took care of the A/C so as to bring the car's interior back to habitable levels before pulling out my cell phone and calling Grace. Now that we had somewhat of a direction to go in, it was time for us to take the necessary steps to get the wheels rolling. Organizing and sorting through the brief of evidence and arranging a bail hearing was at the top of the list, and Grace was the perfect person to take charge of both.

THREE

Linda turned into the office parking lot immediately ahead of me, and we ended up pulling into adjacent spaces. Rather than climb out of her car, she held up a single finger while appearing to continue talking to someone through her vehicle's hands-free system, and I indicated that I would meet her inside. After I saw her finger change to a thumbs-up gesture, I turned for the building's front door.

"You have a bail hearing for Corinne Lucas tomorrow morning at ten," Grace told me when I neared her desk, and after a quick thank you, I headed into my office, where I immediately took off my jacket, hung it over the back of my chair, and took a seat.

There's nothing quite like getting a new case to work on, as far as I was concerned, especially a case as significant as the one handed to me that very morning. To me, it felt like the opening chapter of a good book, the kind already reviewed hundreds of times and found all over social media. I love the anticipation of uncovering hidden secrets, discovering the mystery behind a convincing plotline, and the process of finding each clue and evaluating it while dodging all manner of obstacles.

I barely got my laptop open before Linda walked into the room carrying a half-empty tray of donuts, the rest already distributed among the other staff members.

"I saved you a couple of the custard creams," she said as she set the box down on my desk and dropped onto the chair.

"Hey, thanks." I helped myself to one of the three remaining. "Ready to get your hands dirty with this new case?"

"Always," Linda said with a grin as she took a sip from her water bottle. A few moments later, Grace came in and joined us.

I began to share the details of the case as I saw them, highlighting that I suspected there to be more of a connection between Corinne Lucas and Dale Rich. I didn't have any evidence to prove it, but I did have a gut feeling from my conversation with her. Something just felt off in a way I couldn't explain.

"Grace, I want you to try and see if you can find any connections between Corinne's business and Rich's. There has to be something. The two not only worked in the same industry but also in a very niche market that wouldn't have too many competitors." Turning to my investigator, I said, "Linda, could you first try to get some extra surveillance footage from the area where the murder took place? I just don't feel like the cops have tried to spread their net wide enough."

"Anything in particular I'm looking for?"

"Anyone who might appear to be in a hurry to get out of the immediate vicinity. Try to take it out to at least six blocks in all directions. Somebody killed Dale Rich, and I doubt they would have wanted to hang around for the cops to show up." I was about to turn back to Grace but remembered something else. "Also, see if you can get me a copy of Corinne's phone records. She said she was on the phone with an ex-boyfriend just before the murder. Apparently, the two had been arguing for some time. I'm curious to know just how long."

"All right, I'm on it," Linda said and just like that got on with doing what she did best.

"I managed to find Dale Rich's connection with City Hall," Grace said once we were alone. "Turns out that he not only went to the same college as Deidre Green, but he also dated her for a brief stint during his final year."

"Dale Rich dated the mayor's wife?"

"That he did," Grace confirmed. Inside, I groaned.

Taking on a murder case already garnered media publicity, but to throw in a direct connection to City Hall would elevate the attention even further, not a bad thing when looking at it from a business point of view. Which is probably why a certain boss of mine poked his head into my office at just the right time to join in the conversation.

"I hear you've got one hell of a case on your hands," Dwight Tanner said after knocking on the office door.

"I'm starting to think so too," I said as he took a seat next to his wife. "I don't think it will take long for the media to pick this up, if they haven't already."

"We'll see tomorrow when you show up at the courthouse for the bail hearing," Dwight said, and I nodded in agreement. "You can also bet your bottom dollar that the DA is going to be gunning for a quick conviction. The mayor is going to be breathing down his neck for one."

"Arthur Clements isn't going to have the easy fight he's hoping for," I said. "Corinne Lucas has herself a formidable team behind her, and we're going to make sure we put up a good fight."

"That's what I like to hear," Dwight said with a grin before turning to his wife. "Honey, Wayne Baxter just phoned to ask whether I had time to fly out to Boulder and join him for a round or two this weekend."

Golf, I thought to myself. Of all the possible sports in the world, it was one of the few I had never been able to fully understand. Not the game itself, but the hype around it, the way people almost lived and breathed it like a compulsive obsession.

"We only have the Wilsons' housewarming on Saturday night," Grace said, and for a second, I thought she might dash her husband's hopes of a boys' weekend away. I should have known better. "But I know how much you love the idea of spending time with George and his endless dry jokes."

The immediate grin on Dwight's face was enough to tell me that he'd been allowed to dodge a bullet. I didn't know who George Wilson was or how bad his jokes might have been, but I was smart enough to recognize a reprieve.

"Thanks, love." Dwight pushed himself out of the chair and gave his wife a kiss on top of the head before turning back to me. "Let me know if you need anything for the Lucas case, Ben. This is definitely one I want to see us smash out of the park."

"We'll smash it out of the park, boss," I said with an amused grin and waited for him to leave us alone. "I think you just made his day," I told Grace once I heard Dwight's office door close farther down the hallway.

"You'd understand just how much if you happen to subject yourself to a few minutes alone with George Wilson and his unfunny one-liners."

"That bad, huh?"

Grace not only grinned but also rolled her eyes. "Yes, that

bad." She brushed it aside and pushed herself to the front edge of the chair. "If there's nothing else, I'll go and start probing Corinne Lucas's business records. See if I can find those connections to Dale Rich."

"Thanks, Grace. I appreciate it."

Once alone, I got out of my chair and walked to the window, where I stood in the middle to look out across the limited view. For me, the window gave me a distraction similar to a campfire, my eyes seeing the cityscape and yet completely detached from the mind working behind them. The weird thing is, I wasn't actually thinking about Corinne Lucas or the case at all, but something else entirely. It was Naomi I was thinking of and for very good reason. The anniversary of her death wasn't that far away, a time of year that always hung heavily over me. The thought of how different my life would have been had she not died in a needless hit-and-run is one that constantly plagued me whenever I gave in to the distraction.

"Get your head back in the game," I whispered to myself when I could sense the emotions rising dangerously close to the surface, and after slapping the back of one hand into the palm of the other, I turned and went back to my desk.

For the next three hours, I did what I could to bring myself up to speed on as much of the case as I could, poring over the majority of the evidence sent to me by the prosecutor. I outlasted the majority of the office, and even Grace came in some time after six to ask whether I needed her to stay.

"No, I'm fine," I said and thanked my assistant for another amazing day. "Just going to finish this one statement and head off myself."

"Don't forget the bail hearing at ten with Judge Adams."

"I won't," I said while a silent groan rolled through me.

Herman Adams wasn't my first choice to judge the case.

Our relationship wasn't exactly a breezy one, given the way we'd met some years earlier. Let's just say that a minor traffic incident involving one of us cutting the other off and the subsequent overreaction from one party toward the other had sealed our professional relationship. Adams had been having something of a bad morning, and when I innocently cut him off a few blocks from the courthouse, the man completely lost his shit. Granted, me flipping him the bird after listening to a torrent of abuse might not have helped the situation, but I didn't know who he was at the time. His identity only became clear when he walked into Courtroom 5 of the Allegheny County Courthouse during that morning's bail hearing for a client I'd been representing.

"I'll be coming straight back to the office after the hearing," I told Grace, and after wishing her a good night, I found myself alone once more.

I had lied to Grace about making the statement my last job for the evening. I ended up working my way through the majority of witness testimony that night, finding myself in the zone and not wanting to pass up the opportunity. The zone, as I like to call it, is what you might compare to the place where an author finds themselves able to write hundreds and even thousands of words in one go without ever looking up. It's a place where the flow of information feels like a massive river, with me caught in the current and able to effortlessly consume vast quantities of knowledge. The zone is the place I often hoped to find when settling in for a marathon session, and that evening was one of those times.

By the time I finally popped my head up again, it was just me and our security guy, Marvin, in the building. Even our cleaning crew had already finished.

"Have a great night, sir," Marvin said as I walked through

the foyer, and I wished him the same before heading out into a clear Pittsburgh evening.

I always enjoy driving back to my apartment at that time of the night, the streets almost a polar opposite to the ones I usually battle during the day. By the time I finally reached my bedroom, stripped down to my underwear, and lay down on top of my bed, it felt like I had a pretty good grasp on the case as a whole and was ready to take it to the next level, the hearing scheduled for the following morning. The only barrier standing in my way to winning bail for my client was a certain prosecutor who I knew wasn't about to let me off easily. If Bartell had his way, Corinne Lucas would be going straight to jail without hesitation.

FOUR

When I reached the parking lot of the courthouse, the first surprise of the day hit me the second I saw the media pack already waiting in ambush near the front steps. It didn't take a rocket scientist to know that their intended target was me, given the lack of any other substantial news stories. After first finding a space for the Mustang, I jumped out, straightened my tie to make sure that I appeared presentable, and then gripped the handle of my briefcase a little tighter. I made my way toward the crowd, waiting for someone to notice my approach, and it didn't take long. Halfway there, the first of them spotted me, and after rushing my way, the rest of the mob quickly followed.

The questions began flying the moment the first reporter got to within a dozen yards of me, and I had barely time to answer him before more quickly followed. The majority I ignored, focusing on the ones where I could provide the kind of answer I wanted to give in order to keep control. This was my rodeo, after all, and I wasn't going to be led astray by reporters hoping for an exclusive scoop. All it would take was a slight distraction, a slip of the tongue, and I could effectively ensure my spot on the front page the following morning for all the wrong reasons.

If I were going to get through the media pack in one piece, I would need to keep my cool, remain composed enough to get through the questions, and make a quick escape once I had answered enough of them. As it turned out, the focus shifted from me just a couple of minutes after my arrival when a new target approached the front of the courthouse, this one with a definite taste for the attention. Bartell had always enjoyed the limelight, and that morning was no different. He almost welcomed the first few reporters with open arms, and when it appeared that he was going to give the mob a deeper insight into his case, the rest of the media pack quickly followed those first few.

I grinned as I watched them scurry to where the prosecutor stood his ground, flashing his pearly whites at each of the cameras in turn. He looked like a born natural, putting on a stern expression while talking about bringing a dangerous criminal to justice for the murder of an innocent man. I hung around long enough for Bartell to send a couple of sideways glances in my direction as he spoke, my own grin widening when he mentioned something about people needing to check their conscience if they were going to doubt the efficiency of the justice system.

To me, Bartell looked more like the guys I'd dealt with when buying my latest car, their grins almost as fake as the words they used to try and convince me to sign on the dotted line. Like those lusting for their next sale, Bartell tried to use the kind of hot-button words that pricked the ears of nearby reporters, words like *exclusive* and *inside information*.

Shaking my head, I turned for the doors and left Bartell

standing in the middle of the pack. Once inside the courthouse, I headed straight for Courtroom 3 and took a seat just inside the doors as Judge Adams continued hearing other cases scheduled ahead of mine. He did happen to glance over in my direction during a very brief moment right after denying bail to a previous matter, and the deepening of his frown lines only confirmed his feelings toward me.

When the bailiff finally called our case number shortly after Adams took a quick five-minute recess, I made my way to the defendant's table and took a seat while court security walked my client out. Corinne Lucas looked a far cry from the woman I had left the previous day, the weight of the situation written all over her face. With shoulders slumped and eyes cast down, she took a seat but could barely look at me.

"Do you really think the judge will grant me bail?" The whisper rose barely enough for me to hear her above the ambience of the courtroom and not because she was trying to keep her voice low. Corinne lacked the strength to make herself heard, her fear cannibalizing what little she had.

"I think our chances are better than most," I said, the lie slipping out with almost embarrassing ease.

It wasn't that I wanted to lie to save face for myself but rather to protect what little control Corinne still had over her fears. I had seen first-hand what happens when a client completely loses control of their emotions, and it's not a pretty sight. With the judge already a questionable obstacle standing in my way, I didn't want to risk further exasperating the situation by my client losing her mind right before the hearing.

"Just keep breathing and let me do the talking," I whispered to her when I noticed that the prosecutor still hadn't taken his spot next to us. I looked over my shoulder toward the door and noticed a couple of people run past toward the court-house foyer.

"What if they deny bail?" I heard Corinne ask from behind me, but I barely heard the words as I watched a couple of people in the back row whisper something between themselves before also making a quick exit and heading in the direction of the foyer.

"Let's not worry about hypothetical scenarios until we know for sure," I said, temporarily ignoring whatever was happening out in the courthouse and turning back to my client. "We have to keep focus, Corinne. Assumptions aren't going to help you right now."

The minutes passed by as I managed to keep my client focusing on her breathing while watching the door for any indication of what was going on. It wasn't until a familiar face suddenly came into the courtroom that the situation took a turn.

"Morning, Ben," Elsa Schwarz said to me as she not only shot me a forced grin but also took a seat at the prosecution's table. I took another look toward the doors but had a sudden inclination that Xavier Bartell wouldn't be coming to the bail hearing after all.

"What's going on?" I asked across the aisle, but before Elsa could answer, the bailiff called the courtroom to order.

All I could do was watch as the judge walked out and retook his seat on the bench. After shuffling through some pieces of paper the bailiff handed him, he looked over the rim of his wire-framed glasses toward Elsa.

"I understand we have a change of prosecutor in the following matter?"

"Yes, Your Honor," Elsa said. "Unfortunately, Mr. Bartell

suffered a medical episode at the front of the courthouse just now and has been rushed to Alleghany General." She gave me a bit of a sideways glance but just for a split second before looking back up at the judge.

"Well, let's hope it's nothing serious," Adams said, but something about the way Elsa's face suddenly clenched told me that it was.

The judge wasted little time in getting the hearing underway, and while I did try my best to beat the overwhelming tide pushing against my case, Adams ruled in favor of keeping my client in custody until the trial date, which he set for the first week of June, just five weeks away. I was so sure that Corinne was going to lose her shit that I held her hand for the first few moments to calm her down again.

Rather than have her escorted back to the holding cells, I had court security escort my client through to one of the interview rooms, and once the door closed behind us, I sat down and did my best to reassure a woman living her worst nightmare.

"Now that we know where we're at, we need to stay focused on the job at hand," I said as the tears continued falling from her bloodshot eyes.

"I'm going to end up spending the rest of my life locked up, aren't I?"

"Corinne, don't think like that."

"How can I not?" she snapped as she raised her voice for the first time, her words loud enough to cause me to flinch. "I'm going to spend the next five weeks in God knows what sort of hellhole, and then when they find me guilty, they'll throw away the key."

"I know that's how it might look right now," I said as I lowered my voice to a more empathetic level. "But I have been through this more than a few times, and I can promise you that no matter how bleak it might seem right now, there is always light at the end of the tunnel."

"How can you be so sure that you can win this case?"

I knew that I couldn't pull the wool over her eyes with just some random words. Corinne would see right through them and lose whatever trust she still had for me.

"All I know is that I have the best team available to me, and we will do everything we can to get to the bottom of this. I know it's not much, but I've worked with these people long enough to know that they aren't strangers to miracles."

"Is that what I need, Ben?" She looked at me with eyes that saw straight through into my very soul, searching for any hint of a lie. "A miracle?"

"No," I said. "We don't need a miracle. What we need is to find the truth."

"Then why do you sound so unsure of yourself?"

If she had slapped me in the face at that moment, I think the shock would have been less than what I felt hearing her words, the last thing she spoke to me before court security took her out and back to the holding cells. Corinne took one final look at me just before they led her out of the interview room, and that's when I saw that the tears had stopped falling long before.

While I was sure that Corinne had lost her faith in me, I knew I couldn't let it get to me. I had no intention of throwing the case away, and while I had lost my chance to reassure her, my client's current feelings needed to take a back seat for the time being. I couldn't continue worrying about how she felt as it would only distract me from what I needed to do.

Bail denied was what I texted to both Linda and Grace before leaving the interview room, and when I got back out to the courthouse foyer, there was little evidence of whatever had gone on with Bartell. As it turned out, I didn't need to go looking very far for the answers, as they seemed to find me all on their own, a voice suddenly speaking from behind me as I stood staring at the front doors.

"Can you believe he had a stroke?" I spun around to see Elsa Schwarz standing behind me, the previous look of concern all but vanished, replaced with an expression only too familiar to me.

"Bartell had a stroke?"

The revelation stunned me in a way I can't quite explain. Despite opposing me on so many occasions, I never saw him as the enemy. Quite the opposite, in fact. I held the utmost respect for the prosecutor. Xavier Bartell was a fine lawyer with a brilliant track record. While we might have played for opposing teams, we still played in the same league, and that made us colleagues. He wasn't that much older than me, either, and a stroke taking him down wasn't something I could have ever expected. It rattled me.

"Not sure how bad it is, but he didn't look good when they put him in the back of the ambulance," Elsa said as she took a step closer to me.

What you probably don't know about Xavier Bartell's replacement is that we had something of a history. Let's just say that Elsa Schwarz was shooting smiles and winks at me long before she walked into the courtroom that morning, her interest reaching far beyond the boundaries of our profession. Linda once told me that the potential prosecutor had the hots for me, and if I gave in to her advances, I would probably end up creating more problems for myself.

"Let's hope he has a quick recovery," I think I said just before continuing to the courthouse doors and the media pack still lying in wait for me. I don't know whether Elsa actually followed me outside because I never looked back to check. My insides were still churning from the shock of Bartell's stroke, and turning my attention to the questions flying at me proved the first step in moving on with my day.

FIVE

"Yes, he had a stroke," I told Grace for the second time once we were sitting in my office about an hour later, me leaning back in my chair and staring up at the ceiling. "A full-on stroke, I tell you."

"And he had no symptoms whatsoever?"

"Not according to his secretary," I said, finally feeling strong enough to sit upright again and bring my attention back into the room. "Can you try and get an update for me when you have time? And maybe send some flowers on our behalf."

"Yes, of course," Grace said with a familiar shock in her tone and pushed herself out of the chair.

Once alone again, I opened my laptop and decided to dive into the case to try and get a better understanding of the specifics. Dale Rich proved to be as much a mystery as the man who'd hired me to defend the main suspect, a person who I still wasn't entirely sure about. For one, Dale Rich owned multiple businesses, including men's fashion stores, a Jeep car dealership, and multiple investment properties. Those weren't what anybody involved with the case focused on, though, with his antiques business taking center stage for the most part. He dealt in exotic pieces, often selling ones worth more than most people's homes to global collectors. That also happened to be the business the authorities believed to be linked to his demise.

There appeared to be two theories, from what I could tell. The first was that Corinne had been behind the murder and had coaxed Rich into the alley and ultimately stabbed him after a heated argument. The evidence produced was nothing more than circumstantial, with the most damning of it being the footage of my client having an animated argument during a phone call.

The second theory, which some of the wider media had chosen to run with, was that Rich had been nothing more than an innocent mugging victim, a man caught in the wrong place at the wrong time. The victim's missing wallet, cell phone, and Rolex watch seemed to support the theory. But without any viable footage of a suspect, nor any witnesses, the theory quickly collapsed when put under scrutiny.

From the information at my disposal, I quickly found a man steeped in secrets, a man who while trying his best to remain out of the limelight also seemed to enjoy the unwanted attention, especially from the ladies. One reporter had managed to get an exclusive interview with his purported ex-wife a couple of years earlier, and it didn't paint the high-flying businessman in a very flattering light. Rich had threatened to sue the publication for defamation if it didn't retract the story. Given the source material and the two other women who also came forward, he eventually dropped his threats, letting the story eventually fade quietly into the shadows.

While he might have been a womanizer at heart, Dale Rich never walked away from his responsibilities as a father, the way so many other divorced dads did. He had walked out of the family home and transferred his life to an inner city apartment, where he remained during his final years of life. He and his wife, Elaine, never actually divorced. It was during an interview with an out-of-state magazine that he publicly shared that he never would, not because of any bitterness but because he and his wife had agreed to keep the marriage intact for the sake of their two daughters. Neither wanted to expose their children to the complete havoc divorces tended to bring and had agreed to an amicable split that saw the parents share the responsibilities for their children evenly. The assets remained just as they had throughout the marriage, with the only real change being Rich signing the family home over to his wife.

After spending more than an hour reading about the man, I couldn't help but feel sorry for the family. Yes, Rich did come across as a cheating scumbag, but that one weakness wasn't enough to tarnish the rest of what he did. Womanizing aside, which I might add wasn't what caused the separation from his wife in the first place, he took fatherhood seriously and always maintained a firm grip on his multiple businesses. His employees spoke highly of their boss, with none of the many interviewed having anything negative to say about him.

I don't know why, but something made me suddenly close the laptop, grab my phone and keys, and head out of my office.

I'm going for a drive, I mouthed to Grace as I passed by her desk, and she gave me a wave while speaking on the phone. It wasn't exactly odd for me to suddenly up and walk out at a moment's notice, especially when first taking on a new case. I thought better when driving and sometimes found the car leading my subconsciousness in the direction I needed to go. This time, however, I had an idea of where I wanted to be.

After skirting around the top edge of the city, I made my way to the eastern side of Pittsburgh along the expressway until taking the Fox Chapel Road exit. Just minutes later, I found myself among the kind of surroundings only the city's elite called home. Sprawling estates stretched along both sides of the road, with side streets offering more of the same. The sheer number of European automobiles was enough to make a person wonder which country they were in, given the lack of domestic brands. I eventually found myself on Winterbelly Lane, and a few seconds after turning onto the road, I pulled up in front of the kind of estate most people could only ever dream about.

The first thing that grabbed my attention when I climbed out of the Mustang was the silence, with nothing but the afternoon sun and a slight breeze caressing the suburb. Dozens of mature trees dotted the landscape, both along the road and within the different estates. The two-story Edwardian-style house sitting before me wasn't exactly a mansion, per se, but it did eclipse most of the houses in my own neighborhood in terms of sheer size. It had this weird cottage kind of feel thanks to a number of ornate iron pieces adorning the underside of the main porch.

I actually hadn't considered my visit before arriving and so hadn't bothered phoning ahead to see whether a meeting with the homeowner would be possible, but seeing a white BMW X7 SUV parked in front of one of the three garage doors, it appeared that my hopes would be met. Walking over to the gate, I pressed the intercom, listened to the short beep, and patiently waited for a greeting that came almost a minute later.

"Yes, can I help you?"

I had never met Elaine Rich before that day, nor had I heard her voice, although I could have if I had bothered to follow any number of YouTube links I found scattered throughout several articles during my earlier investigating. Weirdly, I knew it was her the second she answered my call.

"Mrs. Rich, I'm sorry to bother you," I began. "My name is Ben Carter. I'm an attorney investigating the unfortunate death of your husband, and I was wondering if—"

"One moment, please," the voice cut in, maintaining the same level of politeness as the initial greeting. I expected her to send out some sort of security guy to tell me to take a hike, or worse, to call the police and have them escort me away, but surprisingly, the dual gates suddenly hummed, shuddered slightly, and then slowly began to pull in until they stood facing each other.

When I was halfway up the sizable driveway, a lone figure suddenly appeared, walking out of the front door of the house, holding her crossed arms defensively across her chest. She watched me approach and didn't move until I reached the bottom of the half-dozen stone steps when she finally moved forward.

"Thank you for seeing me, Mrs. Rich," I said as I began to climb the steps. She met me at the top with an outstretched hand, and we briefly shook.

"I don't believe I remember seeing you as part of the prose-cution team."

"No, unfortunately I work for the other side," I said, again expecting her to send me marching on my way.

"You're defending Corinne Lucas?"

"Yes, ma'am, I am."

Rather than respond, she gave me a single up-and-down look, took a step aside, and gestured for me to enter the home with a flash of a reserved smile. I made sure to make mine more genuine before following her unspoken instruction and making my way inside. I stopped once in the foyer, waited for her to close the door, and then followed her through into a vast living room that resembled something more akin to a hall.

"Please, take a seat," Elaine offered once we reached the far side of the room, where a couple of leather couches had been positioned in front of a cavernous fireplace, the kind one might compare to those from medieval castles. I swear it was big enough for me to stand upright in, and I might have checked were it not for the present company and the pile of wood ready and waiting in the center of it.

"You have a lovely home," I said as I took a seat on the end of the right-hand couch and immediately wondered how many people had said the exact same thing.

"Thank you," Elaine said as she sat opposite me. "It belonged to Dale's grandfather back in the day, although we did quite a lot of renovating during the past few years."

"Oh, I didn't realize it had been in the family before you moved here."

"We didn't move in until Dale's mother passed away in '06. She lived here alone for the better part of thirty years," Elaine said as she looked around the room, briefly pausing on a wall covered in photo frames of varying sizes.

"That's a long time to be alone," I said.

"I doubt the woman *ever* felt alone," Elaine said as she remained focused on a large photo of an elderly woman I assumed to be the mother in question. "She hated people, especially those she considered responsible for stealing her children away."

"I take it you didn't get on with your mother-in-law."

Elaine scoffed but held her gaze. "Bitterness isn't exactly a trait a person can defend against," she said and finally turned her attention back to me. "But then again, I don't think you came all this way to speak about Dale's mother."

"No, I didn't," I said. "I actually came to talk about you."

"About me? Goodness, whatever for?"

"To try and get a sense of who your husband really was," I said, leaning forward ever so slightly.

"You mean you don't buy all the womanizing articles filling most newspapers these days?"

"The authorities seem to have their minds set on my client murdering him. They refuse to entertain any other possibility despite the lack of evidence."

"You don't think Corinne killed Dale?"

"I'd rather try to find the truth than guess, Mrs. Rich."

"Call me Elaine, please." Her eyes briefly turned up to the same photo again. "*That's* the only Mrs. Rich around here." She looked back at me. "In any case, I stopped using Dale's last name years ago."

"I'm sorry, I didn't know," I said. "And please call me Ben."

"OK, Ben it is."

She paused long enough to reach for a pack of cigarettes I hadn't noticed sitting on the coffee table between us, pulled one out, and delicately placed it between her lips. After pulling a lighter out of the same pack, she chased the tip of the cigarette with the flame before gently puffing a few times.

"So tell me, Ben. Why does a defense lawyer seek out a victim's estranged wife on a sunny afternoon? And don't try and tell me it was to get a better understanding of Dale." She drew on the cigarette, the tip of it glowing brightly enough to reflect from her eyes as she stared at me. "My guess is, you're looking for an alternative suspect. Maybe you think I had a grudge to settle and organized a hit on my husband."

Did I? The thought crossed my mind as to whether that was the real reason for my visit, but I didn't think it was.

"Did you?"

"No, I didn't, since you ask. Dale and I had our differences, sure, but none bad enough to warrant hiring someone to hurt the other." She took another drag, holding the smoke in her lungs for a long time before slowly releasing little tendrils that curled out the sides of her mouth.

"But surely the cheating must have affected you."

That was when she laughed, the sound lacking any hint of humor as she looked up at the ceiling.

"Oh, yes, the cheating." She dramatized the last word, elevating her voice enough for it to echo back at us from the distant corners of the room.

"It can't have been easy," I said, suddenly unsure of whether I was still in the same conversation as the one we had started a few minutes earlier. "Any woman would be forgiven for holding—"

"I didn't hold anything," she snapped, cutting me off as she shook her head in frustration. "The truth is, Ben, I felt bad for him." She paused, looked at the floor, and shook her head. "Guilt is a terrible thing to harbor when you know you're the cause of someone else's pain."

"I'm sorry," I said. "I don't think I'm following." That was when she dropped an unexpected bomb, one I never saw coming.

"When the media first ran with the story that Dale had cheated on me with multiple women, he made me swear to let them go with it. I tried to object, of course, but that was him. Always putting his family first."

"He *didn't* cheat on you?"

"No, Ben, no, he didn't. At least not while we were both still faithful to each other." She grinned again, staring into the space between us as the cigarette continued burning between her fingers. That was when she let out a truth I didn't expect. "*I* was the one who cheated on *him*."

That was when a tear slid silently down the side of her face. It barely made it halfway before she brushed the traitor away with a flick of her finger and scoffed. She took a look at the remainder of her cigarette, considered taking a final drag, and instead stubbed it out in the ashtray before leaning back on the couch with a long sigh.

"I don't understand," I said. "I thought—"

"Yes, many people do assume that the media has it right all the time," she said, again cutting me off. "Does it shock you to know that they had it completely wrong?"

"Then why would he let the story go on like that?"

"Because he couldn't allow them to attack me. He never could. Dale was one of the most loyal men I have ever met." More tears began to spill. "We simply fell out of love, and I think he was politely waiting to see what I would do next. He began staying at the city apartment more and more, and eventually, I told him the truth about me and Henry." Elaine briefly paused to look over her shoulder as if fearing someone eavesdropping, but after a few seconds, she seemed to confirm that the coast was clear and continued. "The girls are upstairs," she whispered. "Henry was just some guy I knew from the weekend market. Nothing serious, just a release, so to speak."

"I understand," I said but wasn't sure whether I actually did.

"In any case, Ben, you can rest assured that you won't find a potential murder plot in this house. I'm sorry for dashing your hopes."

"You haven't," I said, remembering that I was a glass-half-full kind of guy. "You've just reduced my list of possible suspects, that's all."

SIX

WHILE ELAINE RICH PAINTED QUITE A DIFFERENT picture of her estranged husband than the one the rest of the world saw, it didn't take long for that same picture to quickly change for me again just a few hours later. I received a text just a few minutes after leaving her house from Jack Barnes, asking whether I had time to meet him down at The Hose and Ladder for a late afternoon drink. With no other place I needed to be at that particular moment, I sent him a reply almost immediately, saying I'd be there in twenty minutes.

When I pulled into the bar's parking lot fifteen minutes later, I spotted Jack's Pontiac already parked between a couple of Rams halfway up the first row. I found the man himself sitting in one of the many booths running down the bar's right-hand wall talking at his cell phone screen with one hand cradling a beer. After grabbing a beer for myself, I slid into the seat opposite him, and he held up one finger silently asking me to wait.

"Yes, baby girl, we'll go to the game on Saturday, I promise," he told his daughter with the kind of smile only a father could get away with.

"Do you promise?" I heard his nine-year-old ask in earnest. "Because the last time you said you would take me, you didn't, and Mommy said you had more important things to do." I could see the anger rising behind the forced smile as it grew to reveal more teeth.

"I had work to do, sweetie. You know Daddy has to work sometimes. This time, I promise we'll go."

I watched as Jack squirmed his way through a few more minutes of FaceTiming his child before she finally let him go after a final promise to take her to the game. The second the call ended, he dropped the phone to the table with a disgruntled sigh, rubbed his face with both hands, and grunted.

"So the divorce is going well, huh?"

He looked at me through splayed fingers. "The divorce is over with, thank God. Now if I could just get Peterson to convince his new girlfriend that she's only hurting her child by constantly criticizing me, then life would be so much better."

"She's still with Joel Peterson?"

Jack removed his hands and grabbed his beer. "He's already moved in," he said after a long swig from his glass.

"And you're OK with that?"

He looked at me and tilted his head like a puppy. "What's the point in staying pissed off at the situation, Ben? It's not like there's anything I can do about it. And even if I could, why would I want to? She cheated on me. It's not like I could ever trust her again." He took another swallow of beer before continuing. "Besides, I see it as me dodging a bullet. He can have her. As long as my daughter is cared for, then they can have each other."

"You're a stronger man than me," I said and took a large drink from my own glass.

A disagreement between some other patrons briefly diverted our attention toward the bar where the two men looked just about ready to turn their previously-suppressed argument physical. The older of the two, a retired cop named Lance Peterson, slid off his stool with both fists at the ready, his opponent holding up his hands defensively as he took a step back.

"All right, you two," Joel, the bartender, said as he appeared out of a side door and made his way to the argument. "Either take it outside or consider it settled," he said once he stood between the two. A stern eye-balling at each man proved to convince the pair that it wasn't worth it, although Peterson shook his head in disgust, swallowed the last of his beer, and headed for the door. Both his opponent and the bartender watched until he disappeared before continuing with their afternoon.

"Hate seeing Lance like that," Jack said when he turned his attention back to me.

"What do you mean?"

"Been a shell of a man since his wife passed away."

"Alice died? When did that happen?"

"A couple of months ago," Jack said. "Spent the final few weeks in the hospital battling pneumonia before she slipped away."

"I hadn't heard," I said with genuine sadness.

I didn't know the couple well, but I had met them at one of the golfing fundraisers Dwight ran a few times a year. I remembered spending considerable time talking with Alice Peterson a year or so earlier when she'd spotted me arriving in my

Mustang and then proceeded to share her own love affair with the car.

"Bought my first one when I was twenty-eight," she'd told me over a few mocktails, and after listening to her for more than an hour, I understood her passion for the model.

"So how is the Dale Rich murder investigation going?" Jack asked.

"Hasn't really gone anywhere yet," I said. "But then again, it has only just begun."

"I might have something of interest for you."

"Oh?"

He reached inside his jacket pocket and pulled out a folded-up sheet of paper that he held out to me. I reached across the table and took it while eyeing him suspiciously.

"Free info?"

"I figured you could use some help," Jack said and grabbed his beer. "Not sure how valuable it is, but that name seemed to have quite a history with Dale Rich."

"History how?" I asked as I took a look and saw the name Otto Van Hess.

"That there is an Austrian antique dealer slash collector who Rich has been involved with for a couple of years. As it turns out, Dale Rich appeared to make more money from his shady deals than he ever did from the legitimate ones." Jack pointed to the slip of paper in my fingers. "That is one of the men Rich ripped off when he stole a piece and resold it for a seven-figure profit."

"You're saying there's bad blood between them?"

"*Was*, yes," Jack confirmed, reminding me of recent events. "I'm not too versed in the finer details, but I'm sure Linda wouldn't take long gathering some info."

"I'll get her right on it." I refolded the slip of paper and dropped it into my shirt pocket.

I hung out with Jack for another hour or so before he had to call it quits and head home to feed his Labrador, Luke. Once back in my car, I messaged my investigator to see what she was up to and managed to get myself an invite over to her place, where she had just ordered some pizza. I arrived just in time to park in front of the delivery guy and followed him to the front door, smelling the pizza the entire way.

Linda waved me past her when she opened the door and dealt with the delivery guy. I grabbed a beer from the fridge and took it into the living room, where I dropped onto the couch and leaned back with my drink. That first bit of coolness rushing down my throat tasted a little too sweet, and I ended up guzzling at least half the bottle before pausing long enough to watch my investigator walk the pizza box into the room.

"Maybe check these out while you enjoy the fruits of my labor," Linda said with a smug grin as she walked past my spot on the couch and dropped a folder into my lap before setting the pizza box down on the coffee table. The smell of the food filled the room and pushed my sense of curiosity aside as I focused on the food. Cheese pizza was just what I had a taste for, and the first bite confirmed my craving.

"I just met with Jack down at the bar," I said as I pulled the slip of paper from my pocket and held it out to her. "I know you have plenty going on already, but do you think you could add this to your to-do list?" Linda glanced at the name, nodded, and set the note down beside her plate.

"Otto Van Hess?"

"Jack said he has a history with Rich and not the kind that brought them together for drinks, if you catch my drift."

"Potential suspect?"

I watched as Linda pulled a slice of the cheese pizza from the box, one strand stretching impossibly long before breaking loose and dangling in midair. She watched it pendulum back and forth a couple of times before catching it with one finger, winding it around a couple of times, and then slipping it into her mouth.

"Could be," I said as I reached for a second slice after demolishing the first in just a couple of bites. "Jack said there was definitely some bad blood between them but didn't elaborate. Said you'd have a better chance at finding out the gritty details."

"All right, I'll get on it," she said and pointed to the folder sitting on the couch beside me. "Got the phone records you asked for." She leaned forward and picked up something else off the table. "And this."

She got out of her chair and held up a thumb drive, which she maneuvered into the back of the television. Once she retook her seat, a few quick presses on the remote brought up the USB's menu.

"I also managed to get hold of some extra footage from nearby streets on the evening of the murder."

I watched as a couple of different displays filled all eighty-five inches of Linda's brand-new Samsung. Unfortunately, the city's security cameras hadn't been updated in years, which meant the footage failed to utilize the television's potential 4K display. Seven-twenty was about as good as it got, although the majority of the footage looked more like it had been filmed using a potato.

"Went out to six blocks as you asked and did manage to find this guy," Linda said after she fast-forwarded to a section some nine minutes in.

From what I could gather, she'd accumulated various feeds

and copied them all onto the one drive, which she navigated through. The feeds often changed from a single and dual display to sometimes showing four, six, and even eight different screens, depending on the source material. I watched as she hit play, and the screen again returned to just a single feed showing the mouth of an alley.

"Check this guy out," Linda said as she held the remote up, ready to hit the pause button. I watched, and a few seconds later, a hooded figure ran the length of the alley, quickly disappearing around a container behind a café. Aside from the fact that he was running and wearing the hood of his jacket over his head, I couldn't see anything else suspicious about him.

"What am I looking at?" I asked Linda.

"Aside from the fact he seems to be in an awful hurry?" She pointed to the screen. "That's Strawberry Way, just a few blocks from the murder."

"Going to need more than just a guy running."

"How about this?"

She pressed the fast-forward button, and I watched the feeds resume playing by at an increased pace, the display again shifting from a single screen to several before Linda paused it a second time.

"It took me a bit to find this, but watch," she said and pressed the Play button.

This time, the street displayed on the TV screen looked more familiar. I recognized it immediately due to the fountain taking up a large piece of real estate within Steel Plaza. Despite several people using the open space as a kind of thoroughfare, two people immediately stood out to me, and not because they were the only ones standing absolutely still nor because they appeared to be in some kind of face-off, standing some sixty feet apart on opposite ends of the plaza. No, the reason they immediately stood out to me was that I instantly recognized both of them.

The first wasn't too difficult to pick out since I'd only seen him a minute earlier wearing the same hoodie and jeans. The other person standing in the plaza was none other than my client, Corinne Lucas.

"Can we confirm that that's the same guy running out of the alley?"

"I've checked it a couple of times," Linda said. "I'm ninety-nine percent sure it's the same guy."

Corinne appeared to already be on the phone call to her ex-boyfriend, the call she claimed to have been on when entering the alley where Rich would eventually be murdered. As if reading my thoughts, Linda clarified them for me.

"The times check out according to the records I printed for you," she said. "Think these two know each other?"

We continued watching the scene unfold as each person suddenly began walking. When they got to within perhaps twenty to thirty feet of each other, they both turned in the direction of the upcoming murder scene, with the hooded mystery man taking the lead well ahead of Corinne before disappearing completely.

"Rewind it for me," I said once they both disappeared from view.

Linda did as asked. I watched the figures travel in reverse until they resumed their initial places, and when she restarted the scene, I got up out of my seat and moved closer to the screen for a better view. The resolution wasn't the best but definitely not the worst I'd seen during previous clips. Again, the scene played through to the point where both figures disappeared from view, and again, I still wasn't completely satisfied.

"And again, please," I asked of Linda, who did so without question.

There was something about the way Corinne appeared to move during the main thirty seconds of the clip that made me question whether our initial assessment had been the right one. While it might have appeared as if the two people knew each other, the more I looked at my client, the more I doubted my evaluation.

"Do you see the way she keeps shaking her head from side to side while talking?" I asked after gesturing for Linda to repeat the clip a third time. I even stepped closer to the TV so I could point out my observation specifically. "There, see that?"

"I do," Linda said. "She may not even be noticing him at all."

"But he's noticing *her*," I said, trying to get a closer view of the man but knowing I had zero chance considering the resolution of the feed, which must have been no greater than 480p.

"You think he's watching her?"

"I'm not sure," I said as Linda reset the scene one final time. I took a few steps back to try and get a broader view, and while it did help somewhat, I still couldn't get a clear enough view of the mystery man.

"Is there any more footage of this guy besides the two feeds that you found?"

"I've already gone through quite a lot of footage to no avail. These two clips appear to be the only ones that show him."

"So we have no idea where he came from or where he went after that little sprint through the alley?"

The question was purely rhetorical and not one I expected Linda to answer. She paused the feed just as Corinne disappeared from the screen, and I stared at a plaza frozen in time while I continued trying to picture the scene from a different perspective.

"What if this guy intentionally did what he did to try and implicate Corinne Lucas?"

"You mean specifically?"

I hadn't actually considered that far ahead, just more of a spit-ball kind of thought. In my mind, I wondered whether the killer had tried to find someone to take the heat. Not Corinne, but just anybody in general. The idea that he'd targeted my client specifically turned the thought process in an entirely new direction.

"Let's try to find a possible connection between Lucas and Rich that might give us some insight into a possible motive," I said as I returned to my seat.

"You mean in terms of her taking out a contract on him?"

"I'm not sure," I said, dropping onto the couch. "I'm thinking more along the lines of a third party wanting to get between them." I grabbed another slice of pizza, briefly held it in midair, and gave Linda my final thought. "Maybe someone like Hess wanting to rid himself of two rivals with a single crime."

SEVEN

THAT NIGHT, I WENT TO BED FEELING LIKE A MAN caught between two separate mysteries, each part of the same story and yet still substantial enough to be considered its own entity. On the one hand, I had a client accused of the heinous murder of a direct competitor of her business, a man who seemed caught up in a vast number of shady deals, which I still needed to investigate. On the other side, I had the curious man who'd hired me, a man who appeared to be almost as shrouded in mystery as the victim and yet one I somehow needed to trust if I wanted to get to the bottom of the matter.

Dreams weren't exactly a regular thing for me, but this was one night where they didn't hold back, and not just ones surrounding the new case. After I woke up around 2 a.m. from one rather forgettable sequence involving Linda walking down the same alley and attacking me with a knife, I went and grabbed myself a cold drink of water before heading back to bed for Round 2. What followed turned out to be a nightmare of epic proportions, one involving my late wife, Naomi, standing on the same street that had claimed her life years earlier, only this time tied to a lamppost with Dale Rich standing in front of her with a gun pointed at her face. The fact she was also heavily pregnant only added to the terror.

What followed was Naomi pleading for me to save her and our baby, her tears falling almost as hard as the torrential rain as the storm continuously lit up the night sky with ferocious lightning. The thunder would briefly drown out her pleas, each time shaking the ground hard enough to send me stumbling as I desperately tried to steady myself enough to reach her.

"Help me, Ben, pleeeeeease," she cried out, her limp body held up by the rope binding her to the post as her words rolled out again and again.

It was Rich's pistol firing that woke me up with a start. I sat bolt upright in an instant, trying to suck the air into my lungs while fighting to free my legs from the bedsheet wound around them. I half fell out of bed, still fighting to work out the dream from reality, but managed to stop myself from tumbling right off. The beating in my chest didn't begin to ease until I swung my legs out and dropped my feet to the floor.

"Oh, baby," I whispered into the silence of the apartment as the veil of sleep finally began to pull back far enough for me to sense the nightmare drawing back into the shadows.

Reality setting back in always left the same heaviness hanging over me, that same sense of dread when the truth reappeared, always proving the emotional anchor. Naomi's death, her real death, still hit just as hard each time it came back to me. I'm not sure how grief feels for others, but for me, it never quite disappeared completely. It's always there, even if just a step or two back from my attention. While the nightmares about it still hit hard, they pale in comparison to when that painful reality comes back to haunt me.

That morning, I cried about her death for the first time in

quite a while, the emotions proving too strong for me to ignore. In a way, it kind of felt good to finally let them out and not to worry about hiding them. It wasn't as if there was anybody around to witness my temporary breakdown. The morning shower proved to be my weakness. I think the sound of the water combined with that soothing heat stripped away what little resistance I had, and before I knew it, I'd dropped to my knees and began sobbing quietly to myself.

I regained my composure pretty quickly after I let a few tears mingle with the running water and, once out of the shower, got on with my day in the usual manner by following the standard morning routine. Breakfast didn't turn out to be an option, as I made myself a solitary coffee and drank it while scrolling through a few news articles. There wasn't really anything of interest to hold my attention for any significant time, and when I took the last sip, I shut off my cell phone, returned the cup to the sink, and grabbed my briefcase.

Grace was already at her desk when I walked into the office some thirty minutes later, and she greeted me with her usual smile.

"Good morning to you," she said, holding up a couple of envelopes. "Mr. Morris already phoned to ask whether he could see you this morning. Your 9:30 was canceled, so I offered him the spot. I hope that's OK."

"Thanks, Grace," I said, and that was when she tilted her head just enough to convey her curiosity. She didn't say anything per se, but the slight pursing of her lips told me that she recognized something about me that I wasn't about to elaborate on. She could see that I'd been crying.

"Want me to get you a coffee?" It was her way of checking whether I needed something more than just a regular good morning, a neutral ear, or a friendly shoulder to lean on. We'd been there before, of course, and I'd previously taken her up on the offer, but this was one day when I didn't need such support.

"No, I'm good, thanks," I said. "Think I'll go through some of the case notes before Morris shows up."

"OK, but let me know if you need anything."

"Thanks, Grace."

I considered shutting my office door once inside but figured it might give my assistant the wrong impression. Yes, I know it's a bit of overthinking on my part, but that's just me, always aware of the public image I'm portraying. Dropping into my chair, I opened my briefcase, took out the laptop, and set myself up for a quick hour of research before my first appointment. The problem was that Morris had already arrived in a proverbial sense, immediately taking up brain space from the moment Grace mentioned him.

It wasn't unusual for a client to want regular updates on the case, especially one so fraught with possibilities. However, wanting one so soon *and* in person wasn't normal. I'd worked plenty of murder cases during my years, although none quite in the same vein as this one. For one, I had never needed to keep a client in the dark about who had hired me in the first place, and I definitely hadn't felt as awkward about the whole thing either. Morris just felt like an entirely different kettle of fish, a man who I think needed his own secrets exposed. The problem was that I didn't have enough people to cover the extra work hours to do so, which was why I needed to keep my focus on the case itself.

The following hour blew by with me barely able to focus on anything else, those thoughts of Morris and the infinite possibilities dominating my mind. It was only when Grace announced his arrival that I finally managed to break free and deal with the man himself.

"Mr. Morris, good to see you again," I said as we shook hands, unsure of whether I actually meant what I said.

"Likewise, counselor," Morris said and took a seat.

"Can I get my assistant to get you a coffee or tea?"

"No, I'm good, thanks. I'm actually more interested in how the case is progressing."

"Well, it's still in its early stages, as I'm sure you know," I said as I retook my own seat. "The judge unfortunately denied us bail, so that definitely threw a wrench into the works, but we're—"

"Then I take it you haven't heard about the recent demise of one Marco De Baun," Morris said, effortlessly cutting me off midsentence.

"Marco who?" It wasn't a name I was familiar with.

"De Baun," Morris clarified. "He was a junkie found in possession of Dale Rich's personal items."

"Was?" It wasn't the question I wanted to ask, the overwhelming sense of déjà vu again washing over as I prepared for my secret client to again share some significant revelation with me.

"Police confronted him late yesterday afternoon, and after a very brief stand-off, they shot him dead."

"I'm sorry," I said, suddenly wondering whether this was how Morris kept a sense of remaining in control of things by making it seem as if he was the one pulling the strings, so to speak. "Dale Rich's items?"

"The man not only had Dale's Rolex and wallet in his possession, but he had also tried to use one of his credit cards just moments earlier. That was how they were able to find him in the first place. My source told me all it took was for one on-the-ball convenience store worker to summon authorities, and you now have a new lead to investigate."

The questions running through my mind came thick and fast, but again, Morris remained a few steps ahead of the game by foreshadowing them with the answers before I had a chance to ask.

"I have certain contacts down at the police station."

"Why didn't you just phone me with this information? Time is crucial in these types of cases" was all I could think to say.

"I only found out this morning and figured it would be easier to just come and see you for myself. Besides, I was only a couple of blocks away."

My mind again filled with a thousand questions, but instead of giving in to them, I focused on the only one that truly mattered, the one that I knew Morris would bring up next. When he did, I wondered whether he had the ability to read minds.

"I'm no expert, Mr. Carter, but I assume this information would be enough to warrant a meeting with the district attorney and getting the charges against Corinne dropped?"

"You assume correct, Mr. Morris," I said. "It's a call that I will be putting at the top of my agenda."

I lied, of course, although not completely. A call to the district attorney would definitely be on the cards, although not as quickly as Morris might have figured. There was no way I would be going to the DA blindly. First, I would confirm the information just relayed to me. Morris wasn't an idiot, and what he said next again made me question his ability to read minds.

"I suspect you're going to want to check out this information for yourself," he said with a smile and pushed himself out of the chair before holding his hand out to me again. "Why don't I get out of your hair so you can work this new lead?"

"Yes, thank you, I definitely will," I said and shook with him.

"Let me know if there's anything else you need," he said before turning for the door. Just before he reached it, Morris paused to look back at me. "And please remember to keep our business between us. Corinne must never know that it was me who engaged your services."

"She won't," I said. "That's a promise."

He stared at me for a few seconds as if trying to get a sense of deception from me, but my answer had been genuine. Whatever reservations I had about the man himself, I wasn't about to break our agreement.

"Good man," Morris finally said, and after turning back to the door, he disappeared through it, leaving me alone to get on with my next move.

The second I retook my seat, I reached for my cell phone, scrolled through the list of names in my contacts, and hit Call after navigating my way through to Jack. He answered after almost half a dozen rings. Not one to beat around the bush, he skipped the formalities.

"Ben, what's up?"

"Have you heard about this Marco De Baun?" I asked, not sure why I lowered my voice as if needing to hide the question. The only person who would have heard me was Grace, and she was the last person I kept secrets from, especially ones pertaining to a case.

"De Baun, De Baun," Jack repeated a couple of times. I could hear his fingers tapping on the keyboard of his computer. "The one who got himself shot yesterday?"

"A little bird just told me that he was in possession of Dale Rich's—"

"Wallet and Rolex," Jack finished. "Yes, I can see that on the report. Let me check things out and get back to you."

"Thanks, man," I said and hung up.

Twenty minutes was all Jack needed to confirm Morris's story for me, and when he texted me the bullet points of the matter, I knew I had a case to take up with the district attorney, a *significant* case at that. The first thing I did was to ask my assistant to arrange a meeting with Arthur Clements as soon as possible. Once Grace headed off to make the call, I texted Linda the latest update and asked her to add the name to her ever-growing to-do list. I also pondered the idea of hiring a second investigator to ease the pressure off Linda, but I already knew there was no way. If I knew my investigator, there would be no way she'd ever let me do such a thing.

She answered me just a few minutes later, acknowledged the message I had sent her, and returned a reply with a new name of her own: Bryce Lloyd. According to Linda, Lloyd worked with Corinne Lucas directly, and while I hadn't heard of the name before, it would turn out to be one I would eventually get to know a lot better than I could have imagined. Lloyd, as it turned out, was Corinne Lucas's business partner.

———

EIGHT

"I got you a meeting with District Attorney Clements at three this afternoon," Grace told me when she stuck her head in the door a short while later.

"Thanks," I said, already checking through more security footage, including the clip Linda had shown me with the hooded figure and my client in a kind of face-off, or what I still considered anything but.

The footage itself still didn't look any crisper on the smaller laptop screen, but I did manage to adjust the settings enough to make it *appear* clearer, or at least to me. Figuring it was my best bet, I saved the file to present to the DA, as well as the police report Jack had sent through a few minutes after confirming our initial call. Once I had my evidence ready, I turned my attention to other matters while waiting for the time to leave.

At precisely twenty minutes before three o'clock, I closed my laptop, popped it into the briefcase, and left the office.

"Want me to drive?" Grace asked when I reached her desk, and I gave her a nod.

"Sure," I said. "Thanks."

While I knew bringing Grace wasn't going to guarantee me any victory laps, I did know that my assistant was one of the few people who had a way of softening up our district attorney just with her presence. I don't think it was an attraction kind of thing but something deeper than that. The pair had no history, as far as I could tell, but I did notice Clements definitely toning down his aggression whenever Grace was around. This time, I hoped to use it to my advantage while trying to convince the prosecution to drop their charges against my client.

It only took Grace ten minutes to drive us the few blocks to the DA's office, and once inside, Clements' secretary had us take a seat in the waiting room. Grace took a seat near the front of the room while I remained standing nearby, the briefcase dangling lazily next to my leg as I watched the rest of the office continue on with its day. When Elsa Schwarz suddenly appeared and took a quick look at me, I resisted the urge to return her smile. As I did, I felt Grace look up at me while the prosecutor disappeared into the DA's office.

"Guess we know what she thinks of you," my assistant mumbled quietly up at me, and before I could answer back, the secretary cut in.

"Mr. Clements will see you now," she called out to us.

"Thank you," I said and turned for the open doorway.

Inside the office, Arthur Clements sat behind his desk looking down at some papers Elsa appeared to be explaining to him. I stopped a few feet back and patiently waited to be acknowledged, something I knew Clements would take his time with. It was just how he liked to play the game, always looking for some sort of intimidation tactic to use on adversaries.

"Mr. Carter, grab a seat," he finally said, not bothering to look up or even acknowledge Grace as he continued listening to the prosecutor's whispers. I exchanged a look with my assistant, but she remained steadfast, smiling with her usual warmth and taking her seat just the same. When he finally did look up at me, his expression lacked any hint of personality, holding on to a perfect poker face as he continued. "I've asked Ms. Schwarz to join us, considering she's now officially the lead prosecutor in this matter."

"How *is* Xavier?" I asked.

"As well as can be expected," Clements said, his tone rather indifferent as he immediately veered the course of the conversation back to the point of the meeting. "Now let's talk about Corinne Lucas."

"Yes, of course," I said and reached down for my briefcase.

"Twenty-five years is what we're prepared to offer your client for a guilty plea," Elsa Schwarz said before I had a chance to grab my laptop.

"Even with a new and much more likely suspect?" I asked, and Clements immediately fired back.

"You mean some random junkie the police shot after a confrontation?"

"First of all, that junkie had the victim's belongings in his possession at the time of said shooting," I said, finally pulling open my laptop and ready for a fight. Something about the DA's attitude just rubbed me the wrong way, and the tension in the room immediately skyrocketed.

"He could have picked those up anywhere," Clements said, cutting off his prosecutor as she tried to speak. "There's no proof he lifted them from the victim at the time of the murder. And there's no proof that Marco De Baun was anywhere near the murder scene at that time."

"Then explain this," I said, finally able to open the laptop and turn the screen to show them the vision I had of the potential face-off in the plaza. Clements and Schwarz exchanged a look when they saw it, and I couldn't help but detect a hint of snideness about him.

"That, Mr. Carter, is the reason you think we should release your client from custody?" Clements said, surprising me, but I wasn't about to lie down.

"This, Mr. Clements, shows a man who I believe to be Marco De Baun stalking my client before he went and murdered Dale Rich."

"How the hell do you figure that?" Clements asked.

"Because of this," I said and brought up a second window of a crime scene photo Jack had sent me just an hour earlier, one showing a gunned-down suspect wearing the exact same hoodie as the man in the plaza.

"What am I looking at?" Clements said at first, but after studying the scene for a few seconds, he changed his demeanor entirely. "I don't know what game you're playing, Carter, but this shows previous contact with your supposed random mugger, and that, if anything, proves *our* case more than yours," Clements almost snarled at me.

"I tend to disagree," I said, refusing to be intimidated by the escalation of volume.

It always made me laugh when someone figured that simply raising their voice enough would win an argument. While it might have worked on people lacking confidence, the district attorney should have known better than to try the tactic on me.

Clements hung on to his attitude. I noticed that he still hadn't acknowledged Grace in the slightest way, not even with the smallest of sideways glances. It was as if she wasn't even in the same room as us.

"The hoodie De Baun was wearing at the time of the shooting is the exact same one as the one the suspect was wearing in the plaza," I said, ignoring the DA's words. Clements began digging a thumb into one of his temples as he closed his eyes. From where I sat, he appeared frustrated. When he looked over at me again, I could see he wasn't convinced.

"A black Nike hoodie is hardly undeniable evidence proving this man murdered Dale Rich," Clements eventually said. "There must be thousands of that same hoodie in this city alone, let alone the greater state. What we do know is that a man wearing that same piece of clothing eyeballed your client minutes before the murder. We have footage showing your client entering the alley moments before the attack. And..."

Clements paused as he looked up at his prosecutor, and when Schwarz looked down at me, I felt something tighten in the pit of my stomach, a usual indication that somebody was about to drop a boat anchor into it.

"And then we have this," Clements continued when Schwarz handed him a file. He opened it, pulled out two sheets of paper, and held them out to me.

"What's this?" I said as I took them and glanced over each but not seeing any of the printed words.

"That is what we believe to be a motive for the killing," Schwarz said, finally able to make herself heard.

Looking at each sheet of paper closer, I saw a compressed photocopy of a lease on the first, the property looking to be an office in Philadelphia. The second appeared to be the official registration of a company, the name Broadbent Enterprises, not one I'd heard of before. It took me two scans of the page to confirm that I wasn't following its intended purpose. To indicate my lack of understanding, I looked over at both the DA and the prosecutor and shook my head. Schwarz filled me in.

"As you can see," he began, "Broadbent Enterprises recently signed a new lease for an office in downtown Philly. It took us a bit of investigating, but we managed to find that the owners of the business are, in fact, Dale Rich and Bryce Lloyd." Clements unclasped his hands and held them out in a what-now gesture. "Looks like your client's partner was about to share his bed with a new business associate, and given the already-tense relationship Rich and Corinne Lucas had, it definitely proves motive."

The second I heard the latter's name, I felt something cold run up my spine, the dread highlighting the familiarity of the name. Clements must have seen my reaction and grinned.

"Exactly," he said, more to himself than to me, before continuing. "My suggestion is for you to go back to your client, convince her to confess, and take the deal. We have a grieving family who wants answers, counselor. Dale Rich's girls deserve to know why they lost their father, and we intend to give them those answers."

That was when I sensed something more, something the DA wasn't saying but thinking. He appeared to try to hide it as best he could, but I saw through the façade. He looked like a card player holding an unbeatable hand and unable to hide the fact. In other words, his poker face sucked.

"You have something else, don't you?" I asked when the realization grew too strong for me to contain. I watched as Elsa and Clements exchanged a look with each other. "Come on, guys, don't be shy. You have something else."

It was Elsa who broke their silence. "We have a witness who claims to have seen your client arguing with Dale Rich moments before the murder."

"A witness? Who?"

"We will provide a full witness list in due course, counselor," Clements cut in, but Elsa continued.

"She's only just contacted us, Ben, but once we have a chance to speak with this witness in full, we will add her to the official list."

For the first time in a long time, I found myself unable to find the right words. I had been so sure of myself walking into the meeting that I'd totally ignored the possibility of finding myself blindsided by new evidence. It rattled me, and one look at my assistant showed that she could see it.

"Now if there's nothing else," Clements said, rising out of his chair as I handed the sheets of paper to my assistant, who took them. It was comical to watch the man try to lift all three hundred pounds of himself without looking like some walrus learning to skateboard. "Grace, always good to see you," he added, acknowledging her presence for the first time as I also stood.

"You too, Arthur," Grace said, offering him a smile before turning for the door. Clements immediately turned his attention back to me.

"I trust you'll deliver our offer to your client?"

"I certainly will, but I can almost guarantee her answer," I said, not bothering to finish the rest of the sentence.

Only once we were sitting back in Grace's BMW did I speak again, my frustrations ready to boil over.

"Damn it, Grace, she lied to me." I ran splayed fingers through my hair and tried to block the world out. "How can she lie about something so important?"

"Maybe she's just scared and trying to protect herself." I heard my assistant but couldn't process the words on account of my anger.

"This is what happens when a client doesn't understand

the importance of sharing everything with their lawyer," I said as I clicked the seatbelt into place. "I definitely didn't see that coming."

"Want me to take you to the jail?" She checked her watch. "Still enough time for a visit."

"No, I'll go first thing in the morning," I said, figuring it best to hold the interview when not pressed by time. With the jail's visiting hours almost up, I wouldn't have enough time to fully work my client over, and I knew I needed more than just a few minutes.

"OK, then," Grace said, pulling the car out of the parking lot and into the late afternoon traffic. It wasn't long before we found ourselves swamped by the usual snarl, although I barely noticed.

Once back at the office, I didn't bother heading back inside. Instead, I thanked Grace for the ride and asked if she would be OK with me heading off for the rest of the afternoon.

"I'll go and see Lucas before I come in in the morning," I also said. "Maybe see if you can dig up everything you can about this Broadbent Enterprises."

"Yes, of course," she said while locking her car.

Grace gave me a final wave before she disappeared inside while I jumped into the Mustang and sat there with the engine idling for a few minutes, contemplating my next move. Staring into the space between my windshield and the building's outer wall, I wondered just what my client was really holding back and whether she would ultimately be the one to determine her own fate.

When I did finally pull out of the parking lot, I called my investigator to share the details of the meeting with the DA. Linda answered on the very first ring, and it took her all of my first sentence to ascertain my mood.

"Someone doesn't sound happy at all," she said, and I gripped the steering wheel tightly enough for a couple of my knuckles to pop.

"Damn it, Linda, she *lied* to me. She *did* make contact with Dale Rich in that alleyway."

"What? Are you sure?"

"The prosecutor has a witness who claims to have seen Lucas arguing with Rich moments before the murder." I shook my head in frustration while slowing for a red light. "This is going to sink us. And then throw in the newly opened company owned by Lloyd and Rich?" I gazed at the taillights of the car in front and imagined the scene in the alleyway. "The DA is building one hell of a case, and my client continues to try to pull the wool over my eyes."

"I'll look into this witness. See what I can find out."

"Thanks," I said and ended the call.

I don't know if my frustrations eased during that long drive through traffic, but it did keep my mind occupied. I pictured the argument between my client and the victim a thousand different ways and yet still couldn't picture her stabbing him fourteen times. The only plausible scene I could come up with was one where a mugger took over the second Corinne Lucas left the area. If he had, then I needed a lot more than just circumstantial evidence to make my case.

NINE

I WOKE UP THE NEXT MORNING WITH A FEELING I hadn't experienced in a very long time. The day first greeted me with a nauseating drumming in my head, each pulsing stretching down into the pit of my stomach as I remembered the empty bottle of whiskey still sitting on the coffee table in my living room. Hangovers weren't really something I'd ever had to face in my past, and yet that morning, it felt like hell had decided to pay me a visit.

I'd barely managed to roll my ass out of bed before I felt the unmistakable sensation of saliva filling my mouth, the urge to move my legs almost secondary to the panic that gripped me. The body has a funny way of protecting itself, more so when faced with the prospect of vomiting onto a porcelain-tiled floor, and I barely managed to cover the half-dozen strides from my bed to the toilet bowl before my stomach unleashed its contents.

Hot, rancid puke gushed into the crystal clear water as I closed my eyes, content to let both gravity and the convulsions do their thing. The fluid burning my insides on the way out only added to the misery, and I wondered whether giving in to the late-night grief had been worth it. Visions from the previous evening returned while the sound of my vomit hitting the toilet water all but faded out.

I'd stopped off at the dry cleaners on the way home from the office the previous afternoon and picked up a couple of suits I'd dropped off earlier in the week. It was while stuffing them into the closet that I spotted the shoebox sitting on the top shelf. I knew I should have just pushed it back to where it normally lived. At the time, I wasn't even sure why it had moved to the front of the shelf anyway. It wasn't as if we'd had an earthquake roll through Pittsburgh, rattling it out from the spot between a couple of other boxes.

The shoebox held what I like to think of as keepsakes. Naomi used to call it her memory box, an old Nike box she kept years before to store all her little memories in. We're not talking souvenirs or mementos here, or at least not the kind you buy in an airport store. No, these keepsakes went a lot deeper than that. She once took me through the contents of the box when I first questioned the validity of the items. A brief giggle was her only answer before opening it up and systematically taking me through each and every piece in turn, some of the items coming from moments she had shared with none other than me.

One of the more outlandish items she showed me was this small black rock, or pebble, if you will, which she held up between us and stared at with that distant look of hers.

"This came from the top of that mountain we hiked when we visited the Grampians during our vacation to Australia," she said, her words almost fading out before she finished. "It was so hot that day, remember?" I nodded, remembering only too well how close I'd felt to getting heat stroke. The funny thing is, it had been my idea to do the hike in the first place, and she was the one who ended up convincing me to continue to the top despite the scorching temperature.

There was the broken seashell from Miami, the Asahi beer bottle top from Tokyo, and a plain packet of sugar from a diner in Oklahoma. We're talking movie ticket stubs, theater programs, train tickets, all random pieces where each held the power to invoke a rush of memories, each a powerful relic from a life that had ultimately been extinguished far too early.

I had spent the entire previous evening going through that box, eventually needing a stiff drink to help me through the majority of those memories. With the anniversary of her death fast approaching, it proved to be a definite weakness on my behalf. Normally, I would have simply pushed the box back, but not last night. Last night, something had propelled my fingers to grab the edge of it and pull it down, the same energy moving me to the couch, where I summarily went through each item one at a time, holding it long enough to remember the circumstances around it coming home with us.

The bottle of whiskey had been exactly two shots from full when I took my first drink, and when I eventually stumbled the short distance from the couch to the bed several hours later, the same bottle lay empty on its side. Perhaps I didn't feel as intoxicated as I was because of the raw emotions running through me, but I can assure you that the bottle of liquor had done its job. I was drunk, and sleep took me the moment my head touched the pillow.

For some reason, hangovers had never been much of a weakness for me, not even after multiple wild escapades during my younger years in college. Regardless of how crazy the night was and the amount of alcohol I consumed, I would always wake up fit and alert the next morning. Not so this time. This time, all the fabled gods of Hangover City came calling, bringing with them the kind of misery only spoken about in urban legends. I swear my head felt ready to explode, the rhythmic thumping pulsating throughout the entirety of my body.

Only when I was absolutely sure that my stomach had emptied itself and the muscle spasms disappeared completely did I dare try to get to my feet. At first, I hung on to the toilet tank to steady myself, and once I felt more confident, I pressed the button and watched the soupy mess swirl into the abyss.

"Never again, Carter," I mumbled to myself while climbing into the shower, and when the cool jets of water hit me, I closed my eyes and prayed for mercy.

It took all of my energy to remain standing in the shower stall, and at one point, I reached up with both hands and gripped the pipe of the shower head for support. The cold water actually helped a lot, and after a few minutes, I felt the intensity of the head-pounding actually subside slightly. When I climbed back out a few minutes later, I popped a few painkillers with the hope they'd take care of the rest. Thankfully, they managed to work their magic, and by the time I walked into the jail an hour later, the headache had all but disappeared.

"You look like I feel," Corinne Lucas said once her escort left the room and closed the door, dashing any hopes I had that my measures to try and hide my condition had worked.

"Just a long night," I said, forcing a smile that didn't quite rise to the occasion. "How are things with you?"

"As well as could be, I guess," Corinne said, and that was when I noticed the bruise beside her right eye.

"What happened?"

"Just a disagreement with my cell door." I pursed my lips

and tilted my head slightly to show that I wasn't buying it. "It actually was, I promise."

"For real?"

"Yes, for real," she said. "Wasn't watching where I was going and boom, walked straight into it. Hurts like a son of a bitch, too," she said, forcing her own grin that appeared a lot more convincing than mine.

"We have a problem, and I'm not talking about the obvious."

"What sort of problem?" She looked at me curiously, but I couldn't detect any hint of attempted deception.

"The kind of problem that involves a client lying to her lawyer," I said, refusing to sugarcoat the issue.

"Ben, I swear—"

"Save it," I snapped and held a hand up to silence her. "The prosecutor claims to have a witness who saw you arguing with Dale Rich in the alley moments before the murder."

Corinne's jaw dropped open just enough to convey surprise. Her lips briefly moved as if searching for words, but none came.

"I told you from the very beginning how important it was for you to tell me everything... *everything*...about what you know."

For a second, she didn't react, the same look of surprise remaining on her face as I let the silence hang over us. The sound of a door slamming somewhere beyond the walls of our room briefly pierced the air but disappeared again just as quickly. I waited for her to close her mouth again before asking the most obvious question.

"Is there a witness?"

When Corinne finally answered, she did so with a voice

that was barely audible. If it hadn't been for the near-perfect silence, I might not have heard her words at all.

"I was scared they'd pin the murder on me."

I closed my eyes at hearing her confirmation. She saw me and reacted accordingly with the kind of panic that had probably compelled her to lie in the first place. "I knew that if I told them about seeing him, then they would immediately think I killed him based on our history alone. It wasn't as if we were strangers, Ben."

She didn't bother trying to keep her voice down, the panic driving the volume of her voice in the opposite direction. Tears of fear and realization fell from her eyes as the truth reared its ugly head.

"Yes, I spoke with him, and yes, it wasn't exactly a pleasant interaction. I was already angry thanks to that idiot boyfriend of mine, and when Dale goaded me from where he stood, I reacted."

"Goaded you how?" When she didn't answer me, I decided to keep probing. "Corinne, who is Bryce Lloyd?" She paused when she heard the name and looked at me curiously before answering. The tears shut off almost immediately.

"My business partner," she eventually said. "Bryce handles a lot of the more clerical stuff for me. Why do you ask?"

"Because the prosecutor has information showing your partner setting up what could be considered a competing business with Dale Rich," I said and waited for her reaction.

"What?" She looked genuinely shocked by the revelation. "That's impossible. There's no way Bryce would do such a thing to me. How did…"

"How did they find out?" I pulled the evidence the prosecutor had handed to me from my briefcase and slid it across the table.

"See for yourself," I said and watched her eyes run across the page before looking back over at me.

"I don't care what they say. There is no way Bryce would betray me like this. He knows how I feel about Dale Rich, and he wouldn't do this to me."

"That's not all the evidence they shared with me," I said. "There is also footage of you standing in Steel Plaza moments before the murder on your cell phone. Do you remember a man watching you? A man wearing a black hoodie?" She didn't hesitate to answer.

"You mean the guy begging for money?"

"Begging for money?" It wasn't what I expected her to say.

"Yeah, the guy asking me if I had ten bucks I could spare. I didn't answer him, of course. The one thing I've learned over the years is that ignoring those kinds of people will often stop them in their tracks."

"You're sure that's all he asked for? Can you describe his appearance?"

"I didn't really pay attention at the time," she said with a shake of the head. "The hood covered most of his face, and I don't think a bearded chin is going to give the cops much of a lead."

"A bearded chin? That's all you remember?"

"A beard is all I saw, Ben. Honest. White guy, brownish beard, that's all I can share."

I wanted to shake my head in frustration but resisted the urge. Instead, I took back the sheet of paper and dropped it into the briefcase.

"Tell me about Bryce Lloyd and why he would feel a need to go into business with your competitor."

"You don't believe me," she said, this time dropping her eyes to look at her fingers as they wrestled with each other.

"Look, Corinne, I've said this before. Holding things back from your lawyer isn't the smartest move right now. You're facing serious prison time, and if you ever hope to—"

"Damn it, Ben, I already—"

"AND IF YOU EVER," I said, amplifying my voice above hers before silently staring at her while letting the echoes of my words fade out. I continued after a few seconds of uncomfortable silence. "If you ever hope to see the outside of a jail cell again, then you need to tell me everything, and I mean *every-thing* there is to know about your life, including your business, your secrets, and everything in between. I should have known about the interaction with Dale during our first meeting, but instead I found out about it from the prosecutor. How do you think that makes you look when they can see you holding things back from your own lawyer?"

For a moment, we sat there, draped in complete silence again, me watching Corinne as she continued staring at her fingers. I could almost hear the cogs and wheels working inside her head, her brain assessing my request and trying to find the right words to throw at me. Personally, I think she was just a victim of her own persona, a fiercely private woman thrown into the limelight while facing a sink-or-swim dilemma, the sinking part also meaning the end of her life.

"I understand this is hard for you," I said, lowering my voice to a far more empathetic level. "It feels like the world is watching, and every move you make could be manipulated."

"I feel so alone," she suddenly said, her words barely above a whisper. "It's a strange sensation considering I spend the majority of my days on my own anyway." She looked across at me for the briefest of seconds before lowering her eyes again. "I guess it's one of the upsides of working predominantly online." She grinned. "Or maybe it's a downside. The only time I have to deal with people is when I'm actually showing a piece that the client requests to see. For the most part, it's just online communication."

"You don't have a gallery where you display the pieces?"

"Yes, but it's not an open walk-in kind of gallery. It's by appointment only, which means I'm limited to those moments when I have to meet a client face to face, which wasn't often, as I did most of our buying over the Internet."

"What about Lloyd? Did he ever deal with clients face to face?"

"Yes," she said with a shake of the head. "Bryce is the face of the company, if you will, a genuine salesman with the charm to go with it. He has the contacts and the industry connections to help us move some valuable artifacts."

"So I'm guessing that without him, you'd have a hard time keeping your business afloat," I said, thinking out loud.

"Lloyd is a valuable asset to the company, yes, of course, but he isn't the be-all and end-all, if that's what you mean."

It wasn't that I was trying to make her feel bad, which is how I think she took it. Instead, I was trying to think of the situation from the prosecutor's point of view. They already had the information that Bryce Lloyd had effectively signed up with Dale Rich, and if they figured Lloyd to be a critical part of my client's company, then it would only confirm the smoking gun they already claimed to hold.

"What would you have done if you did find out that Lloyd joined your competitor?"

"He didn't," Corinne snapped back at me.

"I know, but let's just pretend he did," I said, maintaining a controlled tone. "How would you have proceeded?"

She looked at me with a near-vacant expression as if not understanding the question. I waited for her to answer, and when she saw I wasn't about to change the question, she sighed loudly.

"It's not something I've ever actually thought about, Ben. Bryce has been a valuable partner of mine for many years, and I've never considered him betraying me."

"Tell me what you know about a man named Otto Van Hess." I could see by her reaction that she knew the name. "Is he someone your business partner dealt with as well?"

"No, Otto was *my* client, not Bryce's." It didn't surprise me to learn that she knew the name. "I've sold Otto several pieces in the past. He's what you might call a flipper."

"Flipper?"

"When it comes to his personal collection, Otto is what you might describe as a kid with ADHD. He can never hold on to pieces for very long. What interests him today will bore him tomorrow, and so he tends to resell a lot of his pieces when he grows tired of them."

"From what I've been told, Hess also knew Dale Rich. Is that correct?"

Corinne grinned back at me, but the expression lacked any humor. "The way I heard it, Otto hired someone to steal a recently excavated piece of Roman pottery from a dig site in southern Italy. Quite an *expensive* piece, I might add."

"How expensive?" I asked.

"Well, let's just say that when Dale Rich hired his own thief to steal it from Otto's thief, he ended up selling it to a client for one point three five."

"One point three five *million*?" Corinne nodded as if the number was just a throwaway one. "And they got away with it? The authorities never caught up with them?"

"Aside from the actual find, none of it was official. The numbers are merely a rumor, but I have a trusted source who assured me that was the sum Dale Rich received. As far as the rest of the world is concerned, that particular piece is considered missing, and nobody is quite sure where it is right now."

"That's a lot," I said. "No wonder he and Van Hess had a falling out."

"That wasn't the only time the two had crossed paths, but it certainly was the most expensive transaction."

I shook my head in disbelief, and while we continued talking for almost twenty minutes more, the rest of the conversation paled in comparison to the stolen piece sold by Dale Rich. I did feel a little disjointed walking out of the jail after our conversation, having not received the answers I was looking for, but in hindsight, it did steer me in an entirely new direction, one that would ultimately open up a fresh set of leads.

TEN

Yes, I should have gone into the office when I finished interviewing my client at the jail, but the truth is, my mind still hadn't returned to its usual switched-on state. The case should have been at the forefront of my mind, but the reality for me was that there was something much more powerful drawing my attention away in another direction, a direction sitting way back in my past.

I first sent Grace a quick message advising her that I had finished my visit to the jail and had another errand to run. *No problem* were the only words she texted back to me, and I turned the Mustang in the direction of a place I knew I'd eventually end up anyway, especially with the approaching anniversary. The cemetery proved to be one of the few places where I didn't feel guilty about letting my grief run wild. I actually grinned, thinking back to the one counselor who'd managed to break through the walls on the subject. It was because of what Tanner Bowden had told me on the subject that I no longer struggled with trying to contain my emotions.

"Crying is nothing more than a release valve for the soul,"

was how he'd put it, and his words just resonated with me in a way no others had before.

Despite all of the raw emotion coursing through my body, not a single tear fell during that drive to the cemetery. Don't get me wrong; I expected to feel the familiar dampness in the eyeballs, followed by that delicate tickle of a tear or two tracing a neat line down my face, but none came. Instead, I felt my teeth gnashing against each other as I watched the traffic ahead of me, occasionally reacting to brake lights popping on and off as if on autopilot. Only when I eventually turned off the main road and pulled into the graveyard's near-empty parking lot did I feel the familiar lump in my throat shift position.

Once I found a space and killed the engine, I sat there in silence for a few moments and just stared out into the nothing-ness filling the void between me and the gates. A couple stood next to a Toyota Camry parked a few spaces closer to the entrance than I was while talking with someone sitting in the driver's seat, but I barely noticed them. My mind still struggled to ease the grip it had on the rest of my senses, that vise-like hold hanging on for dear life.

It took a few deep breaths for me to ease the beating in my chest enough to open the driver's side door and climb out. The Camry's taillights indicated the vehicle's intention to reverse, and I made sure to cross well before it pulled out of its spot. The couple I had seen earlier standing by the vehicle's side had magically disappeared, and looking both ways along the ceme-tery's front, I saw no trace of them. A vision of them being ghosts began to play through my mind as I walked through the gates, and I had to stop myself grinning when I pictured them heading back to their respective plots and lying back down in their eternal resting places.

"There's no such thing as ghosts," I whispered to myself

just as I reached the first few rows of graves, and that was when a different voice cut in, this one also familiar to me as being the voice of reason. "Oh yeah? Then why do I sit at my wife's grave talking to her for hours on end?" The question came out so suddenly that I nervously looked around to see if anybody living had heard it. Thankfully, I couldn't see anybody and so continued walking, reminding myself to keep the whispering to a minimum, although the voice did make a good point.

By the time I reached Naomi's grave, all questions and answers had faded away completely. After giving her headstone its ceremonial kiss, I stepped over to my usual sitting place and dropped to my knees, where I took a moment to reflect on the location. As if summoned by the dead, or perhaps even the living, the sun emerged from behind a rather ominously dark cloud and immediately lit up a large portion of the cemetery. The brightness felt particularly concentrated around the spot where I sat before my wife. I looked up at the sky, closed my eyes, and let the warmth build on my skin, enjoying the moment, which I took as a sign from beyond.

"I'm glad to see you, too," I whispered as a rogue gull began screeching furiously somewhere over by the tree line. It faded out just as quickly when I opened my eyes again, and I looked upon the picture of my wife staring back at me from her headstone.

At first, the words refused to play ball, and I just sat there staring at the image while my brain continued throwing forth random images for me to process. Visions from the day she died, the morning she shared her pregnancy, the night when we first kissed, all intermingled into a whirlwind of grief. It all seemed to hit me at once, and I felt the lump in my throat slowly slide down until it filled a heavy void in my chest. The sensation felt all too familiar, but I barely managed to tighten my emotional response to avoid the tears when something interrupted me. Movement caught my eye, a blur of energy running straight at me before a warm drooling tongue began bashing my face from multiple directions. I tried to fight the attacker away, but the speed of my hands paled in comparison to the four-legged intruder.

"Jonesy, what the..." a voice cried out somewhere beyond my scope of attention. The dog continued bathing me in slobber despite my attempts to push it away, and at one point, visions of my face on the six o'clock news crept in, the anchor sharing details of a vicious and fatal dog attack. It wasn't until the stranger finally pulled his animal off me that I saw why it had broken free in the first place.

"Mister, I'm so sorry," the stranger said with a grin that conveyed embarrassment over humor. "He just forgets his size sometimes."

"I can see why," I said as I watched the man struggle to pull the excited St. Bernard out of reach.

The man trying to control the beast looked to be about half its size and was definitely not a picture of strength and stability. Instead, he could have fitted a saddle to his animal and looked half normal riding it like a horse. He stood at no more than five feet tall, his arms trying to keep the dog under control, shaking with visible exertion.

"Fabian Telford," he suddenly said and leaned forward as he let go of the leash with one of his hands to shake with me. Seizing the opportunity the second he sensed an opening, the drooling behemoth again lunged toward me, this time adding several excited barks to his attack. Telford immediately pulled back his hand and tried to regain control.

"Ben Carter," I said with a bemused grin and stepped forward enough for the dog to reach me so as to reduce the strain on the owner's arms. I let Jonesy jump up and put his paws on my shoulders, closing my eyes as the tongue went to work.

"I'm so sorry," Telford repeated with an added laugh and stood by as his dog bathed my face with slobber.

It took a few minutes to happen, but once Jonesy got his fill of fresh human, he finally dropped back down on all fours and sat. Telford watched as his dog simply stared at me, perhaps confused by the lack of retaliation.

"Sometimes it's easier just to play along," I said as I began to wipe the moisture from my face with the back of my arm.

"You have a dog?"

"No, but I grew up with one just as excitable as yours," I said. "Maybe not as big, but definitely as enthusiastic."

"I do have to apologize, though. I know this isn't the place to have a crazy mutt run free, annoying people trying to grieve in silence, but it's just that I like to bring Jonesy to come along to visit my son for his birthday." He looked over his shoulder and tried to point to one of the rows near the back, but the leash only gave him so much room to play with. I also noticed his face tightening at the mention of his son.

That was when a few pieces seemed to all fall into place at the same time. Something about the man's name had already stirred up a small sense of familiarity, as had his face, but when he mentioned his son, the final piece brought the other two together.

"Wait, you're not Fabian Telford the comedian, are you?" He managed to hold both hands up and out in front in a kind of surrender and grinned widely enough to show teeth.

"Guilty as charged." He looked around as if searching for eavesdroppers, and then whispered, "but this is my day off, so don't tell anyone."

"I promise I won't," I said, lowering my voice to match the volume of his and then with a normal tone, I added, "although I doubt the mob would attack you in this place."

"Ha," Telford blurted out with genuine amusement. "You'd be surprised."

"Really?"

"I can show you newspaper articles contradicting your belief, Mr. Carter."

"Ben, please," I said. "Really?"

"Absolutely, but maybe that's a story for another time." He tried to take a step back as if retreating, but Jonesy's lack of support kept the step to a minimum. Telford ignored it and pointed to Naomi's grave. "I'll let you get back to your loved one."

"Thank you," I said, honestly appreciating the gesture.

After another couple of strenuous tugs, the man who had managed to build an entire comedic career on making fun of his own small stature finally convinced his canine friend to retreat with what dignity it had left. Jonesy gave one last attempt to rebel but lacked the same kind of conviction as previous tries. I watched the pair walk off, but after less than half a dozen strides, Telford stopped just as suddenly and looked over his shoulder.

"Why don't you come and check out my next show?" he said as he reached into his pocket and fumbled around for a bit. He eventually pulled out a couple of what looked like business cards and held them out as he tried to take a couple of steps back toward me.

"Thank you, I will," I said when I closed the distance to save him from trying to change the dog's direction and accepted the offering.

"I'm on stage this weekend, in fact." He grinned again

before adding, "Bring a friend," which he accompanied with a finger pointing at me.

This time, when he turned, Jonesy showed no sign of disobeying, and I watched Telford head back to where I assumed his son's final resting place to be. When I returned to my previous position sitting on my butt before Naomi's grave, I looked at the cards in my hand and found the same man staring up at me with the very same grin on his face. What I saw in that grin wasn't amusement or happiness but rather something else entirely. It was empathy that I had found in that grin, the same emotion I'd felt during our current chat.

Curiosity got the better of me, and I pulled out my cell phone to try to answer the lingering question dominating my thoughts. It took me only a few seconds to find the answer I was looking for; the first news report was enough to share the details. Telford's nine-year-old son, Zac, had died just a few days after Naomi in a hit-and-run. Chills ran through me as I continued reading the story. The similarities between his tragedy and my own ran almost in parallel, with more than a couple of details eerily familiar. The single father fought with authorities for months trying to find the person responsible for his child's death, but to no avail.

When I saw Telford walk past some thirty minutes later, he only offered me a brief wave and a suppressed smile. I returned the gesture with a wave of my own, adding a slight nod of the head, and watched until he disappeared from view. A few minutes after disappearing, a final bark from Jonesy came from somewhere in the parking lot, and I imagined the man trying to get the beast into his car, the scene just another comedy routine in his day. I could have stood to check and watch them for myself, but I remained seated.

While Telford and his slobbering companion may have

given me a bit of a distraction, there was no getting away from the reason for my visit. The weight in my chest might have faded for a few brief moments, but now that I was alone again, it returned just as quickly. A distraction wasn't what I had come for. This visit had been one I needed to do, perhaps for a lot longer than I'd believed, and now that I was there, words had to be spoken, although I'll keep them to myself. There are just some things that need to remain between a husband and wife.

ELEVEN

Linda contacted me a couple of days after my visit to the cemetery, asking if I wanted to meet her for lunch down at Vinny's, one of the city's premier hot dog vendors. I agreed, of course. Not only did I need an update from my investigator, but the idea of a footlong with mustard proved impossible to turn down, and so I headed down to the river-front around one.

The day wasn't exactly spectacular, given the thick blanket of clouds I'd woken to, but the rain that had fallen for most of the morning appeared to have tapered off completely. By the time I climbed out of my car early that afternoon, most of the dampness had already disappeared, and I was sure that a few rays of sunshine might actually break through at some point.

"Hey, boss," Linda called out to me from where she sat on a park bench, tying a rogue shoelace. She didn't look up but rather gave me a brief wave before she quickly returned to taking care of business.

"You just get here?" She looked sweaty and was dressed in

the kind of clothes people generally ran in, which gave me the idea she'd already been there for some time.

"Nah, went for a jog. Had an hour to kill." Finishing wrestling the lace, she stomped the shoe on the ground as if to wake the foot inside up and stood. "Should have come earlier. We could have gone together."

"Wish I could have," I said, which wasn't a lie. "Had a meeting with a client."

"Maybe next time."

"Yes, maybe." I pointed to where a couple of people stood waiting in front of the Vinny's food cart. "Hungry?"

"Starving. Skipped breakfast and probably shouldn't have."

"Well, make up for it with lunch," I said and began walking toward the vendor.

"Got some info on Hess, if you want it."

"Anything worthwhile?" When she didn't answer, I slowed and turned to look at her. The eye roll she gave me indicated something juicy. "That good, huh?"

"Let's just say the man's no stranger to the authorities."

"An antiques dealer?"

"More like a cartel leader," Linda said, lowering her voice as a couple walking their husky went by. She stopped and eyed them until they had pulled ahead a bit before continuing. "Got himself quite an operation. Suspected of smuggling everything from art to cash and everything in between."

"Oh, so a regular Al Capone, then," I said. "And has *he* ever been convicted of anything?"

"Not Hess personally, no, but plenty of people working for him have."

We reached the food cart before she had a chance to continue, and once the former customers cleared, I waved her forward and let Linda order before me. We both watched the vendor do his thing in silence, my own insides already growling a low rumble in anticipation of what was to come. Neither of us opted for any of the fancy condiments, preferring plain old mustard and nothing else.

We took our food back to the original bench where I had found Linda sitting when I'd first arrived and proceeded to take care of the food, again in silence. There's just something about sitting out in the open air, consuming food and watching life pass by. Each of us sat within our own bubble, much like the cars passing by before us, containing their drivers, each encapsulated within a temporary existence that separated them from the rest of the world, if only for a provisional moment in time.

It may have taken less than ten minutes to eat our lunch, but to me, those ten minutes were well spent. What traffic there was barely registered, and it was great to spend the time not thinking about the case or the rest of the world. We could have talked, I guess, but I think Linda appreciated the silence as much as I did and didn't speak again until she'd swallowed her last mouthful.

"I need to come here more often," she said while wiping a bit of mustard from her chin with the napkin.

"You and me both," I replied and washed the final bit down with the last of my Coke. "Can't put a price on a decent bit of solitude."

"My thoughts exactly."

"Tell me something," I said. "This million-dollar deal Dale Rich apparently stole from Hess."

"You're going to ask me if I think it may have been enough to get the man murdered."

"Something like that, yeah," I said as an ambulance with lights flashing zipped past. Linda also watched it fly by and didn't respond until it disappeared from view.

"I've already tried to see if any of Hess's other competitors met with suspicious endings, but from what I can tell, the only foul play I could find was the non-lethal kind, if you get my meaning."

"No mysterious disappearances then?"

"Some serious intimidation, sure, but no murders, I'm afraid."

I'd seen an image of Hess and couldn't ignore the striking resemblance to the former owner of Microsoft, albeit without the glasses. I imagined Hess to be a man nervous while standing in a stiff breeze, his body not the kind capable of athletic feats. He looked more like a pen pusher, a man prone to use his brain over brawn.

"What about hired muscle?" I asked. "Surely he's using some? Maybe one of them could be capable of killing Rich."

"Capable, maybe, but there'd still have to be an order from Hess," Linda said, "and I'm not finding anything to indicate that he might give that kind of order."

"Keep looking," I said, shaking my head. "I'm not convinced that Lucas had him killed. Anything on this witness the DA claims to have found?"

"The one claiming to have seen your client arguing with the victim? No, nothing yet. I'm assuming it might have been someone from the Chinese restaurant, but I need more time."

"You got it," I said and leaned back on the bench.

I felt confused...scattered, almost. My brain just didn't seem connected with the case, almost as if too much had been going on. Too many things had already happened since Morris walked into my office and handed me the case. I felt like the bits of information Grace and Linda had already found and given to me just didn't connect. I saw everything from the middle of a storm, with most of the information whipping past in a few brief seconds before disappearing again and being replaced by something else.

"I need a reset," I suddenly said.

"You OK?"

I looked at Linda sitting at the other end of the bench as she stared at me through her Ray-Bans, the eyes barely visible behind the dark lenses.

"I'm fine," I said. "Just a few things on my plate, that's all."

"Been to the cemetery yet?" I briefly grinned. The woman didn't miss a thing and, having been with me for a number of years, knew the time of year and what it did to me.

"A couple of days ago, yes." That was when I remembered the tickets handed to me by a certain comedian. "Hey, you want to go check out a show with me?" She raised her eyebrows with surprise.

"Are you asking me out on a date?"

"No, silly. It's just that I met this guy at the cemetery, and he gave me some tickets to a show." I didn't think it was possible, but the eyebrows raised a little higher.

"You *met* someone?"

"Not like that," I said and jokingly slapped her leg. "This guy's dog attacked me while I was sitting with Naomi, and he turned out to be Fabian Telford."

"Get out of town, for real? Man, I love that guy."

"Yes, for real. Got two tickets for this Saturday night. One's yours, if you want it."

"Hell yes, I'll come. Thanks."

"Don't mention it. I'll pick you up around seven."

We changed the direction of the conversation back to one involving more familiar names like Bryce Lloyd and Otto Van Hess, the thirty-five-year-old Bill Gates clone, but other than me sharing information told to me by Corinne Lucas, there wasn't much else to talk about. Linda promised to continue looking into both men and would update me accordingly. With not much left to say, I thanked her for the information, and after we exchanged a fist bump, we each climbed into our respective vehicles.

When I got back to work, I asked Grace to join me in my office, and once inside, we closed the door. I took off my jacket, loosened my tie, and took a seat.

"How was lunch?" Grace asked from her side of the desk.

"Just as good as ever," I said, dropping into my chair. "But I think I found an issue that needs some attention."

"An issue?"

"I need to go back to basics with this case, Grace. I feel like a lot of the information is nothing more than disconnected bits. My brain just isn't processing it the way it should."

"I was wondering how long it would be before Naomi's anniversary would hit you."

If you ever find yourself wondering what makes a great workplace, let me give you a bit of advice. It's not the money, although that part is nice. It's not the perks or the benefits. Hands down, it's the people. In all my years of working, nothing has ever felt more genuine than the people I worked with since joining Grace and Dwight's firm. They were my family.

"I wasn't sure you'd..." I stopped, suddenly aware that the next words might sound more like an insult. "Of course you remembered," I said instead.

"Dwight asked about it this morning. He wondered whether you might need a couple of days to—you know."

"Nah, I'm fine. And besides, the case is exactly the kind of distraction I need. Which is precisely why I called you in here. Let's get the basics down so we can see where we stand."

"All right, let's do it," Grace said with a nod of the head and tapped the screen of her iPad.

I nodded, opened my laptop, and navigated my way through to the folder containing all of the updated information on the case.

"OK," I began. "We have Walter Morris hiring me to defend Corinne Lucas. The DA has refused to release her despite evidence showing someone in possession of the victim's belongings."

"Rolex and wallet," Grace added.

"Yes, correct. Marco De Baun, also deceased. Was found in possession of Dale Rich's wallet and Rolex," I confirmed and shook my head with an air of frustration.

As if needing confirmation, I brought up De Baun's most recent mugshot onto the screen of my laptop.

"Charming looking fellow," Grace said when I turned the laptop around far enough for her to see.

"I take it you're not a fan of facial tattoos?" The photo showed a sliver of them running across the man's forehead, hinting at more covering the rest of his head and probably most of his body.

"Not even facial hair, Mr. Carter," Grace said with an amused grin. That was when I stopped, something inside me stirring awake. My assistant noticed the change. "Did I say something wrong?"

"He has facial hair," I said, the words barely above a whisper and meant more for myself.

"That's not a good thing."

"No, no, it's not that," I said. "Corinne Lucas told me that the man who appeared in the plaza that day, asking her for money, had a beard. Aside from his clothes, it was one of the few things she remembered. A brown beard."

"But the DA has already dismissed De Baun as a suspect because of Corinne Lucas being seen arguing with Rich, have they not?" I ignored the comment as something new took over.

"Grace, make a note for us to recheck all the footage we have of the suspect entering and leaving the alley. Also, ask Linda to expand the search. There's got to be more footage." Knowing how easily I could have the case against my client dismissed with the right piece of footage frustrated me to no end. "Damn it, the city has so many cameras up around the place and they're telling me none of them captured this scene?" I shook my head in disgust. "There's got to be something."

"I've made a note," Grace said before turning our attention back to the point of the exercise.

At one point, Grace got out of her chair, left the office, and returned a few minutes later, wheeling in one of the whiteboards we kept around the place. With me remaining in my seat, she grabbed a blue marker and began to make a list of names, writing each in a particular position and then joining them with lines to highlight their connections. Bryce Lloyd, Corinne Lucas, Dale Rich, Marco De Baun, Otto Van Hess, and even Walter Morris found a place. When it was done, she stood back, and we both just stared at the bunch of notes.

"Let's focus our efforts on Hess for now," I eventually said. "I know Linda hasn't found anything to indicate the man's capable of murder, but I'm not convinced. I think if anyone had a motive to kill Dale Rich, it's him."

"What about Bryce Lloyd?" Grace asked.

"I'd like to meet with him. Set up an appointment, would you?"

"I'll get right on it," Grace said, and after I thanked my assistant for her help, she left me alone in the office to ponder some more.

Some cases just felt a little too similar to onions. Each layer one peeled just brought more tears with it, and this one seemed to have many layers. I hadn't ever peeked inside the world of antiques before, but from what I had already seen, it appeared to be one hell of a ruthless business, driven by nothing more than greed and money. I chuckled at the thought, knowing money to be behind the majority of crimes committed every day. For some reason, however, I just didn't feel that this crime was one of them. In my heart, I still believed the murder of Dale Rich to be something much deeper.

TWELVE

Everyone needs a form of tension release, and I'd found a new form just a few months earlier when I joined a local gym and began hitting the weights quite hard. OK, so I'm not talking about bulking up or trying to imitate a certain Austrian actor-turned-politician, but I found that it actually helped me in a lot more ways than just turning some of my flab into muscle. For one, I found that I slept much better after spending a couple of hours pumping iron. Secondly, I found my confidence also increasing, not a bad thing for a lawyer defending clients on a daily basis. But the best part? The anger.

There's something unique about having the ability to stand in the middle of a room full of people and internally screaming endless abuse while burning through multiple repetitions. Weightlifters also performed in front of a mirror, which gave me the added benefit of staring at myself while venting silently through my clenched teeth. It definitely felt cleansing, although maybe that's just the way I viewed it.

When I hit the gym early that evening, I followed the same routine I'd gotten used to during the previous months, namely working my way through several weight stations, then hitting the free weights for the majority of the time before finishing with a good twenty-minute burn on either a treadmill or bike. I preferred the latter but opted for the treadmill this particular evening, and after a decent run, slowed the pace down to a brisk walk. It was during these walks that I often ran current cases through my head and let thoughts run freely to see if anything would drop. I'd barely walked a couple of hundred yards when I remembered De Baun's demise. Something that had never been clear to me was how a man working in a store would spot a stolen credit card when the suspect only tapped it to pay. Morris described it as a switched-on storekeeper, but at the time, I didn't question it on account of having a substantial development to decipher. I was still thinking about that curiosity after walking close to a mile before I suddenly felt a tap on my shoulder.

Looking around, I was surprised to see a familiar face staring back at me, one I had only really ever seen while dressed in a professional suit.

"Hey, Elsa, how are you?" I asked as she hopped on the treadmill next to me.

"I didn't know you trained here," she said with a grin. "Been coming here long?"

"Just a few months," I said. "Only discovered it after I moved into my new apartment."

"You live around here, too?"

Suddenly aware that I might have just given a little more information than I would have liked, I answered her with a simple nod while pausing the music on my phone. Beside me, Elsa increased the incline of her machine to Level 4 before starting her walk.

"How is Xavier doing these days?"

"Still in the hospital," she said. "I heard that he should be able to go home next week."

"Fingers crossed," I said as a shudder ran down my spine.

It still shocked me to think that Xavier Bartell had suffered a stroke in the first place, and the idea that he'd dodged an absolute bullet was definitely a relief. Being just four years older than me meant that it hit a little close to home, if you know what I mean. I tried to ignore another shudder, but it gripped hard as my upper body briefly shook. Elsa didn't miss it.

"Someone walk over your grave?"

"Something like that," I said, suddenly feeling an urge to go. "I'll see you in court, all right?"

"Leaving already?" She sounded disappointed, but I ignored it. "I thought we might grab a drink after."

"I can't," I said. "And besides, I doubt your boss would approve of you mingling with the enemy." I didn't wait for her response and wasn't expecting her to give one, but Elsa Schwarz had never been one to shy away from anything.

"Maybe next time," she called after me. I didn't look back but did casually wave at her over my shoulder.

I had a sudden urge to get the hell out of there. Something about the prosecutor reminding me of Bartell's stroke just hit me the wrong way. The air inside the place felt unbreathable, with me laboring through each breath while heading for the locker room. I wouldn't call it a panic attack as such, but when I finally pushed through the door, I took a moment to pause and focus on filling my lungs.

When I got back to my locker, I first sat down and leaned back against the wall while imagining Bartell collapsing to the ground in front of the courthouse. Did someone happen to catch his head before it hit the concrete path, or had he suffered a secondary injury as well? What caused the stroke in the first place? Did he lose feeling in either side of his body? Was there permanent damage?

The thing is, I should have already gone to see him, even if just out of professional courtesy. Yes, we worked on opposing teams, but we were still part of the same club, right? Why hadn't I swallowed whatever apprehension I had and gone to visit him, just to satisfy my own curiosity?

"I'll go and see him," I whispered to myself as I stood and opened my locker, and then, as if needing my subconscious to hold me accountable, I added, "You promise yourself to go and see him."

Elsa was already gone when I walked out of the locker room. It wasn't as if I was actively looking for her. It's just that the gym's entrance was at the other side of that particular area, and I had to walk almost directly past the treadmill I had just used moments before. I could hear an aerobics class going on in an adjoining room, but when I reached a point where I could have seen the participants, I didn't bother looking and continued toward the exit.

Something about the fresh night air hitting my lungs caused me to stop and look up into the night sky briefly. Stars weren't exactly in abundance in the middle of a large city, but I did appreciate what few I could make out. I also spotted flashing lights almost directly overhead as some unseen airliner soared forty thousand feet above me. I stood my ground for a few moments and watched those distant flashing beacons until they eventually disappeared behind a nearby building, the plane's precious cargo a few minutes closer to their destination.

The one thing I'd always found myself doing whenever spotting a jet plane soaring through the sky was imagining myself aboard, on my way to some exotic island in the middle of the ocean. I was still picturing landing in one of these tropical locations when I reached my car in the nearby parking garage. I think that slight distraction is why I never saw the three men approach me; their presence only became obvious when the first spoke.

"Nice car, man," the gruff voice called out from about forty feet away. His voice echoed off the concrete ceiling enough to get my attention. I didn't slow but looked behind me to see the three of them walking in a neat line toward me. The second I spotted them, something inside me tightened, and I knew trouble had found me.

"Thanks," I said, and while I could have tried to cover the last ten feet or so and climb into the driver's seat, it was obvious they were ready for me to do so because a fourth man suddenly appeared on the other side of the Mustang, this one sporting the kind of grin meant to intimidate.

"It's a 2022, isn't it?"

I didn't bother looking back at the first guy. Engaging in conversation wasn't exactly a priority for me.

"Yes, it is," I called back over my shoulder and gripped the handle of my gym bag in anticipation of using it as a weapon. As it turned out, I never got the chance.

The fourth guy walked menacingly around the front of my car, his eyes never leaving mine. From the looks of him, I'd say he'd probably been pumping the weights for a lot longer than I had, the sleeves of his T-shirt struggling to contain the girth of his biceps. When he reached the driver's side, he pointed to something on the windshield and nodded, and stupidly, I missed the cue, his distraction working perfectly. By the time I turned to ask what he meant, his friends had already closed in.

"What do you—" was all I managed to get out before a fist robbed me of the end of that sentence. Every hint of air left my body with a punch violent enough to lift me off my feet. I'd barely returned to the ground before another slammed into the side of my head, a third cracking a rib.

All four set upon me, blows peppering my body as I struggled to suck the air back into my lungs. It's funny how your brain will prioritize itself, even when under extreme duress like I was at that moment. I should have probably tried to protect myself, but the need for air somehow took precedence, and that was the only thing I could focus on.

Someone's steel-capped boot smashed into the side of my knee, bringing me closer to a complete collapse. I coughed as an uncomfortable warmth ran down the side of my neck. I'm not sure which cut the blood came from, but curiously, it was the one thought I remember having as my other leg collapsed underneath me and I fell to the ground hard. Unfortunately, someone had a hold of one of my arms, and it twisted in a way that shouldn't have been possible. Something audibly popped before an unbelievable pain shot through my entire upper body. What felt like a white-hot poker ripping directly through my chest stole what little strength I had left.

A voice called out from somewhere in the distance, but none of my attackers paid the slightest attention. I remember hearing the echoes from that voice bouncing through the air as a few final blows continued raining down on me. Just before I lost consciousness, a calm voice whispered something into my ear, and I remember detecting the slight hint of weed on the man's breath.

"Lucas is guilty. Lose the case or we'll come back" was what that voice whispered to me. I don't know which of the men had knelt down to speak to me, but it wasn't the one who'd initially asked about my car.

In the minutes following the attack, all contact with the outside world felt like nothing more than second-guessing. The noises I heard didn't seem to follow standard patterns. Footfalls sounded as if they both approached and departed at the same time, the sounds of the boots clopping on the concrete floor fading out before suddenly reappearing. I tensed up in anticipation of a fresh round of kicks and punches, but instead heard a voice asking me if I was OK.

I'm not sure how much time actually passed before the ambulance finally arrived, but I do know that the pain never receded, not even slightly. I felt like vomiting more than once, and I actually may have, but thankfully, my brain doesn't recall that part of the night. I'm surprised I still remember as much as I do, given the amount of punishment I took, particularly to the head. I may have even passed out completely at some point because the moment between me seeing a stranger's face looking down at me to then lying inside an ambulance with a paramedic fitting an IV into the back of my hand happened in the blink of an eye.

What I do remember thinking during that ride to the hospital, though, is the message itself, the one whispered to me by one of the attackers and spoken with a hint of deep Southern drawl. It hadn't been a random mugging, after all, which is precisely what I'd thought it was at first. The only two questions I had were who had sent the message and why it had to be delivered in such a brutal manner. Perhaps I would find the answer in the latter, the obvious nature of the attack the biggest clue of all.

THIRTEEN

I SPENT TWO DAYS IN THE HOSPITAL. THE WORST OF my injuries turned out to be a dislocated shoulder, and it is the moment it popped that I remember as being the worst pain I'd ever experienced. OK, the worst *physical* pain I've ever experienced. Quite a number of people came to visit me that first afternoon, including Dwight and Grace, who stayed for almost an hour. Grace sat on the edge of the bed while Dwight took the only available chair and pulled it closer to the bed.

"You look like shit, kid" is how my boss essentially greeted me, and if it hadn't been for the three stitches holding my top lip together, I might have grinned at him. Grace slapped her husband playfully on the chest as her cheeks turned bright red. "What?" Dwight said with a shrug of the shoulders as Grace set a bunch of envelopes on the bedside table. "He knows it to be true."

"Maybe he does, but you don't have to point out the obvious, Dwight Tanner," Grace said sternly to her husband and then to me, "I thought you might like your mail."

"Thanks," I said before receiving a very careful hug from my assistant.

"I hope you managed to land a few punches of your own," Dwight said as he sat down, and I wish I could have told him I did, although I doubt I landed a single finger on any of them. My lack of reply answered for me. Dwight picked up on it, and I watched him purse his lips. "At least you're alive," he said before Grace changed the subject.

"Who would have thought that both you and Xavier Bartell would end up in the same hospital at the same time?"

"Xavier is still here?"

They both nodded in unison. "He's at the end of the hall, second door from the end," Grace said. "He actually looks pretty good."

"He's in better shape than you," Dwight added, and this time, when Grace gave him a look, he sank coyly into his chair. "Sorry, dear."

The next visitor to come and see me walked in thirty seconds after Dwight and Grace's departure. Linda also happened to carry one of the aforementioned hot dogs from a certain vendor we'd visited just a couple of days earlier in one hand, and if it hadn't been for the condition of my lips, I might have enjoyed it a bit more.

"Oh geez, Ben, I'm sorry," Linda said when she saw me grimace with the very first attempted bite. "I wasn't thinking."

"It's fine," I said while staring at the bun in my hand. "It's perfect, and I really don't care if it takes me the rest of the day to finish this."

I wasn't kidding either. Hospital food just didn't quite cut it for me, and the truth is, I was starving. The hot dog couldn't have come at a better time, and I wasn't about to pass up the chance to fill my belly even if it felt like every part of my body opposed the idea. Linda took up Grace's previous position at the foot of the bed and watched as I made quite a job out of her gift, but my efforts paid off. Almost thirty-five minutes after commencing the meal, I slipped the final sliver of bun into my mouth.

"Linda, that was incredible," I said, carefully leaning back against the headboard. My shoulder throbbed, but somehow, the lingering taste of mustard overshadowed the misery.

"I was hoping it might cheer you up."

"That it did," I said.

"Good, and now, maybe you can tell me who the hell jumped you." She leaned slightly forward as if leaning in for the answer.

"I wish I knew," I said. "It all happened so fast, I didn't even get a good look at them."

"None of them?" I closed my eyes and thought back to the initial moments before the attack, the seconds before the world turned painful.

"Maybe one," I said. "The guy they used to distract me. The one standing behind my car when I got there."

"What about him?"

"Tattoo," I whispered. "A tattoo on his left forearm." I scrunched my face up, trying to zoom in on the image in my head. "It was of a female vampire." I opened my eyes again and looked across at Linda. "Maybe the security footage can help. The cops told me they were in the process of trying to get a hold of it." I'd barely finished the words before Linda shook her head.

"Unfortunately, the ones on that particular floor weren't functioning." Inside, I groaned.

"Of course they weren't," I said with a hint of amusement.

"But there are plenty of others. Just a matter of time before we find them. Are you sure it wasn't just some random beating?"

I shook my head, remembering the one detail impossible to forget.

"They all but confirmed it for me with their words."

"What words?"

"The words one of them whispered in my ear after they finished breaking my body," I said, but before I could share them, approaching footsteps drew our attention to the door.

That was when another visitor walked into the room, although Jack Barnes paused when he saw Linda already sitting on my bed.

"Oh, sorry, guys. Don't mean to interrupt," he said with an apologetic hand held up before him.

"You're not interrupting," I said and waved him closer with my good hand.

"Geez, they really did a number on you," Jack said as he walked closer and remained standing. "At least you get the good drugs, though, right?"

"I'd rather avoid the beating, if I was going to get a choice in the matter." Both Jack and Linda quietly laughed at that.

"Here, I brought you this," Jack said and pulled something out from his jacket. "This should bring a smile to your face."

"What is it?" I asked, but I could have saved myself the question as I took a look at the photograph.

"You mean, *who* is it?" Jack said, finally opting for the seat and dropping down into it. "Are those your guys?"

That tightening inside my stomach returned when I saw the faces of the four men walking along the sidewalk just outside my gym. Two of them appeared to be taking sideways glances through the plate-glass windows where I probably stood just a few feet away, busy walking or running on the treadmill. It wasn't the clearest image, unfortunately, but the grainy scene did show enough details for it to be useful.

"That's them," I whispered. Jack gave me an appreciative nod and looked at Linda.

"We haven't identified them yet, although I think I know this one here," he said while pointing to the tallest of the four, the one sporting the female vampire on his forearm. "Pretty sure that's Danny Glick, a well-known thug who works security for a few bars around town." Linda had leaned over to get a look at the photo.

"Any chance he'll talk?"

Jack looked at her and nodded. "I might be able to convince him. From what I remember, he's one of those types of guys who shows a lot more bark than bite."

"My body says otherwise," I said with a groan as the throbbing in my shoulder stepped up to the next level. I winced while trying to shift myself into a more comfortable position, but it didn't help. Linda leaned back to give me room and frowned at my discomfort.

"Want me to call the nurse, Ben?"

I shook my head. "Nah, I'm good. Just a nuisance really."

"All right," Linda said, but she sounded far from convinced.

It was Jack who ended up leaving first but not before giving me one final rib about the beating. It was a guy thing, of course; none of his words held any malice. If we had been in a bar, I might have slapped him playfully on the shoulder, but given my condition and current location, I stuck to calling him a few choice words instead.

"All right, I'd better get back to it, folks," he finally said and squeezed my hand before leaning down and planting a kiss on top of Linda's head.

"Let us know how you do with talking to our friend," she said. Jack cocked his thumb at her, gave me a nod, and walked out into the hallway. Linda and I sat in silence for a few moments listening to his footfalls gradually fade out before resuming our conversation as if it hadn't been interrupted in the first place.

"One of them told me that Corinne Lucas is guilty and for me to throw the case or they'd come back," I said. Linda recognized our previous conversation and nodded.

"I guess that's confirmation enough," she said and looked toward the door. "Let's hope Jack is right and he knows one of them. Shouldn't be hard tracking him down." She was about to say something else on the matter but then clicked her fingers as a new idea came to mind. "Oh, that reminds me. I tried to get in touch with this Otto Van Hess."

"How did you do?"

"Refused point blank to talk to me. His secretary stonewalled me from the get-go."

"Give me a few days and I'll give him a try. Maybe I'll have better luck."

My investigator stayed for almost another hour before having to leave again. She wished me well and told me to try to relax as much as possible and heal myself, but I could already feel an urgency to get back to work. Injuries or not, I had no intention of throwing the case because of the beating, and I wasn't about to let those assholes intimidate me. Besides, Corinne Lucas deserved the very best defense, and I planned on being the one to provide her with it.

"And how is the pain level for you, Mr. Carter?" a voice suddenly said, pulling me from my thoughts. I looked up to see a new nurse walk in.

"My shoulder is firing up again, but the rest of me feels fine."

"I'll get you something just as soon as I finish my checks," she said and proceeded to run her usual tests on me.

While most of my vitals appeared normal and Nurse Chadwick promised to return with some pain relief shortly, she still hadn't done so a half hour later, and feeling like the bed might be the cause of my discomfort, I ended up climbing out to see whether standing would offer me some relief. Surprisingly, it did, and I spent the first few minutes gently pacing back and forth around my room. Awkward is the only way to describe how I moved due to random bolts of pain shooting through my body with certain movements. I guess, in a way, I saw it as more of a lesson on how I could move correctly to avoid it.

At one point, I popped my head out into the corridor to check the foot traffic. It wasn't exactly a busy area of the hospital. I saw a few people walking back and forth between rooms, as well as the front section of the nurse's station halfway up, but no visible nurses. I did see one briefly walk out of a room a few doors down from me, but then she immediately entered another and disappeared again. That was when I remembered what Grace had said, and I decided to go exploring for myself.

Nobody paid me the slightest attention as I made my way down the corridor, not even when I reached the nurse's station, where a lone doctor appeared to be checking a patient's file on one of the three computer terminals. He briefly looked at me over the rim of his glasses but then dismissed me just as fast when he returned his attention to the screen. As for Nurse Chadwick, I didn't see her during that initial outing, and I ended up reaching my destination without being questioned by anyone, not that I was in prison. I just figured that, being a fresh admission with a suspected concussion and various other injuries, someone might have tried to force me back into bed.

Xavier Bartell looked to be in far better condition than I was, sitting up in bed with a James Patterson book in one hand and a blue metallic drink bottle in the other. He didn't see me standing in the doorway watching him at first, but he did when I took another couple of steps into the room.

"I'm sorry, friend, I think you have the wrong room," the prosecutor said while looking at me with suspicious eyes.

God, just how bad do I look? was what I thought to myself before stopping to let him get a better look at me.

"Ben Carter? What the hell happened to you, man?"

"Got into a bit of an altercation," I said, trying to grin, feeling like my lip would tear itself open, and changing my mind on the matter, all within a split second.

"I'll say. And I thought I was in bad shape."

"You look good, Xavier," I said, approaching the bed. "Sorry for not coming in sooner to see you. It's just that—"

"You don't have to apologize," he said. "We both know how busy things can get in our part of the universe. Who would have thought I'd end up in here for the reasons I did, huh?" He sounded surprisingly jovial.

"It did shock everybody, that's for sure," I agreed. "Have you heard anything about when you might get out?" I knew the answer, of course, but asked anyway for the sake of small talk.

"They're telling me next week, but to tell you the truth, I'm ready to go home now." He lowered his voice and added, "Not the biggest fan of hospital food."

"I know what you mean," I said. "Just had Linda bring me in a Vinny's footlong." Bartell raised his eyebrows before shaking his head.

"I'd kill for one of those right now," he said but immediately changed direction. "So how's my replacement doing?"

"Elsa? I think she'll certainly put up a good fight." I didn't bother adding the sexual tension that existed between us, figuring it to be a minor detail between her and me and nobody else. Bartell had other ideas.

"You know, I heard she has quite a thing for you." Again, he lowered his voice. "Probably shouldn't be telling you this, but I'm pretty sure that's why Arthur put her on the case."

I mildly snickered. "That doesn't surprise me one bit. Guess he thinks a distraction might help his case."

That was when Bartell's face turned a little more serious, his lips briefly pursing as he considered me standing there.

"I doubt very much anybody has ever told you this, Carter, but the DA actually respects you more than he would care to admit." His words surprised me.

"Clements respects me? Geez, you really did suffer a stroke," I said with a forced grin, and by forced, I do mean forced. My top lip already felt stretched to capacity without even *trying* to smile.

"No, I'm serious," Clements said as he doubled down. "I personally heard him say it more than once. I know for sure he'd love for you to join our side."

"And leave the firm?" I couldn't even imagine doing such a thing. Bartell sensed my apprehension and held a hand up.

"Relax, Carter, this isn't an official offer to bring you across. I just don't like seeing a man judge another without knowing all the facts. All I'm saying is there's a lot more respect for you inside the DA's office than you might think."

We both just looked at each other in silence for a second while a couple of unseen people walked past the door. Only when their footfalls faded out again did I acknowledge the prosecutor's words.

"If that's your way of saying I'm a great lawyer, then I thank you" was what I said, and I meant it.

The conversation felt forced from that point on, almost as if both of us remembered our position within the great game of justice and subconsciously retreated back to our respective sides of the fence. When Nurse Chadwick suddenly appeared at the door and questioned why I was out of bed, she effectively killed the conversation in its tracks. I wished Bartell a speedy recovery before allowing myself to be led back down the hallway to my own room, where the aforementioned painkillers sat waiting in a small cup beside my bed.

While I lay in bed waiting for their effects to kick in, I grabbed the small pile of messages Grace had brought with her. I found a couple of random envelopes mixed in with them, of which one caught my attention immediately. Unlike the three others, this one hadn't been printed but hand-written. The name the sender had written also immediately grabbed my attention for one specific reason.

Ben is how the majority of my friends and colleagues addressed me. Some even opted for plain old B or Carter, while others used Mr. Carter for more formal correspondence. There had only ever been a single person who'd used the name on that envelope: my wife, Naomi.

To Bennie Carter was how the top line read, but my eyes couldn't get past that first name, the one that shouldn't have been there. The shiver rolling down my spine lacked any hint of curiosity, the immediate fear eclipsing every other sensation at that moment. I had to briefly pause when I couldn't quite tear the top off the envelope because of my shaking fingers. A couple of deep breaths did the trick, and what I pulled out changed everything in an instant.

FOURTEEN

"I'M TELLING YOU, HE KNOWS SOMETHING," I TOLD Linda for the third time as she opened the passenger side door of her truck for me. My obsession with Riccardo Costa's card had only intensified since it fell into my lap the previous day, and now that my investigator was picking me up from the hospital, I could no longer keep it inside.

"Why would he wait all this time to bring it up?"

Linda sounded far from convinced, and I couldn't blame her. My week had already been dominated by the emotions surrounding the anniversary of her death, so it's fairly understandable that I'd jump on anything even remotely linked to it. But this wasn't just anything random, and in all the years since that fateful day, I had never heard anybody call me that name.

"Who knows, but I can feel it," I said once she climbed into the driver's seat and slammed her door closed. "I can *feel* it."

"OK, I hear you," she said with a hint of annoyance.

"You don't believe me, do you?"

"I know how hard this time of year is for you, and I also know how gut-wrenching grief can be, but believing Costa knows something about Naomi's death?" She hesitated to reverse out of the parking space and instead turned to me. "I know how much you want to change things or find a reason for her death, but Ben, it was an accident."

Looking at her, I knew that wasn't the time to try and plead my case, if there was even a case. Maybe this was one of those times when the best course of action was *in*action. Perhaps it was best for me to let things go, or at least make it seem as if I was letting it go, but in reality, continue looking into things on my own.

"Maybe you're right," I whispered and turned to stare through the windshield. "Maybe this is just me hoping for more."

Linda watched me for a few more seconds. I peripherally saw her give a brief nod before turning her attention back to the vehicle. A minute later, we pulled out of the parking garage and shortly later, joined Pittsburgh's midday traffic. We drove in silence for the majority of the way to my apartment and only talked again when Linda stopped the Jeep in front of my building.

"Want me to come up with you?"

"Nah, I've just got the one bag," I said.

"And you're sure about the flowers?"

"Yes, please, you keep them. I don't think anybody will hold it against me for giving them away."

"OK, but only because you said so," she said and gave me a nod. "And you'll be sure to rest?"

"As instructed by the doctor," I said, throwing in an awkward salute with my good arm.

"All right then. I'll pick you back up at seven. Hopefully, this Telford guy will put a genuine smile back on that face of yours."

"Let's hope so," I said and closed the door.

I remained standing on the sidewalk until Linda's car disappeared from view. My shoulder had begun throbbing again, indicating the need to pop a couple of fresh painkillers, but I wanted to resist the urge. Knowing how easily people became hooked on them, I didn't want to rely on them so quickly. During the short elevator ride up to my floor, I made the conscious decision to cut back on taking them until predetermined times, and even then, only if the pain truly called for it.

When I reached my apartment and closed the door after stepping inside, I briefly stood motionless with the bag in my hand, listening to the silence of the room. Actually, it wasn't just the silence I sensed, but also the smell of the place, the very feel of it. I had only lived here for a few months, and something about it still didn't quite feel like home. I wasn't sure what part about it held me back, but something definitely lacked.

Unsure of what I was waiting for, I took the bag to the laundry, emptied its contents into the washing machine, and started the cycle. Next, I went to the kitchen and started the coffee machine. I'd recently purchased myself one of those pod things, and it definitely added some much-needed sunshine to my day. The sales guy even threw in a couple of boxes containing various flavors, and I'd been having a great time exploring the assortment. Caramel vanilla latte quickly became a new obsession of mine, although Colombian mocha wasn't far behind.

The other thing I loved about pod coffees was that they took just seconds to make. I'd barely gotten myself a bottle of water out of the fridge before the cup had already filled.

"Damn, that's good," I muttered to myself after a quick sip

to test whether my tastebuds hadn't also taken serious damage. Thankfully, the full flavors of the beverage hit home.

I took the water and the hot drink over to the couch, where I set them on the table before grabbing my laptop. For me, things were about to get both personal and emotional, which is why I wanted everything on hand for when I would need it. I left the pills in my bag, which I had sitting on the floor next to my feet. Those little suckers could stay there until I absolutely needed them and only then if I found myself rolling around on the ground in agony.

While the laptop ran through its start-up sequence, I pulled the card Costa had mailed me from the envelope and spun it around to the image on the front. It showed Roll Safe, the guy from a classic Internet meme, tapping his head. You've probably seen it yourself, as there are hundreds of iterations about it, but the premise is always the same. The guy taps his head and points out something obvious, like not needing to answer a message if you don't open it in the first place or being unable to get mugged if you never go outside.

In this instance, the words printed above the man's head read *Can't point the finger if it was just an accident.* Secondary chills ran through me when I read them again, the same tightening invading my stomach as the first time I saw them.

"How can you not see it?" I whispered into the silence of the room, thinking back to when I showed the card to my investigator. To me, it looked obvious, plain as day. The man had sent the card to goad me, and he was doing one hell of a great job. But more than that, he had also opened up a can of worms that I had been struggling with for years.

The problem with an accident stealing my life in the blink of an eye was that I had no one to blame. Yes, I could have vented my frustrations at the driver, but since a hit-and-run stole Naomi away, I didn't even get the satisfaction of that. A faceless unknown person had effectively killed three lives at once. The subsequent police investigation fell flat on its face not long after, leaving me with nothing more than a broken soul for company.

Once the laptop appeared ready, I opened up a web page and navigated my way to a saved folder I kept at the very front of my Bookmarks Bar. The article I clicked on opened in a heartbeat and immediately brought with it memories I'd struggled years to contain.

Local woman succumbs to injuries after hit-and-run, read the headline, and my eyes darted across the first few lines of text before I absently scrolled through the rest of the article. I didn't need to read any more. The words lived in my head rent-free, memorized from countless readings throughout the years.

The year 2017 had been the kind most people would rather put behind them, but in a way, I had never felt an urge to try to forget things. To me, it became more of a necessity to learn to live with the pain instead of trying to remove it. That way, it didn't feel like I was cutting out an important part of Naomi's existence from my life. I know it sounds weird, but that's just how I saw things.

That particular month had also been particularly bad for hit-and-runs as a whole. Six happened within the space of just four weeks. I'm no expert on accident statistics, and this isn't the time to go into them, but that sounds high to me. Fabian Telford's son happened to be one of the six. It wasn't the kind of connection I wanted to share with anybody, but I guess a comedian might have been the best option if I had to have one.

Next, I opened a fresh page and typed in Riccardo Costa. His message made it sound like he knew something about Naomi's death, and I had a lingering suspicion that he might have even been responsible for it. All I had to do was find a possible connection between the two of them. Yes, it felt like throwing spaghetti at a wall and seeing what stuck, but I had virtually nothing to go on, and in my present mental state, I wouldn't stop until I found something.

Costa's name brought up thousands of hits, just as I expected the search to. Google worked its magic in a matter of seconds, and I quickly found myself scrolling through page after page of news articles, forums, social media pages, and lots of other hits. The man certainly lived a precarious life. Some might even consider him to have something of a cult following. It's funny what people gravitate toward these days.

I must have spent at least three hours going through dozens of pages sharing details about the mob boss, but when the throbbing in my shoulder eventually forced me to divert my attention away, I didn't think I had made the slightest headway. If Costa did have some sort of connection to my wife, then it remained somewhere hidden beyond the scope of my investigation and would take much more effort to find.

After heading to the bathroom and relieving myself of two cups of coffee and half a bottle of water, I used the remaining water to wash down a couple of painkillers. I hesitated taking a second, but the pain just hit differently when I pushed myself off the couch, and after holding it in midair, just staring at it, the misery won. I popped it into my mouth and swallowed it along with a mouthful of water.

"Next time it's just the one," I told my reflection and again made a mental note of sticking to the promise. If I didn't, who knew where this little diversion might lead me?

While I hadn't planned on it, I did end up taking another slight detour from the day I had planned for myself and headed for the bedroom. With varying parts of my body starting to follow the damaged shoulder, I wanted to try and maybe sleep through some of the pain and give the pills some time to kick in. I must have needed it, because I ended up passing out almost the second my head touched the pillow.

It was the cell phone lying on the bed next to me that jerked me awake a few hours later when Linda messaged to say she was on her way.

"Shit," I groaned as I rolled out of bed, mad at myself for not setting an alarm to save me needing to rush.

It wasn't until I jumped out of the shower a few moments later that I noticed the distinct lack of pain in my body. I even raised my bad arm almost up to my head without so much as a twinge before realizing why. The pills continued working their magic, the same kind that could suck a person in and hook them for life. I shuddered at the thought of needing to rely on them and almost longed for a hint of discomfort just so I knew they weren't quite as powerful as I feared.

A knock on the door left that test for another time, and with a towel wrapped around my middle, I went to find my investigator standing out in the hallway.

"You're not ready yet?"

"Fell asleep," I said as I waved her inside. "Won't take me long. Grab a drink, if you want."

I left Linda to her own devices while I returned to the bedroom and got dressed. Let's face it, guys have it a lot easier than the ladies when it comes to prepping for a night out, and five minutes later, I followed Linda out of my apartment.

"How's the pain?" she asked once in the elevator.

"Bearable," I said, not wanting to sound overconfident. I had made a mental note not to take another pill until at least morning, regardless of the pain level.

"Careful of those things," she said without me needing to

mention the reason why I felt OK. We exchanged a look that didn't need words.

The traffic turned out to be a lot nastier than we had hoped for, and we didn't get to the show until after the posted starting time. Telford had already taken the stage and appeared to be just getting through his opening greetings, which caused Linda and me to sneak to our seats in the very front row. Of course, Telford noticed and made sure to highlight us, but thankfully, he let us off easy. One decent laugh from the rest of the audience was enough for him to continue with his regular stint.

The man knew how to make people laugh, and for one brief moment, I was actually thankful for popping the pills. Who knows how miserable my night would have been if I had arrived without the safety net of medication? They don't call them rib ticklers for nothing, and my cracked one sure could have flared up multiple times if it weren't for good old pain relief. Much like me, Linda laughed so hard that visible tears rolled down her face on more than one occasion, and by the time the final applause rose into the air, I felt physically dehydrated from crying so much.

While the rest of the audience began to stream out of the place, a lady working for the club came and asked us if we wanted to head backstage and meet the star of the show. I couldn't exactly refuse, having been invited there in the first place, and so Linda and I followed this woman through a side door, down a dimly lit corridor, and finally into some dingy backroom where Telford stood surrounded by half a dozen other guests.

"Geez, and I thought people didn't like *my* act," Telford said with a concerned grin as he assessed the damage from a distance. "I should see the other guy, right?" He excused himself from the group and immediately walked over, shaking both our hands when he got close enough.

"The other four," I said with a laugh. Telford raised his eyebrows and looked at Linda, who nodded to confirm the number. "It's not as bad as it looks," I said, more than happy to tell the lie while a hint of throbbing in my shoulder supported it. I didn't show my dismay at feeling the pain return, but then again, I'd been almost longing for it just a couple of hours earlier.

It felt good to be invited into the place, and the more Telford talked with us, the more I could feel our connection grow. I wasn't sure whether he knew about Naomi or not, but there was something about him that felt different from the day when I met him and Jonesy in the cemetery. Perhaps he had taken the time to do a little research himself and discovered our tragic link. If he had, I wasn't sure how to go about asking him.

When Linda drove me home later that night, I should have felt better than I was. The laughing alone should have filled me with enough dopamine to last me well into the next day, but unfortunately, that couldn't have been further from the truth. In fact, it was being in close proximity to Telford that actually brought me back down to where I now found myself, which was lost and desperately needing answers.

"Listen, Linda, I know you're not going to agree, but I need you to put the Lucas case on hold for me and turn your attention to Riccardo Costa."

"Costa? Why on earth would you want me to pause the Lucas..." She paused mid-sentence. "It's that card. He's gotten into your head, hasn't he?"

"So what if he has? If he knows something about Naomi's death, then I need to find out what it is."

She sighed and didn't bother trying to hide it. I felt heat

rising from within at the sound of it and questioned whether I had indeed fallen for nothing more than some sick ploy.

"This is something I truly need," I finally said as I looked down into my lap. "He knows something, Linda. I can feel it in my bones."

When she finally answered, she did so with a tone I neither recognized nor understood. At first, it sounded as if she had pity on me, the words almost condescending in nature, but that's not who Linda was.

"If you want me to look into this, then I will." It almost sounded like she was doing it purely because I was her boss and paid her bills. Only that's not how she meant them, her follow-up words much closer to the truth. "Just be sure your employer knows you're moving resources from a case. I'd hate for you to risk your job."

She was right, of course. While I might have been the one to pay Linda, it was Dwight who paid her indirectly through me. She was also my only investigator, which meant I had nobody else to fall back on. The Lucas case should have remained my priority, but at the time, my thoughts weren't exactly using common sense. Emotions have a tendency to turn small matters into monster storms, and Costa's card had created one of the biggest of my life. Maybe I should have devoted a few extra minutes to make sure of my decision, but then again, hindsight can be a bitch.

"Do it," I told Linda, and she answered with a single head nod. In the end, it took just two words for me to derail one investigation, and the second I spoke them, I knew I had risked everything.

FIFTEEN

When I woke up early the next morning, the first thought that came to me was enough to pull the veil of sleep fog from my brain in a matter of seconds. My investigator was going to look into a matter closer to my heart than any before, a case that shouldn't have existed in 2023. The reason I still felt tired was because of a nightmare I'd woken from at two that morning, one where Dwight drove around town in a huge Ford F-650 with Naomi tied to the front of the truck Mad Max-style.

When I checked my cell phone, I found a message from Grace asking whether I'd be coming into work that day. She said she had something going on and wouldn't be in until midday, to which I replied that I would be in later. Given that I still didn't feel a hundred percent, I wasn't about to push myself for the sake of an opening statement, which was perhaps the biggest job on my current agenda.

When I did eventually walk into the office after dropping the Mustang off at the service center, the looks on the faces of my colleagues were ones I had seen before. This wasn't, after all, my first time as the victim of a beating. I guess you could say that the prospect of one came with the job, a definite inherent danger when dealing with potential life sentences. I probably reacted the same way as I had the first time, acting all nonchalant like it was nothing and saying that it looked worse than it felt—a blatant lie, of course.

Dwight didn't see me walking in, but he did come and pay me a visit shortly after I dropped into my chair behind the desk. I'd barely gotten the laptop open before he popped his head through the door and shot me another one of his empathetic comments.

"You didn't walk into any doors on your way in, did you? I wanted to update our health and safety protocols before you returned."

"I did, and I'm going to sue the pants off you," I said with a grin.

"Oooh, I like when you talk dirty," Dwight said and subsequently grabbed a seat before me. "So how are you feeling, kid?"

"Been better," I said and gave my bad arm a half-attempted rotation. Having not taken any pain relief that day meant I felt every minute twinge. Dwight saw me grimace and winced.

"Looks painful just watching you. Maybe you should take an extra couple of days."

"I would if I could, but I have a trial coming up, and I don't think my boss wants me to risk losing it."

"Your boss would rather you win the case but not at the expense of your health," Dwight said and leaned forward far enough to grab the edge of the desk. "All jokes aside, Ben, if you need some more time, just say so. There are plenty of people able to step in."

I held a hand up and shook my head. "I'm fine, honest."

"And Linda? How is your investigator doing?"

That was when I felt a twinge in my middle but not from any damaged muscle. I hated lying to my boss, and this one felt a little too close to the heart.

"She's doing great. Working on a man named Otto Van Hess. We think he might be directly involved in the Dale Rich murder."

"A suspect?"

"Possibly," I said and wondered how long it would be before he found out that I had taken Linda off the investigation to chase up something completely unrelated.

"All right then," Dwight said with a thumbs-up. "Keep me posted."

"That I will," I said and watched my boss leave the room. I expected him to stop in the doorway and turn back with another comical remark, but he never did. Instead, I heard him whisper something to someone else before that mystery person took his place in my office.

"You *do* look much better," Grace said as she took the same chair her husband had sat in just seconds before.

"Well, it's about time someone gave it to me straight," I said with an air of humor.

"I managed to get you an appointment with Bryce Lloyd for next Tuesday at eleven, if that's all right with you. According to his secretary, he's currently out of town and won't be back until late Monday night."

"Perfect," I said. "Do you think you could drive me, by any chance? I might have to drop the car off at the shop, and they told me it might take a few days, so I'm not sure I'll have it back by then."

"Broken?"

"Not sure. It's struggled to start a couple of times now, and

I think it just needs a bit of attention. It's still under warranty, so I'm not too worried."

"Yes, I can drive you, but he actually works just a couple of blocks from here."

"Really? I didn't know." I genuinely hadn't, and it caught me off guard. Call it my suspicious mind, immediately looking for clues.

"From what I can tell, he's opened a new showroom in the past couple of weeks."

I made a mental note to look into whether it had been prearranged with his business partner, the one currently incarcerated and waiting for a trial.

"Interesting," I said, but before I could elaborate, Grace surprised me with what she said next.

"Listen, I didn't want to make it feel like I'm prying, but I saw the letter Riccardo Costa sent you." She smiled uncomfortably. "I almost held it back for a more appropriate time, but then I knew you'd want to see it right away."

"I wasn't sure whether you noticed it," I said, her words catching me completely off guard.

"Considering that comment he made to you outside the courthouse that day, I wasn't sure whether it might have something to do with that." An uneasiness rolled through me, recalling that long-ago moment with Costa's off-the-cuff remark just after getting arrested.

You know something, it's rare to lose a loved one through an accident are the words I remember most from that day, especially the final few. He didn't say them for the hell of it or to quote facts. He said them for a single reason...to taunt me. Those words sat with me for weeks before I finally managed to push them into the background, but they didn't go far.

Rather than tell Grace about the card, I instead pulled it

out of my briefcase and handed it over. She looked at the image for a long time before handing it back and asking the one question I knew she would.

"Do you believe him?"

"That he knows something about Naomi's death? Absolutely. Yes, I do."

I wasn't about to lie about it, not when I could feel the truth in my teeth. I saw Grace's reaction immediately, the expression on her face remarkably similar to what I had seen on Linda's.

"I just don't want to see you unnecessarily hurt," Grace said when it looked like an uncomfortable silence would take hold. "People like that enjoy hurting others. They manipulate them to further increase their suffering. Don't let him do that to you, Ben."

I could see the genuine concern in her eyes and thought about telling her that this wasn't like that, but I knew that much like Linda, she had already made up her mind, and I couldn't really blame any of them. It was me they were concerned about. To them, Naomi was dead, and nothing I did would bring her back, but I wasn't, and to them, I mattered.

"I know I'm going to sound like a broken record, Grace, but I really think he knows something, and if there's even the slightest chance that he does, then I'm going to take it."

She could see that I had made my mind up and didn't try to talk me out of it again. In fact, she asked me if I wanted to double down and pay Costa a visit myself, something that took me by complete surprise.

"I can arrange a visit, if that's what you want."

For a second, I wasn't sure whether I should agree to one, not because I didn't think it would be worth it but because I wasn't sure whether I could emotionally handle it. What scared me was getting into an interview room with someone playing me. What if both Linda and Grace were right and Costa was just toying with me, hoping to add to my misery by using Naomi's death for his own enjoyment? That was when a thought came to me, one that I swear I'd never expected before that moment.

"Let's see if we can make it for Thursday," I said.

Grace's expression didn't change, almost as if she hadn't heard what I had said. I was about to repeat it when she beat me to it.

"Thursday? As in *this* Thursday?"

"Yes, why not?" I said, only too aware of the day's significance.

I had spent the first day of June every single year since Naomi's death at her graveside, usually passing the majority of the day mourning my loss. Never in a million years did I expect myself to be arranging to meet with someone on that very same day who might open a door to a mystery I'd held close to my heart every waking hour since that fateful night.

"If you say so," Grace said uneasily.

"It feels almost fitting, if you ask me. If he does, in fact, know something, it seems only appropriate for me to find out about it on that day."

Only when she was sure that I wasn't pulling some weird prank on her did Grace leave the office to arrange the interview with Riccardo Costa. Less than an hour later, she confirmed the appointment, informing me that I would be meeting the mob boss at eleven on the morning of June first, just two days away.

The truth is, I felt numb when she told me. Perhaps it was the conflicting emotions running through me, each a product of the nightmare I'd spent years navigating my way through:

the fear of being played, the anticipation of finding something new, the angst of finding out something much darker than even I could have imagined during the darkest moments of my grief. I guess the strongest emotion of all was hope, hope that I would one day find the person responsible for the death of my wife and our unborn child, maybe their unmasking providing the closure I still knew I needed.

It wasn't easy spending the rest of the day trying to focus on one case while distracted by another. Corinne Lucas still needed my attention, but when compared to the prospect of finally getting my hands on some information about Naomi's death, the latter just had a much stronger hold over my consciousness. Who could blame me, right? I did manage to get the first part of my opening statement written. It might have only been a rough draft, but it did read quite well, and given that the trial was still a few days away, it didn't need to be perfect.

When Grace popped her head in just after five, it took her a couple of attempts to grab my attention, thanks to the video feed playing on my laptop showing an interview Corinne had given a media crew the previous year. The reason for the interview was due to an exotic statue she'd sold to a renowned collector named Yasin Saleh, a man supposedly well known within Persian antiquities.

"I'm heading off unless you need me for anything else."

"No, I'm good, thanks, Grace," I said while delicately stretching after a marathon afternoon. "I'll see you in the morning."

She gave me a wave before disappearing from view. Feeling a need to also stretch my legs, I pushed myself out of the chair and walked over to the window, where I watched Grace cross the parking lot and head over to the waiting Mercedes of her husband. I remained at the window watching the car pull out into traffic before turning my attention to the continuing sunset. While there weren't a lot of clouds hanging in the sky, those that did became the focal point of brilliant color, the westerly edges a fiery blend that seemed to glow even brighter with each passing second.

My cell phone vibrating on the desk is what eventually pulled me back into the room. Linda's message was just a single word, the question mark turning it into a complete sentence. The second I read it, my stomach reacted with a loud growl as if directly linked to my eyes.

Dinner?

It sounded like the perfect invitation, but halfway to Linda's house, my cell phone again interrupted me, this time with a call from Jack Barnes. I hit the answer button and greeted him with enthusiasm.

"Jack, what incredible news do you have for me this evening?"

"Hey, buddy. I thought you might like to know that I managed to track down Danny Glick." I didn't immediately recognize the name, and Jack picked up on the pause. "One of the guys who beat you up."

"Oh, yes, of course," I said, the conversation from the hospital returning. "I think I blocked that event from my mind."

"Glick dropped a name when I threatened to bust his ass for a lot more than assault."

"Go on."

"Winston Parker. Said he's done a couple of jobs for this guy." I scanned my memory banks for the name but couldn't come up with anything.

"Do we know who he is?"

"I've run the name through the database, and aside from a mugging some years ago on an old guy with that name, nothing popped up. I'm thinking it's nothing more than someone's alias."

"How old?"

"Eighty-two," Jack said.

That was when a thought suddenly hit me, Jack mentioning the mugging reawakening a thought I'd never gotten the chance to fully investigate.

"Marco De Baun," I blurted out without any self-control. The name caught Jack by surprise.

"Huh?"

"Can you do me a favor?" I heard the question and grinned. "Sorry, could you please do me *another* favor, Jack?"

"I'm here to serve," he said with abundant sarcasm.

"How did the cops know about Marco De Baun trying to use Dale Rich's credit card? I heard it was the storekeeper making a call. Could you confirm it for me?"

"Sure thing," Jack said. "I'll add it to my to-do list for the morning."

"Thanks, man," I said, and after wishing him a good night, I ended the call.

SIXTEEN

LINDA SOUNDED JUST AS SURPRISED AS GRACE HAD when I shared with her my intention of meeting with Costa on the very anniversary of my wife's death.

"But why *that* day, Ben? Why not wait and give me a chance to work things over?"

"Call me superstitious, but there's just something telling me that's the day for it," I said, biting into the first slice of pizza.

I could feel Linda's eyes watching me from her side of the couch, but I wasn't going to react. I had made my mind up, and nobody was going to sway my decision. I think she knew that, which was why my investigator didn't dwell on it. Instead, she turned her focus to the slice in her hand and went to work on it. A few moments later, the movie began, and not long after that, each of us spread out on our respective couches and enjoyed some classic Indiana Jones.

When I got home shortly after eleven that night, I immediately went to the bathroom medicine cabinet, pulled out the box of painkillers, and popped two into my mouth. A couple of handfuls of water from the faucet helped wash them down, and closing my eyes, I hoped they wouldn't take long to take effect. I'd stupidly forced myself to suffer a lot more than I should have and hadn't taken one since the previous morning. With my body not having nearly enough time to heal, it probably wasn't the smartest move, but the fear driving my decision remained absolute.

In my mind, prescription pain relief remained one of the most common reasons many normal people turned into full-blown addicts. Just ask Norman Roe, a client of mine whom I'd defended two years earlier for a manslaughter charge after the pistol he used in a gas station robbery accidently discharged, killing the young attendant manning the counter that night. The thing was, it hadn't been Norman's only run-in with the law. Another accident five years earlier had turned his life on a dime. He woke up one morning after an eleven-day coma to discover he'd hit and killed a five-year-old boy after a drunken fight with his ex-wife.

Good old Norman thought it a brilliant idea to jump into his Chevy Tahoe after spending all day in a bar and confront his former wife about their divorce from almost nine years earlier. After assaulting the woman on the doorstep of her current home, Norman fled the scene, managing to drive all of three blocks before he slammed head-on into a Toyota Corolla driven by Cooper Manning's mother. While the much smaller hatchback remained crumpled in the middle of the street, the Tahoe mounted the sidewalk, struck a tree, and flipped three times before coming to a halt half inside the entrance to a 7/11.

The accident left Norman with a broken spine and pelvis, and while he recovered physically, he never quite freed himself from the painkillers the doctors prescribed to him, so much so that he quickly developed quite a taste for them. His habit became so bad that he even resorted to stealing prescription pads so he could write his own.

Norman Roe's guilty verdict, along with the two previous ones against his name, gave the judge presiding over the case reason to award a life sentence. I can still hear the man's sobbing when the judge spoke the words, but rather than object to them, my client welcomed the sentence almost as if he wanted it that way. Just before the court officers led him away, he whispered something to me about finally being able to let go of his hate and anger.

When I hopped into bed that night, I imagined Roe lying in his own bed a few miles south of me, his cell somewhere near the man I would shortly be visiting. He was the reason I couldn't bring myself to give in to the pain. I would rather suffer in silence than willingly take a drug to dampen the pain. Call me over the top, but Norman Roe's life had spiraled out of control so fast once he gave in that he had no chance to turn things around again, and I wasn't about to risk doing the same.

The same thought continued rolling around my brain the following day when I popped just a single pill in the early evening after trying to get a hold of Otto Van Hess but having the same kind of luck as my investigator. By then, the throbbing in my shoulder had turned vicious enough to bring on a sweat, and I didn't feel an ounce of guilt for giving in. Thursday morning began with a slight twinge in the problem shoulder, but when I stood in the parking lot of the jail just a few hours later and gazed up at the rows of recessed windows dotted across, the discomfort had all but faded away.

Maybe the moment itself managed to distract me from the pain, but the thought of taking a pill just in case of a flare-up hadn't crossed my mind. Instead, Costa's sneering face from the last time I'd seen him, being dragged away by the cops in front of the courthouse, filled my head, those final words still ringing loudly. Goosebumps broke out across my skin as I imagined him sitting in his cell, waiting to be escorted to the interview room. I wondered whether he shared the same kind of anticipation I did, although obviously for a different reason. I wanted answers, while he wanted...

"What do you really want?" I muttered to myself while still staring up toward the top of the building. My eyes settled on one window in particular, but I had no clue whether it played any part in Costa's life. If it did, then it was nothing more than a coincidence.

It was while sitting in the parking lot of the jail that my cellphone vibrated from the seat beside me. Jack's message contained just five words, the answer to my previous evening's request throwing yet more questions than answers at me. *Regarding your question...Anonymous tip* was what he sent through, and I immediately began to wonder who would have made the call.

I waited until ten minutes before the top of the hour to walk into the jail and submit myself to the usual admission process. Because I'd been through the motions plenty of times before, I barely heard the instructions, going through them as if on autopilot. The only moment that truly stood out to me was when I followed my escort down a corridor and listened to the sounds of the jail echo from almost every corner.

Once we reached the interview room, the officer told me to grab a seat while he went to get Costa. I did, and that was when I noticed just how hard the beating in my chest felt. If it hadn't been for the unbearable silence inside the room, I might not have noticed it, but with nothing else to distract me, my nerves really came to light. Even my breathing felt labored, almost as if I'd run to the room at full speed. Each time I heard the tinkle of keys or the rattle of a door opening somewhere down the corridor, my stomach tightened to such an extent that I had to physically take a deep breath to calm myself again.

When several sets of boots on tiles suddenly echoed some distance away, I knew they weren't just headed in my direction but coming for me specifically. The louder they grew, the heavier the unease within my middle as multiple scenarios played out in my head, each involving Costa's initial response to seeing me. In some, he grinned widely; in others, he winked at me. Just before the footfalls reached the doorway, I imagined Costa breaking into salacious cackling, then blowing me kisses for falling into his trap. I was so sure I'd imagined every possible scenario that when he did finally step into view, he had no chance of surprising me.

Strangely, Costa didn't react to me at all. The poker face he had when I first saw him remained throughout the process of the guard sitting him down in the chair opposite and fixing his handcuffs to the metal bar running the length of the table between us. He did stare at me from the moment he sat down, though, maintaining eye contact as the guard did what he had to before finally going out and locking the door behind him.

An uncomfortable silence rolled over the room when the final echoes of the steel door slamming closed disappeared. I expected Costa to speak first and so held my tongue. I actually feared him hearing the uncomfortable beating in my chest, which had again reached fever pitch.

"You look nervous, counselor," Costa finally said, effectively breaking the silence between us.

"I am," I said and immediately wondered whether it had been a mistake to admit it. It was also at that point that I wondered whether it had been a mistake to come at all.

"I'm not a scary guy," Costa said with an air of arrogance.

"No, but you do hold information I need."

"What information is that?"

That was when the first hint of a grin poked through. I imagined his train of thought at that moment, the bait he'd thrown out into the universe finally getting a nibble.

"Why did you send me the card?"

"Card?" He tried to sound surprised, but it didn't take hold.

"You didn't go through all of this just to now play dumb," I said, shaking my head. "And I doubt this is just a game. You *know* something." I leaned forward enough to place my forearms on the table. "You know something about my wife's death."

He didn't answer immediately, his eyes returning to their previous gaze behind that poker face. I felt him probing my mind, trying to get a glimpse into my very soul to see just how hard I'd taken the bait.

"I hear you're defending Corinne Lucas" was what he said next, and to be honest, the change in direction surprised me, as did hearing my current client's name.

"What does that have to do with the card you sent me?"

"Absolutely nothing," Costa said nonchalantly. "I just like to keep up with current affairs. Damn shame for her to have you representing her during this difficult time." He lowered his tone to a more patronizing level. "Why would you even consider taking on such a case when you know you don't perform well at this time of year?"

"Who I take on is none of your business," I said defiantly. "Now quit playing games and tell me what you know."

Instead of talking, Costa let out a slight chuckle as my frustrations intensified. My consciousness barely registered the heat growing inside me as I kept my focus on him.

"If you're thinking of trying to convince me to help you get out of here, then you're in for a shock because I'm not helping you." He tried to look surprised and even held his hands out in a what-if kind of gesture as the chains linked to his cuffs jangled against the metal table.

"I don't need your help to get out of here. I'm at peace with my fate, counselor. Are you?"

"What the hell does that mean?" The arrogance behind his words picked away at my self-control, and that was the first time I wondered whether he would actually break me. I could hear both Linda's and Grace's words echoing in my head, their unheeded warning coming back to haunt me.

"I'm just asking whether you can live with the way things are in your life. You lost a lot the day that car hit your woman. What was her name? Naomi?" The grin widened enough to show teeth, but that wasn't what irritated me.

Hearing him speak her name rubbed me the way finger-nails on a chalkboard did for some people. I felt my insides churn with anger, the inability to react tormenting me the most. I wanted to lunge for him, to slap the ridiculous grin off his face and make him talk. Unfortunately, we both knew that wasn't how the script would play out. We each knew our part in the game and would play it until the inevitable conclusion when either he or I called for a guard and the interview ended.

Was he playing me? I could no longer tell. That previous feeling I had of somehow sensing that Costa knew something about Naomi's death no longer remained. Instead, doubt flooded my senses. An uneasiness began to take hold as I felt color rising in my cheeks. The words from both my assistant and my investigator echoed louder now that my own positivity was dwindling.

"Why did I send it, you ask me?" He shifted in his seat

while looking directly at me. "Let's just say that I don't feel as confident about my future in this place as I did while on the outside." He looked up and around as if seeing beyond the walls of the interview room. "Maybe I just wanted to screw with you a bit more before the reaper comes calling," he said and grinned widely enough to show teeth.

The faint echo from his words had barely faded out before a new one replaced it, mainly my fist smashing against the bridge of his nose. I jumped up and launched it so fast that it caught Costa completely by surprise, although it did me too. Something inside my brain snapped when I saw that grin, and the punch was a direct side effect. In a way, the feeling of connecting with his face far outweighed the immediate pain shooting through my hand, a bittersweet agony I more than welcomed.

Costa looked shocked as I pulled back and forced myself to sit. I expected him to call out for a guard or to begin screaming at me for the attack. It wasn't as if he could move far or retaliate. His hands remained chained to the table while I could have gone in for a second helping. Rather than cry out, Costa at first appeared to understand what had just happened. A thin line of blood ran across the part of his nose where I'd broken it, another thicker line running from his right nostril.

"That's one hell of a hook, counselor," Costa said before the same grin took form, stretching a little wider when he saw me react again. "Looks like I do get to play another game after all."

"DAMN IT, TELL ME WHAT YOU KNOW!" I screamed, and this time, the guards did make an appearance, brought to the room by my outburst.

"What's going on in here?" one of them asked as he surveyed the situation. One look at Costa and the visible blood told the story. "Did he strike you?" the guard asked as he took a position close to my side. I could barely breathe, my brain fighting the urge to jump across the table for a second time.

"No, I just bumped my head on the table," Costa said with delight and shot me a wink.

The unbearable realization that I'd been played finally took hold of me. That was when I lost control and again lunged for him, but this time without much success. Thankfully, the guard standing immediately beside me reacted with lightning speed and grabbed the back of my shirt before I had a chance to turn the situation into a complete shit storm.

"Get him out of here," the first guard called while Costa continued grinning at me. He did call out something else while the second guard dragged me from the room, but my own screams drowned out his words and saved me from further humiliation.

SEVENTEEN

CALL IT A DUMB MISTAKE OR EVEN JUST AN oversight made by a man blinded by grief, but when I sat near Naomi's grave a couple of hours later, I knew I'd screwed up. All I could think of was the perfectly good advice given to me by people I not only *paid* to give me such advice, but who also cared enough to give me the very best. I should have listened to Grace and Linda. Not only that, but I should have drawn on my own experiences and realized that men like Riccardo Costa loved nothing more than to toy with men like me.

"I screwed up big time, babe," I told Naomi while sitting cross-legged before her.

Luckily for me, Costa had declined to press charges, and during my brief meeting with the warden, my own professional career hung in the balance while he considered all options available to him. It only lasted a few minutes, during which time Bruce Greene threatened to ban me from the jail indefinitely if I couldn't control myself. Thankfully, the man not only knew my situation but also my boss, and I'm fairly certain he phoned him before having me brought to his office.

"I'm going to cut you some slack this time, Carter," Greene said when he finished explaining the ramifications of striking a restrained prisoner. "But you pull another stunt like this and I won't be as forgiving."

When I walked out of his office after that little lecture, the color in my cheeks didn't come from the hot-blooded anger I'd felt walking into the place. No, that primal rage had long abandoned me when I realized I'd fallen for one of the oldest games in an inmate's handbook. That color was nothing more than a neon sign advertising my humiliation. Costa had gotten me good. He'd used my grief against me and gotten the reaction he hoped for. I imagined him sitting back in his pod, surrounded by other inmates and having a good laugh as he regaled his friends with the story.

"I screwed up," I repeated with a whisper as the warmth in my cheeks returned at the thought.

I did spend a couple of hours with my wife and child, but while I normally would have gone home afterward or maybe even visited a bar for a bit, I ended up heading back to the office. I felt like I owed it to Corinne Lucas and her case, given how easily I'd strayed for my own benefit. I'd barely managed to walk in the door before Grace directed me to Dwight's office. The look on her face told me she not only knew about my recent activities but also didn't agree with them.

I sighed long and hard as I dropped my briefcase on the desk and headed back out into the corridor. Dwight's door stood open, and when I knocked on it, the man himself simply waved me inside without looking up from his cell phone screen. It definitely felt like I'd been called to the principal's office, and I took my seat ready for a dressing down.

"Just had a call from Buster Greene, champ," Dwight

began after making me wait in silence for a few moments. "Can't say he was impressed with your work down at his jail."

Guess I got my time frame wrong. I'd assumed the warden would have made the call before seeing me, not afterwards.

"Dwight, listen, I know I screwed up."

"You screwed up all right, Ben." He set his cell phone on the desk and leaned back. "Hitting an inmate?"

"He taunted me," I cried out defensively and again felt familiar heat in the tips of my ears. Dwight just stared at me, and I knew I'd screwed up again. "I got played," I whispered. "I got played, and I know it."

"Why the hell would you even go down there? Costa isn't your client, and as far as I recall, you're the reason he's in jail in the first place. Man's serving twenty-five years thanks to the evidence you and your investigator provided."

I wanted to tell him about the card but realized he probably already knew, given that his wife was my assistant. That's when it dawned on me that Dwight hadn't called me into his office for an explanation. Things had gone beyond that point already.

"I've got half a mind to pull you from the Lucas case and send you on a much-needed vacation. The only thing saving your ass right now, and the only reason Buster agreed to sweep this under the carpet is because of Naomi. We all understand how tough it is for you today." He leaned forward again, the chair creaking in protest from the weight. "But rest assured that there won't be such empathy next time."

The guilt running through me far outweighed the embarrassment at that point. I felt like I'd let down my best friend, my family. In truth, I probably deserved to be pulled from the case and suffer the consequences.

"I promise it will never happen again, Dwight," I said, and it was a promise I intended to keep.

"I hope so, kid, because I don't intend to have a conversation like this again. You're better than this, and brighter than any dumb inmate like Riccardo Costa. Next time you get someone claiming to have information about your wife, you can come and see me personally, and we'll figure it out together." He shot me a wink to convey the seriousness of his offer.

"I promise I will," I said and took my leave.

When I passed by Grace's desk on my way back to my office, she looked up at me in a way that told me she knew exactly what I had just sat through. I didn't see any judgment, if that's what you think. I think if we had been anywhere but the office, she might have even gotten out of her chair and hugged me. To show her that I understood, I squeezed her shoulder on the way past and apologized in my own way.

"I should have listened to you," I said before continuing on into the office. No other words needed to be said, and I was thankful we could leave that particular episode behind us, considering I had more important matters to deal with. Five minutes later, we were back on track when Grace summoned me through the intercom.

"Ben, I have Walter Morris on line 2 for you."

"Thanks, Grace," I said and took a deep breath as I picked up the phone. "Mr. Morris, hi, it's Ben."

"I hope you're feeling better after your unfortunate incident," he said, and it took me a moment to realize it was the beating he meant and not the more recent incident at the jail. As if trying to help me remember, my shoulder briefly throbbed a couple of times for the first time that day.

"Feeling much better, yes, thank you."

"And you're all good for the trial? Anything you need from my end?"

"No, I think we're good," I said. "We're still following up on a couple of leads, which I hope to wrap up before the end of next week."

"As long as we're set by then," Morris said, and I couldn't help but feel like the man would have micro-managed the case if given half a chance. Something about him still didn't feel right, but I decided to let the thought go. I had had enough of assumptions that day and wasn't about to follow a second one down a rabbit hole.

"Corinne will have the best chance on the day, Mr. Morris, I assure you."

"Well, all right then. Call me if there's anything else you need. I'm available night and day."

"Thank you, I will," I said and hung up the phone.

The next call I tried to make was to my investigator, but she didn't answer, so I opted to text her instead. I'm kind of glad she didn't take the call. Rather than apologize over the phone, I much preferred to do it in person, and so I asked if she wanted to meet down at the Hose and Ladder for a quick drink after work. Her response came through almost immediately with a simple thumbs-up emoji, and when I walked into the bar a few hours later, I found Linda already sitting in one of the booths under the huge antique forty-foot ladder suspended from the ceiling.

I barely made it to the bar to order my drink when a hand fell on my shoulder, and a voice immediately reminded me of an unfortunate incident from earlier in the day.

"Heard you tried to get a contract on yourself with Riccardo Costa today, Carter," Nick Brewster mocked as he stood next to me at the bar. "Good job." Brewster worked as a defense attorney for Lyle and Holmes, a similar firm to the one I worked for. Nick and I often ran into each other at the court-house and often ribbed each other over losses but didn't really interact outside of work.

"How the hell did you hear about that?" It genuinely surprised me that he knew about the incident.

"The guard who pulled you back is my brother-in-law," he said and gave me another clap on the shoulder. "I told him he should have turned the other cheek and let you give that son of a bitch another smack. Lord knows he deserves it."

"Thank your brother-in-law for me the next time you see him. He probably saved my career." I grabbed my beer and headed to where Linda sat waiting for me.

"How are the knuckles?" she asked me before I even had a chance to sit.

"Oh my God, you too?" I looked around the bar as if trying to find the next person to grill me about the interaction with Costa.

"Did you really think you could keep it a secret?"

"No, I guess not," I said as I slid into the seat opposite. "Just didn't expect the world to find out so quickly."

"You're a well-known attorney, Carter. What did you expect?" She had a point.

"Yeah, I guess so, but it would be nice to keep some secrets, you know?" She laughed at that and took a drink from her glass.

"Listen, Linda, I'm sorry for—"

"Don't even start," she said with an upheld hand. "It is what it is, and now it's done, as far as I'm concerned. I don't want to hear another word about it. Besides, I found some-thing that might get your attention back on the Lucas case."

She pulled out a folded sheet of paper from her jacket pocket and slid it across the desk.

"What's this?" I asked and picked it up.

Linda didn't speak as I picked it up and unfolded it. Only one side had anything on it: an image of an airline ticket. I looked over at her, and she filled in the gaps.

"Otto Van Hess came to Pittsburgh for a visit three days before Dale Rich's murder and left again the very same day as the killing. He prepaid a round trip."

"This doesn't prove he had anything to do with the death, though," I said.

"No, but I also have it on good authority that Hess met with Rich on the morning of the killing and, according to Rich's secretary, they had one hell of an argument."

"She told you that?"

Linda nodded. "She did."

"Would she be willing to testify?" I felt a sliver of hope, but Linda shook her head.

"I tried to convince her, but she remained adamant that she knew nothing else and didn't want to *go through hell on the stand* is how she put it." Linda even used her fingers to air quote the unseen woman's words.

"I'll go and see her," I said without hesitation. If there was even the slightest chance that Hess had something to do with Rich's murder, then I needed to uncover it.

"She's been staying at her parents' house out in Somerset," Linda said, and I quickly made some mental calculations.

"I could head down that way on Wednesday after finishing with jury selection," I said after remembering my scheduled meeting with Bryce Lloyd on Tuesday.

"Want me to tag along? It might help if she sees a familiar face."

"If you have the time, sure. I could always use the help. Anything to get her defenses down." I paused to consider a drink but had another thought. "Listen, see if you can find any connection between Van Hess and De Baun."

"Think Hess might have hired him?"

"Something like that," I said and picked up my glass. "I had Jack check how the cops knew about De Baun in the first place. Turns out it was an anonymous tip." I held the glass in midair and pondered. "If Van Hess really did hire De Baun, then maybe it was also he who tipped off the cops to silence him. Can you get a hold of some voice samples for me?"

"Yes, of course," Linda said without hesitation.

I took a large swallow of beer, and when I looked across the table again, I found Linda watching me with a look of curiosity on her face.

"What?"

She didn't answer immediately, but when she did, the question hit directly home. "You want to tell me about it, don't you?"

I could have played dumb, I guess, but then I wondered what the point would be. Linda knew me better than most people, and she had this uncanny ability to look right into my soul.

"It's not like I can talk to anybody else about it," I said.

"So just how obnoxious was he?"

"Very," I said, remembering Costa's grin that finally broke my self-control. "He played me like an absolute fool."

"Don't beat yourself up for it. He just happened to understand your most vulnerable point, that's all. And besides, given that it was you and I who pretty much secured his arrest, he was always going to come after us."

"Yeah, well, I guess he figured me to be the weaker link in the chain, given how he came after me."

"Not weaker," Linda said. "Just more vulnerable."

Someone once told me that life is about lessons, and while taking another drink from my glass, I understood the latest one to find me. While I'd always seen Naomi's death as a tragedy, others found it to be a useful tool capable of manipulating me. I never realized just how much of a weakness her death was for me, but now that I had, I made sure from that moment on that nobody would ever use it against me again.

EIGHTEEN

THE MUSTANG TURNED OUT TO HAVE NOTHING MORE than a bad case of dirty fuel. When it broke down completely on Monday morning, the place where I had it towed confirmed the problem within an hour of receiving it. I swear it pays to know people in the industry.

"I'll give it a complete flush after lunch and have it back to you before the end of the day," Brent, my technician, told me when he called me after making the diagnosis. By then, I had already caught a cab back to the office, where Grace was in the middle of filling me in on the details of a witness from the restaurant who was there when Dale Rich was murdered right behind it and when Corinne Lucas walked through without stopping.

We spent the day going through quite a few of the witnesses, mainly the ones we continued bringing together to help build our defense. Grace had managed to convince two of Lucas's regular clients to testify in relation to her character, while she continued working on a third who worked regularly with both Lucas and Bryce Lloyd. It was the latter person that

Grace and I began to talk about first thing the following morning in anticipation of our meeting.

"It will be interesting to see how he feels about his partner sitting in a prison cell," I said when we prepared to head out of the office for our meeting. Despite my having the Mustang back, Grace insisted on us walking the three blocks or so. She said something about me needing to stretch my legs a bit more after neglecting my gym membership since the beating, and I couldn't help but agree.

It actually felt good to spend some time walking in a straight line. Having spent most of the previous few days sitting on my butt, I hadn't noticed just how stiff a lot of my joints had become. I'd managed to lay off the pills completely, but that was only because I'd forced myself to ignore the aches and pains. The doctor did prescribe me something a lot weaker, but I still hesitated to consider it.

The walk would have been a lot more enjoyable with less traffic filling the air with a constant stream of exhaust smoke and incessant honking. Grace and I walked mostly in silence, speaking only when we stopped at traffic lights and even then just making casual small talk. She did point out an ad on the side of a bus about some resort in Phuket, Thailand, and revealed that she had recently bought a package for her and Dwight for their anniversary.

"Twenty-three years, isn't it?" I asked just as the pedestrian light turned green.

"Twenty-five," Grace said with a kind of triumphant tone.

"That deserves like an Academy Award these days," I said. "Should be putting your names up in a marriage hall of fame or something. You guys should be proud."

"We are, but it's still hard work. Even after all these years."

For the next block and a half, Grace shared her personal

secrets to making a marriage successful, almost as if I needed to take notes in case I joined the ranks at some point in the future.

"I first need a partner," I said when we finally reached our destination. With exactly zero prospects at that very moment, I figured the chances of my getting hitched any time soon were practically zero.

"You'd be surprised how fast it can happen," Grace said while pushing the elevator button.

"I'll take your word for it."

When we reached the seventh floor, what we found wasn't the kind of layout we'd expected to see. The place resembled more of an art gallery with an open layout stretching across the length and width of the building. One corner of the floor appeared to have a couple of designated offices set up with a reception desk positioned neatly between the two flanking doorways. To get to it, we had to walk past multiple glass antique displays of varying time periods, and I noted that none of the pieces showed any hint of a price tag.

"Ah, you must be Benjamin Carter and his lovely assistant, Grace," a voice called out from somewhere to the side. At first glance, I couldn't spot where it came from, thanks to the weird acoustics of the place, but then a tall figure emerged from behind one of the larger display cases.

"Bryce Lloyd, I assume," I said when the man neared us and held out my hand.

Given his height, Lloyd actually had to lean slightly forward to take it, even though I held it considerably higher than I would typically have. He gripped my hand tightly enough for me to notice but not enough to crush my knuckles together. His smile reminded me of Walter Morris, a similar kind of warmth that immediately drew a person in. I guessed his height to be somewhere above six feet seven at least, and I wouldn't have been surprised if I had found it to be closer to seven.

"Why don't we head to my office, where we'll be a lot more comfortable," he said after shaking Grace's hand.

"This is an interesting place you have," I said, pointing to a couple of pieces as we passed by and stopping next to one. "This is Greek, isn't it?"

The display featured an ancient helmet that I thought I recognized from a recent movie I'd seen, one featuring Brad Pitt as one of the most famous warriors of all time.

"You have a keen eye, Mr. Carter. Athenian, yes. Notice the intricate owl on its lower right faceplate."

I leaned down to get a closer look and found myself surprisingly fascinated. I guessed that it was made from bronze, although I wasn't sure why the metal looked almost black instead of the usual golden sheen. While I'd seen plenty of Roman helmets featuring some kind of red hair as a crest, this one appeared solid, the thin dorsal fin curving across the top and down the back of the helmet.

"How much would something like this go for?" I don't know why, but for a brief second, I actually pictured it sitting in a display case in my apartment. Lloyd's answer instantly popped that bubble.

"The last one we sold went for twenty-five thousand even, and that one didn't have the owl."

"Do you do credit?" I laughed at my own joke, and while Lloyd did offer a grin, he wasn't about to let the chance of a sale slip him by.

"We do, actually." He looked over to where a woman sat at the reception desk. "Trudy will be more than happy to take you through the application process."

"Maybe another day," I said and gestured toward his office.

I recognized Bryce Lloyd in an instant. Not him personally, but his demeanor, his existence, if you will. He reminded me of the guys I spoke to at the dealership whenever I went looking for a new car. They, too, went out of their way to be friendly, welcoming, and understanding. Nothing I could say would have offended him; the man switched on like a searchlight, always hunting for the next customer to close.

When we reached his office, Lloyd first asked Trudy to hold all his calls and then held the door open while ushering us inside. He did offer us generic refreshments, but we both politely declined, as I think he expected us to. Grace and I took the two seats on the near side of a huge desk while Lloyd slowly walked around the far side before dropping into a luxuriously padded chair. The antique leather actually creaked as he relaxed all of his two hundred and fifty-odd pounds into it.

"I was surprised to find a man like you willing to take on such a complex case," Lloyd began. "And for free. What's the catch?"

"No catch," I said, wondering how much research the man had put into me and the firm. "It's not unusual for our firm to take on select cases from time to time. Corinne's case just happened to come in at the right time."

"That's very generous indeed."

"My husband came from an extremely poor background and feels it his duty to give something back to the community," Grace added.

"That's right," Lloyd said with exaggerated surprise. "You're part owner of the firm."

"Yes, I am," Grace said. "Although I prefer to stay away from the pointy end of the business."

"Best place to be," Lloyd agreed. "But your business isn't why you came to see me today, is it?"

"No, it's not," I said, retaking charge of the conversation. "I'm in the middle of trying to clear your partner's name, Mr. Lloyd, and have a few questions for you."

"Please call me Bryce. I prefer to keep things informal when discussing in-house matters. Do you prefer Ben or Benjamin?"

"Ben is fine," I said. "I'm curious how you came to be partnered with Corinne in the first place."

"We actually met during an exhibition in Rome some years ago. We both happened to be interested in the same piece, a very rare sword, if I remember correctly." He chuckled as he looked up at the ceiling and leaned back.

"Who won the bidding?" I asked.

"Unfortunately, it wasn't that kind of exhibition. We both ended up putting in offers a few weeks later, but neither of us ended up with the piece. It went to a collector from France."

"I'm guessing this is one extremely competitive industry," I said, and Lloyd agreed.

"You don't know the half of it. I think that's why Corinne was so keen for us to join forces in the first place. She knew I had the connections and the showmanship, while she brought the ability to build our inventory."

"So you sold whatever she brought in."

"That's pretty much the long and the short of it...yes."

"And what about Dale Rich?"

I expected him to squirm somewhat, to get caught by surprise and show an uncomfortable reaction to the question. Unfortunately for me, Bryce Lloyd remained every bit the salesman, able to meet the question head-on and never flinch a bit.

"Ah, yes, I was wondering how long it would take for you to ask about him. I'll tell you the same thing I already told the district attorney. Dale Rich tried to get me to join a business venture I had no interest in joining, and that fake signature he used to try to convince me will not stand up in court."

"You deny signing up with him?"

"Vehemently," Lloyd said as his face turned to stone. "I take my professionalism very seriously, Ben, as I'm sure you do too. Dale Rich approached me on three separate occasions, trying to entice me away from Corinne, and each time, I refused."

"What about the office in Philly? The lease looks to have your signature on it."

"Yes, Dale showed me the lease during our final meeting and said that he would show it to Corinne if I didn't agree. To tell you the truth, I didn't expect him to be capable of blackmail, but I should have expected it given his refusal to accept my decision."

"Can you tell me why he was so adamant about you joining him?"

Lloyd didn't answer at first, instead leaning back in his seat as he considered me. He narrowed his eyes, studying me for whatever reason. Personally, I think he wanted a few extra seconds to consider his answer.

"This business relies on obtaining stock," Lloyd said. "Without it, you might as well choose a different line of product and set up an eBay store. The rarer the stock, the more profitable the business."

"But I thought you said it was Corinne who brought in the stock, and you sold it."

"Yes, and while he did try to convince Corinne to allow him to join us as an equal partner, she flatly refused to even meet with him. In the end, he went for the next best thing." He folded his arms across his chest defiantly.

"He wanted you to betray your business partner and use what knowledge you had about her contacts."

"In a nutshell, yes," Lloyd confirmed. "I spent years building up connections and know exactly how hard it is to form those relationships. While Corinne and I had been in the business for more than twenty years, Dale Rich had only gotten involved with antiques during the past three, a far cry from what is needed to play with the big guns."

"You mean to tell me Rich did all this because he wanted to cut corners?" I was beginning to see the picture a lot clearer.

"Precisely. That man didn't have the same passion for antiques as Corinne and I have. We take pride in what we do because we share the same kind of enthusiasm as those who buy our wares. Rich was nothing more than a businessman looking for an extra buck. He couldn't care less about what he sold. His sole purpose was to make as large a profit as possible."

"Isn't that yours?" I didn't bother sweetening the question.

"Yes, of course, as it is for anyone in business, but we turn a profit through mutual respect with our clients. We share a passion for antiquities and, in turn, we provide more of a service than just a straightforward sale of a product."

"Have you ever heard of a man named Otto Van Hess?"

"Otto? Yes, of course. He's one of the more colorful characters within our industry. He's also one of the few who plays on both sides of the fence when it comes to artefacts."

"What was his relationship like with Dale Rich?"

Lloyd's face turned dark with an edge of humor. "I doubt the pair would have clinked glasses, if that's what you're asking. Dale's double-cross of the man didn't leave a lot of room for pleasantries, and no, before you ask, I don't think Otto had him killed."

"What makes you think I would ask such a question?"

"Because you're here looking for an alternative motive than the one the district attorney has on Corinne."

Bryce Lloyd had an answer for everything, and it didn't take long past our initial exchange for me to ascertain that he'd probably rehearsed a lot of his answers. When Grace and I walked out of the building after the interview, I waited until we reached the first set of traffic lights before reflecting with her.

"Do you believe he really didn't sign up with Dale Rich?" I asked once the traffic around us slowed enough to hear again.

"Hard to say," Grace said. "He certainly put on the charm, that's for sure."

"And that charm is precisely why I think he's hiding something," I said before a nearby cab's honking drowned out my words.

We didn't speak again until we returned to our building, with me taking a short detour to the bathroom while Grace headed to the kitchen. We caught up again a few minutes later in my office, where I laid out the plan for the following day. I hated the idea of needing to take a drive after what I assumed would be a long day of jury selection, but I couldn't ignore the possibility of gaining a potential witness.

"I could drive you to Somerset, if you like," Grace offered, but I shook my head.

"Linda has already agreed to come," I said, "and since she's already met the woman, it might be best to take her with me."

"Totally," Grace said in agreement, and once that part of the day had been settled, we moved on with the rest of our plans.

NINETEEN

When I walked into the courthouse with Grace beside me the following morning, I did so with an extra bounce in my step. For a lawyer, there's just something special about walking in knowing there is an entire trial waiting to play out with me one of the key players. Sure, lawyering involves more than just standing in a courtroom, just like race drivers go through a whole process to get to race day, but once they sit behind the wheel and that green light flashes, their sole purpose comes to the forefront. I might have spent weeks and months preparing for a case, but that's nothing compared to the moment when I finally got to present our case in court and fight for my client.

Elsa Schwarz stood just inside the entrance, talking with one of her colleagues, and she gave me a wave as I walked past. I returned it but didn't slow, anxious to get to the courtroom and start the process of selecting jurors. Grace, however, didn't miss an opportunity to point out the obvious.

"I think someone has the hots for you," she whispered to

me once we were far enough away from the prosecutor, and while I did look at her with a grin, I didn't bother responding. The look of glee on her face was enough to tell me that any response would have been futile.

Once inside the courtroom, we took our respective seats and waited for the process to begin. Elsa and her associate took up their seats a few minutes later before the bailiff called the court to order, and the judge joined the party. While I couldn't recall the same three parties ever coming together prior to that morning, it still felt like a reunion of sorts. This was our domain, the place where justice lived. While all three of us might have served a different purpose, we all needed each other if the great wheel of justice was going to turn.

OK, so it might sound a bit dramatic, but the law excites me. Being a lawyer in an office feels a bit like that racecar driver without a track. I could spend countless hours building a case, interviewing clients and witnesses, meeting with investigators and assistants, but until I actually stepped into a courtroom and fought for my client, nothing else mattered. The courtroom is where I truly earned my price tag, and it's the one place I actually felt at home, much like that driver yearns for the track.

Corinne, on the other hand, couldn't have looked more uncomfortable if she'd tried. The fatigue on her face conveyed more than just a lack of quality sleep. She looked like she'd aged at least a decade since I last saw her with more defined lines running over various areas of her face. Even the grays in her hair looked a lot more pronounced than before. When she looked at me the first time while walking toward our table, I couldn't help but notice the fragility of her steps. The woman looked to be walking on her toes as if trying to avoid making the slightest noise that might draw attention. When she sat next to me, she almost hovered above the chair for a few seconds before finally relaxing into it.

"I need to get out of here" were the first words she whispered to me while looking down at her hands. Each word sounded like an effort for her, and I couldn't help but feel guilty for losing the bail hearing.

"And you will," I said. "Just as soon as we prove your innocence." I nodded toward the group of people sitting in the gallery. "Today, we decide on who gets to sit on the jury, and tomorrow we begin fighting for you." I leaned a little closer to make sure she heard my whispered words. "You'll get through this, Corinne. It may not happen today or tomorrow, but you *will* get out of here."

I hated making promises I had no control over, but I also knew that one of the most powerful tools for a defendant was hope. If I could just convince her to hang on, then it would go a long way toward helping her remain composed enough for me to take on the physical fight. While I didn't see any visible reaction to my words, Corinne did seem to relax a lot more. Once the morning got underway, she quietly followed each part of the process and even made a couple of observations about potential jurors.

We had only managed to secure half the number of jurors needed by the time Adams called for lunchtime recess, but I was happy with the ones chosen. Some jury selections can drag on for an entire day, so locking in six in just three hours gave me hope of an early afternoon. Thankfully, we secured the rest within just a couple of hours after our return, which meant that we still had plenty of daylight left by the time Linda and I hit the road for our drive to Somerset.

While Linda drove, I sat in the passenger seat with the

laptop open and resting on my lap. I'd been going through a number of witness statements again, namely the one from the bellboy who found Rich in the back alley. He stated that he didn't begin screaming immediately because he didn't want to be known as a scaredy cat. Given that the kid was still a few months short of nineteen, it made sense that he wanted to avoid a ribbing from his colleagues should they find out.

I only screamed for help because I felt like someone was watching me was what he told the interviewing officer. *I swear I could see a shape in the broken window of the old storeroom, and it freaked me out.*

"That old storeroom the bellboy mentions," I asked Linda at one point. "Did you ever happen to go and check it out?"

"I did, yes. Looks ready to fall down and probably should have been pulled down years ago. I didn't find anything of interest inside, though."

"Do you think someone could have been watching him?"

"It's possible, but I'm not sure whether it would have been the killer. If it was the guy we saw running a few moments later, then he'd have to be an Olympic sprinter to cover the distance."

Linda had a point. Even if the killer decided to hang around, why would he risk getting caught? I'd known some perpetrators, namely those who killed for the thrill of it, get involved in investigations, often remaining close to the crime scene to keep the thrill alive for as long as possible. Maybe Toby Walker had also known about such a trait and figured the killer might have remained nearby. Either that or he was genuinely scared for his life.

We didn't speak again until Linda pulled up out the front of a quaint-looking home on the town's outskirts. It sat in the middle of a rather large block of land, and I could see an older woman tending to a vegetable patch near the front. From the look of the various garden beds, it was obvious someone in the home had a rather addicted green thumb.

"Can I help you?" the woman asked with a thick accent when Linda and I walked through the front gate and waved to her.

"I'm Ben Carter, Ma'am, here to see—"

"Mr. Carter, hi," a second voice called from the house, and I looked over to see a young woman standing beside a half-open door. When Linda gave her a wave, Marina Osmeier returned it with a smile that lacked all hint of emotion.

After thanking the woman still standing in the middle of her ample crop, I followed Linda onto the porch, where the woman greeted us with a handshake each before inviting us inside. The home felt a lot smaller thanks to a dominating hallway that sealed off a lot of the rooms. It appeared as if the main bedrooms were at the front of the house, and Marina had to walk almost the length of the home before reaching the small living room.

"Please, take a seat," she said and gestured toward the couch. A fireplace dominated the far wall with a huge photo of a castle hanging above the mantle.

"That's German, isn't it?" I asked as I sat on the leather couch.

"Austrian. My parents grew up in Salzburg."

"Oh, *Sound of Music* country."

"Yes, it is."

"Have you been there yourself?"

"Not yet, but I'm hoping next year. My father is over there currently," she said, but instead of taking a seat on the opposing armchair, Marina instead pulled a rocking chair closer to us.

I could see the discomfort in her eyes. She wasn't exactly shaking with fear, but there was definitely a lot more emotion in her than I would have expected. Rather than prolong the agony for her, I decided to cut through the small talk and get to the point.

"Thank you for seeing me, Marina. I understand this is a difficult time for you, so I appreciate you agreeing to talk to us."

"I just hope that they find whoever killed Dale. He didn't deserve what happened to him."

"That's what I'm hoping to do," I said. "Linda told me that you saw Dale meet with a man named Otto Van Hess on the morning of his murder, is that correct?"

"Otto, yes. He seemed like such a sweet man when I spoke to him on the phone to set up the meeting. Even when he first walked in, he came across so warm."

"What happened?"

"What happened is he flipped like a switch the second he saw Dale. He didn't even bother waiting until they were in the office. The guy just lost his shit, flew into a rage about how he'd been ripped off and how Dale owed him." She sat on the very edge of the chair as she spoke, and I could see her fingers tremble ever so slightly. Linda and I exchanged a brief look when Marina looked out through a window to see whether her mother was still busy gardening.

"Did Otto threaten Dale at all?"

"More than once," she confirmed. "Dale just about dragged Otto into his office, and despite him closing the door, I still heard every word. Told him if he didn't pay up, he'd end him. Said that he wasn't a violent man, but Dale's actions had turned him into one."

"This was over the statue Dale supposedly stole, am I right?"

She nodded. "Dale told me it was his fair and square. Said that Marcus, the one in possession of it, asked him for twenty thousand dollars and he would hand it over."

"Marcus worked for Otto, right?"

"I don't know about that, but Dale did say that Otto had been shady about the statue from the beginning. He said that the man working for him hadn't been paid and that if Otto couldn't look after his staff, then he was more than happy to." Marina looked out the window again, and when something caught her eye, she excused herself.

"Just give me a second," she said before leaving the room.

"What are you thinking?" Linda asked me once we were alone.

"I'm thinking that Dale Rich seemed to open up an awful lot to his secretary," I said, watching as Marina appeared outside, talking to her mother.

"Think she was more than just a secretary?"

"I'd put money on it," I said. "Regardless of that, though, I need her to testify. I'm starting to think that Otto Van Hess has a lot more to do with this killing than we have been led to believe."

Marina reappeared before Linda could answer me, and once the woman retook her seat, I decided to change tactics. Instead of asking, I decided to assume and see where it led me.

"Marina, I know you and Dale were close. A lot closer than people might assume." She looked at me curiously. "It's OK, we're not here to judge. As far as Linda and I are concerned, you two shared nothing more than a professional relationship." I pushed myself forward to get closer to her. " But if you cared for Dale at all, then help me save an innocent woman from a life sentence. Testify." She slowly shook her head, but I ignored it. "Tell the court what you heard so that the truth will come out. If Otto Van Hess really threatened to kill Dale, then the jury needs to hear that."

"I can't, honestly." Tears filled her eyes, the first few rolling down her cheeks as she tried to wipe them away. "Please, I can't. Dale's wife already suspects, and if she sees me up on that stand, I'm afraid she'll see right through me."

I could have left the girl's illusion intact, but I couldn't risk my case on account of her feelings. This was about so much more, and sometimes, people needed a good old reality check.

"You weren't the only woman Dale saw outside of his marriage, and his wife has always known, Marina." Her look of shock surprised me as I didn't think she was quite so gullible, but her reaction confirmed it.

"What do you mean?"

"I mean, if you're really scared of how Dale's wife might perceive you, take it from me when I say that she isn't going to care. Like you, she only wants to find the person who stole her children's father away. This isn't about infidelity or betrayal. It's about murder, nothing more."

When the sobbing finally took hold and it became obvious there was only one course through the storm, Linda walked over, knelt down in front of Marina, and hugged the woman. The second she did, the woman's sobs turned to unbridled crying, her body shaking with each wave of emotion. Thankfully, I could see the mother continuing to enjoy the fruits of her labor through the window, which meant she wouldn't be interrupting us any time soon.

It took ten minutes and half a glass of water for Marina to calm down enough for the conversation to resume. I left the room to give them a moment of privacy, but more so for my investigator to work her magic, and it ended up paying off. By the time I came back into the room, Linda had built enough of a bond with the woman to convince her to help, and when I asked the question, Marina agreed to testify. By the time Linda and I jumped back in the car to return home, I had another name added to my witness list, a list that still needed more if I was going to have a shot at winning the case.

TWENTY

It's funny how a person perceives time. The days leading up to the anniversary of Naomi's death felt as if they were dragging so badly, and yet the moment the day itself passed, the days leading up to the trial just about flew by. Waking up on the morning of the first day, the first *official* day, always felt a little like a general waking up for a major battle. I'd seen such scenes in plenty of war movies where the general watches his troops prepare for the fight to come. While I didn't exactly have a battlefield to explore or troops to walk among, I did feel much the same emotions.

For one, I went through my paperwork while sitting at the kitchen table, my research acting as a kind of weapons cache. My opening statement could be seen as the first salvo, the initial line of attack, designed as a doorway to enter the conflict. I had witnesses, of course, but they wouldn't come until later, not until the prosecution had a chance to present their own. Each one of theirs could be seen as an individual attack that I needed to repel. As for my direct opponent, any so-called *hots* the prosecutor might have had for me prior to that day would be firmly switched off. She might have had a thing for me, but whatever advantage that might have gotten me out of the courtroom would no longer be in play.

I reread my opening statement in its entirety during the first coffee of the day, and I ended up changing a couple of lines to make them sound a little more sincere, but other than that, the rest of it sounded perfect. Once I rinsed the cup and packed the paperwork back into my briefcase, I headed back to the bathroom to finish preparing the rest of myself. I selected a tie given to me by Grace earlier that year, a menthol green design with floral emblems scattered across it. When I was sure I looked the part of a genuine defense lawyer, I went to the wall mirror inside my walk-in closet and checked the reflection.

"Now go get the job done," I told myself after making sure I didn't have any stray threads or a crooked tie. I actually looked pretty sharp, aside from the faint shadow of a bruise near my left ear.

When I reached the parking lot of the courthouse, the first thing I noticed was the dozen or so reporters already surrounding a certain prosecutor. Elsa Schwarz wasn't exactly a tall woman, only standing around five-two, if that, but I could still make out her perfectly styled blond hair between a couple of bald heads. I stood by the Mustang for a few seconds and watched her continue answering questions before she politely held up a hand and excused herself. Those who took the hint quickly began to scour the area for the opposing counsel, and I knew it was time to make an entrance.

"Yes, we do plan to bring up the fact that the police have not located the murder weapon," I told one reporter after his question, while another asked about Corinne Lucas's current mental state. "Imagine how you would feel being locked up for a crime you're innocent of and then forced to defend yourself" was how I answered that one.

After half a dozen quality questions and answers, I, too, thanked the crowd for their interest in the matter, promised that justice would prevail, and continued my way into the courthouse. Grace met me just inside the door, and I gave her a more in-depth update on the meeting Linda and I had had the previous afternoon, adding to the brief text I'd sent her during the drive back. I also asked Grace if she could try working on Van Hess's secretary, maybe try to find a way for me to talk with the man.

We headed straight for the courtroom, where the general public had already begun to fill up the gallery. Seats at a murder trial were always in hot demand, especially one where the media took a keen interest. I saw a couple of familiar faces among them, including Elaine Rich sitting with a man I didn't recognize. While I didn't know his name, I didn't think it looked like the kind of friend you'd pick up at a weekend market for sex and then bring along to your husband's murder trial. And that ruled out Henry.

Elaine saw me and gave me a wave. I returned it and wondered how much of that smile would remain if I proved Corinne's innocence. That's the thing about murder trials. Everybody always assumes that they're designed to convict killers, and yet this one, like so many before, was designed to prove the guilt or innocence of my client. If I proved her case and the jury found my client innocent, the family grieving one of their own would end up empty-handed, all sense of closure torn away by the lack of answers. That's why defense attorneys are generally considered the mortal enemy of victims' families. We try to clear the names of the people they hope to convict.

"Best of luck, Elsa," a random woman called to the prosecutor from a couple of rows back, although not quite loudly enough to echo across the courtroom.

I looked over and saw the prosecutor looking my way after acknowledging the person, the same grin as always on her face. Behind her, the district attorney also looked in my direction but without any hint of warmth. That was a man who knew the enemy and made sure to keep his emotions in check. Clements had been playing the game for decades, was seen as a genuine veteran, and I guess he had earned his professional arrogance, if you could call it that.

When the bailiff finally called for the courtroom to rise, it took one of the security guards to get the attention of a small group near the back to comply. I don't think they heard the official instruction on account of laughter after someone clearly made an ill-timed joke. When the rest of the room turned to see what the hold-up was, the three women stared back red-faced with embarrassment.

Judge Herbert Reginald Adams entered the courtroom at precisely 9:02 that morning, took his seat, and immediately brought out the defendant. The silence that hung over the room during the judge's entrance seemed to gain weight when Corinne Lucas was brought out, the breath of the crowd somehow inhaled and held until she took her seat next to me. You could have heard a pin drop from the next room. I gave my client a nod of assurance, which Corinne mirrored back to me.

The first thing I noticed about her was the stark contrast to the woman who'd been seated next to me the previous day. When she entered the room, Corinne walked with a sense of purpose the likes of which I hadn't seen before. Head upright, she gazed into the crowd a few times along the way, no doubt meeting the eyes of several people and yet never shying away. She displayed the kind of confidence I had hoped for weeks ago. Even her skin looked better, the make-up looking almost professional.

"Are you ready for this?" I asked her once she was sitting next to me.

"Ready as I'll ever be," she said and nodded again, more to herself than to me.

The jury emerged next, each of the twelve people making their way out of the side door and immediately taking their seats. Most of the five men and seven women looked across the courtroom to where the defendant sat, but Corinne didn't lower her eyes for any of them. She met each of their gazes in turn. Two of the women turned their attention to the public gallery instead of the defendant, perhaps searching for a familiar face. I had never served on a jury before, but I have heard that for some people, it can be pretty frightening to be placed in such a position of power. Throw in dozens of strangers watching from the sidelines, and the concept can become truly overwhelming.

With all the pieces now effectively stacked into position, Adams set the wheels of justice in motion by calling for the prosecutor to deliver her opening statement. After shuffling through a few pieces of paperwork, Elsa Schwarz rose from her chair, took a final look in my direction as if acknowledging the challenge between us, and then made her way closer to the jury. Halfway across the floor, she began to address the group directly.

"Ladies and gentlemen of the jury, my name is Elsa Schwarz, and I have been a prosecutor for the city of Pittsburgh for almost nine years now. And during that time, few cases have shown such heinous violence as this one." She came to a stop about a dozen feet from the front of the jury, enough space to ensure she could meet the eyes of each and every person seated before her.

"The family of Dale Rich deserves answers. His wife, his two teenage daughters, who've been left traumatized and struggling to understand why their husband and father died in such brutal circumstances, deserve to have the person responsible for their loss sent to prison for the rest of her life. We intend to prove that Corinne Lucas had both the means and the motive to orchestrate such a heinous crime. She not only shared a professional relationship with the deceased, but also a personal one, a relationship that at times crossed the boundaries of moral decency."

Elsa played her cards well, keeping the jury's attention on her while slowly striding back and forth while talking. I could see why Clements favored her over others. She was not only attractive, but the prosecutor had a gift for speaking and could make any statement sound almost poetic.

"We will show how Corinne Lucas managed to confront the deceased in a dark alley and brutally stab him multiple times before callously leaving him there to die. We will show how the victim tried to convince the defendant's business partner to leave and join an opposing company, something Corinne Lucas saw as the greatest betrayal for which she made Dale Rich pay the ultimate price."

Elsa stopped to turn and look in Corinne's direction, holding my client's gaze for just enough time before turning her attention back to the jury. Like I said, she knew how to put on a show.

"The defense will have you believe that Ms. Lucas is herself a victim of circumstances, but once we present the necessary evidence, you will find that there can be no question about this woman's guilt. Corinne Lucas is a killer, and it is your job to make sure she is never capable of hurting another human being in her life."

Adams waited until the prosecutor had retaken her seat before he handed the floor over to me. I took a final look at Corinne, gave her an empathetic smile, and pushed myself off the chair. Like the prosecutor, I waited until I had crossed most of the floor before beginning my opening statement. But while Elsa Schwarz might have set the benchmark quite high, I had every intention of surpassing it.

"Ladies and gentlemen of the jury, my name is Ben Crater, Corinne Lucas's defense attorney. The case before you today is not the crime of passion and industrial sabotage that the prosecutor is leading you to believe. It is not a case of a woman protecting her business or reputation that you might be led to believe. No, this case is so much simpler than that. We will show how Dale Rich was nothing more than a man caught in the wrong place at the wrong time, a victim of circumstances who faced the unhinged wrath of a desperate individual looking for a quick buck."

I paused to get eye contact with almost half the jurors as I slowly walked to one side before returning to the middle.

"We will show how the prosecution will try to prove that circumstantial evidence is enough to convict an innocent woman. We will prove beyond a reasonable doubt that Corinne Lucas had neither the will nor the capability of such a heinous crime, but that she is herself a victim in this matter."

I paused again for dramatic effect, getting eye contact with those not covered during my first pass. Someone in the crowd coughed profusely for several seconds before the previous silence returned.

"As jurors," I continued, "it is not your job to point the finger of blame at Corinne Lucas, nor is it your duty to convict her based on your personal feelings. This is a case where facts matter, and unfortunately, the prosecution lacks the facts needed to prove my client's guilt beyond a reasonable doubt. Remember those words, ladies and gentlemen...*beyond a reasonable doubt*. Circumstantial evidence does not warrant a guilty verdict without concrete proof, and what you will not find here is the malice or intent for my client to commit such a horrendous crime. We will prove beyond a shadow of a doubt that Dale Rich's murder happened on the spur of the moment, a mugging, which unfortunately doesn't fit the prosecution's narrative. Once we present our side of the case, ladies and gentlemen, you will find my client's innocence abundantly clear and will have no choice but to vote for a not guilty verdict. Thank you."

The silence in the courtroom remained until I returned to my seat, by which time the judge briefly paused to gather his notes. A faint hum rolled across the room until he looked up again, at which point the silence returned. This time, when the judge spoke, he did so with words that sounded like music to the ears of every criminal lawyer in the world.

"Ms. Schwarz...you may call your first witness."

TWENTY-ONE

IT WASN'T UNUSUAL FOR A PROSECUTOR TO FOLLOW A similar pattern of specific witnesses when it came to a murder trial. They usually began with someone who could set the scene for the jury, someone who knew the layout of the area and could share enough about the crime to bring the jury up to speed. So when Schwarz called the first police officer on the scene to the stand as her opening witness, it didn't surprise me.

"The prosecution calls Officer Daniel Morales to the stand," the prosecutor called. It took a few moments for the cop to show up, but when he did, he walked with the kind of purpose one displays when late for an appointment. He kind of rushed across the floor, and during the swearing in, it wouldn't have surprised me if he had asked the bailiff to hurry it along, given the way he nodded along to each word spoken to him. He appeared to suffer from a severe case of impatience, although I'm not sure if that's how he actually felt.

"Thank you for coming today, Officer Morales," Schwarz said once the witness was turned over to her. She stood but remained behind her desk. "Could you please introduce yourself to the court?"

"I'm Officer Daniel Morales, currently assigned to Zone 2, where I've been stationed for the past two years."

"You were the first officer on the scene, were you not?"

"Me and my partner were, yes, ma'am."

"Could you describe what happened?"

"Jimmy had just...I'm sorry, Officer Morgan had just finished writing out a citation to someone for jaywalking when we received the call over the radio asking us to check out a disturbance in Garland Way. This was at..." He pulled a notepad from his shirt pocket, flipped through a couple of pages, and pointed to a specific point. "This was at precisely 6:04 in the evening. We were only a block down on Sixth, and so it didn't take long for us to arrive."

"What did you find when you got there?"

"One older male on the ground, another nearby in a highly distressed state."

"The one in a distressed state, was he the one who called the police?"

Schwarz moved out from behind her desk and started to slowly walk across the floor toward the witness.

"No, the call came from a bystander near the other end of the lane. Several people had begun gathering on account of the screams for help."

"Go on. What happened next?"

"My partner went to the distressed person, whom we ascertained to be an employee of the hotel, while I knelt beside the man on the ground. I checked for a pulse but found none, and given the large number of stab wounds, I made the decision not to perform CPR."

"How many stab wounds are we talking here?"

"Objection, Your Honor," I said. "Question calls for speculation."

"Sustained," Adams said without pause.

"I'll rephrase the question, Your Honor. Officer Morales, how many stab wounds did you see from your initial position?"

"Maybe half a dozen, all to the upper body. There was a significant amount of blood pooled under the body."

"Did you happen to see a murder weapon at all?"

"No, none. My partner told me that he asked—"

"Objection, Your Honor, speculation."

"Sustained. Please just answer the question asked."

"Sorry, Your Honor," Morales said to the judge, and then to Schwarz, he added, "No, I didn't see a weapon."

"Did you happen to see any visible signs of a struggle?"

"No, not at that point. From what I could see, it looked like the man had been attacked and left for dead. One of his pants pockets had been turned inside out, and I couldn't see any personal belongings. No wallet, no cell phone, nothing to help identify him."

The prosecutor continued for a few extra questions, and when she finally finished, the judge handed the witness over to me.

"Thank you, Your Honor," I said and pushed myself out of the chair. Halfway across the floor, I asked my opening question.

"Officer Morales, could you tell the court how many people you saw standing around at the bottom of the alley where you said the person who made the call stood?"

"Maybe a dozen? I didn't really pay them that much attention at that point, as I was too focused on the victim. When I did take another look, the crowd had probably doubled by then."

"Would you say that the spot where you found the victim could be described as quite isolated?"

"It's fairly remote, yes."

"So not visible from the street?"

"No, it's more in an alcove of sorts."

"You mean like the kind of place where someone might wait for a potential victim to walk past and then call them in?"

"I guess."

"Thank you, no further questions."

The judge excused the witness and waited for the officer to leave the courtroom before he handed the floor back to the prosecutor.

"You may call your next witness, Ms. Schwarz."

"Thank you, Your Honor. The prosecution calls Margaret Pierce to the stand."

The woman who entered the courtroom next took a lot longer to reach the stand due to the cast on her right leg. When it came to crutches, some people could use them, and others couldn't, with both the woman and me firmly in the latter camp. I remember breaking my ankle a few years earlier and needing to use some. People make using them look so easy, and yet when I tried, I resembled a three-legged dog trying to rollerblade. No matter how much I tried to follow the instructions, I just couldn't get the hang of them. From what I could see of the crime scene investigator, neither could she.

Margaret Pierce eventually made it to the stand, and once the bailiff finished swearing her in, the prosecutor immediately walked over to begin her questioning.

"Mrs. Pierce, how long have you been a crime scene investigator for the city of Pittsburgh?"

"Twelve years."

"And during that time, how many muggings resulting in murder have you attended?"

"Seven," the witness said. "Two of those in the past year."

"And thinking back to each of those scenes, would you say that the crime scene involving Dale Rich is comparable to any of those seven?"

"No, none." The prosecutor appeared to look surprised at the answer, so much so that she animatedly looked from the witness to the jury and back again.

"None? How so?"

"Each of the seven happened on an open street. They usually involved the victim being followed for a certain period of time before being attacked."

"And this crime scene?"

"This crime scene is much more isolated than the usual type. It would take quite a bit of luck for someone to lie in wait and have just the right kind of person walk by. It is, after all, a driveway leading to a disused loading dock."

"Could you share your findings about the specific scene with the court? Any signs of a struggle, any physical evidence left behind?"

"No signs of a struggle. From what I could find, the attack happened very fast, with all of the blood splatters falling within an area no larger than two feet by two feet. My guess is that the attacker came from behind, stabbed the victim several times before the victim collapsed to the ground, and the attack continued. One stab wound grazed the side of the victim's stomach and left a dent in the concrete, indicating quite a frenzied attack."

"Was there any evidence to indicate the attacker was waiting for their victim for any length of time?"

"No, none. I did manage to find several discarded cigarette butts, but none of these appeared recent, nor did they match brand-wise."

"Thank you, Mrs. Pierce. No further questions," Schwarz said when she finished her examination of the witness and returned to her seat.

"Your witness, Mr. Carter," Adams called down to me.

"Thank you, Your Honor," I said and picked up where the prosecutor left off.

"Mrs. Pierce, that area *was* used as a smoking area, though, wasn't it? By several hotel employees, I mean?"

"Yes, I believe so, although they tended to keep to the very end of the driveway. It's quite a long space."

"About how long, would you say?" I'd reached the witness stand and taken up position on the far side so that I could maintain eye contact with both the witness and the jury.

"Forty-three feet."

"So you measured it?"

"I did," Pierce said. "The area has a slight bend, which keeps the far end closest to the hotel hidden from view."

"You mean the area where the hotel employees tend to spend time smoking?"

"Yes." She nodded as if needing to back up her answer.

"So if somebody stood near the end, they wouldn't normally see somebody standing near the entrance to the loading dock?"

"No, they wouldn't."

"Would you say Garland Way was a popular shortcut for people?"

"A shortcut?" She paused to think. "Yes, I guess it would make for a decent shortcut, although I don't know how popular it might be."

"So it wouldn't be entirely out of the question for someone to lie in wait for an unsuspecting victim, given how isolated the area is?"

"It wouldn't be entirely out of the question, no."

"Thank you, Mrs. Pierce, no further questions."

"The witness is excused," Adams declared before I reached my seat and then continued with, "Let's make it a ten-minute recess." He brought his hammer down for a single smack, the echo shooting across the courtroom like a gunshot.

To me, the case would be a simple one, on paper at least, although proving it not so much. After going through all the available evidence again and again, I couldn't see past the fact that it might have been nothing more than a straightforward mugging, and that was the path I would pursue. Yes, I still believed Otto Van Hess to have had something to do with the murder, but without even a shred of evidence, I didn't want to commit to a theory I had no way of proving. The mugging made so much more sense.

The prosecutor, on the other hand, had just a single path forward. To prove my client's guilt, she would need to build a picture in the minds of the jury, a picture that showed Corinne Lucas as a cold and calculating killer who went to extreme lengths to rid herself of a competitor. My guess was that Schwarz would follow up her initial witnesses with a couple who knew Lucas, witnesses who would describe the kind of person who would fit the prosecution's case perfectly. It was those witnesses whom I would need to discredit as much as possible.

Not needing a break, I remained at my desk with Corinne, who sat silently staring into her lap. When I began writing some notes, she turned to look at the people sitting behind us, perhaps just to pass the time. I didn't pay much attention until she whispered something that interrupted my train of thought.

"What the hell is *he* doing here?"

I turned to look at her, and her eyes remained fixed on some point a few rows back from us. Following her gaze, it took me a few moments to find the person she'd zeroed in on, and I finally understood her surprise. Sitting almost near the back and partially hidden behind a very large woman was Walter Morris.

"What is he doing here?" Corinne repeated, this time with a lot more conviction. I did feel a moment of hesitation when I spotted him, unsure of how to respond. Seeing him also caught me by surprise, given our arrangement.

'You know him?"

"That's Walter Morris, my old neighbor," she said. "Guy has a history of stalking me."

"I take it you don't appreciate seeing him then?"

"No, I certainly don't," she snapped and turned back to face the front of the court. "I don't suppose there's any way to make him leave."

Given that he was sitting in the very back row and appeared to try and keep himself from being spotted, I couldn't figure out why he'd bother being there in the first place. Up until that moment, Morris had relied on my updates, and given that the trial had only just begun, it wasn't as if he would miss out on crucial information. So why show up and risk exposing himself?

"Let me go and have a word with him," I said, and not waiting for a response, I rose out of the chair and began walking down the aisle toward the exit door. A few steps in, Morris saw me coming and left the courtroom ahead of me but didn't go far once out in the hallway.

"Follow me," I quietly said when I got near him, not wanting to advertise our interaction. I wasn't sure whether he heard me until I walked into the closest available interview room and he walked in behind me.

"Close the door," I said, to which he complied. I waited until the door closed before confronting him. "Do you want to explain to me why you're in the courtroom?"

"I thought I'd check out how things are going," he said, completely oblivious to my own tone of frustration.

"Corinne saw you, and she definitely wasn't pleased by your appearance." I lowered my voice. "What if she finds out about our little arrangement?"

"She won't." He waved the possibility away. "As far as she is concerned, I'm just another member of the public interested in the case." He pointed a finger at me. "You offering to come and talk to me is more likely to raise suspicion. Especially if I comply with you asking me to leave."

He had a point, one that I hadn't considered before offering to talk to the supposed stranger. Why *would* he agree to leave the courtroom if asked by the defense attorney? It wouldn't make sense.

"Fine, go back in," I said. "I'm not sure what purpose you came here to serve, but I guess it's too late to ask that question now."

"I actually thought it would be strange if I *didn't* make an appearance, given how Corinne thinks I feel about her." He shrugged and held his hands up. "I don't admit to being the sharpest tool in the shed, but if she thinks I'm obsessed with her, then it makes sense that I would want to come and check out her murder trial."

Point 2 made, and rather than answer, I just nodded and walked to the door and paused.

"Give me a few seconds to go back inside." I opened the door and headed back to the courtroom.

"I'm not sure where he went," I told Corinne once I was back sitting beside her, the lie rolling a little too easily off my tongue. "He didn't go to the bathroom, anyway."

She looked over her shoulder and scanned the galley. After I watched her eyes work their way left and right several times, she turned back to face the front, at which point, the bailiff brought the courtroom back to order. I don't know whether Morris had retaken his seat nor whether Corinne saw him at all. All I know is that I turned my attention back to the things that mattered, and there it remained for the rest of the day.

TWENTY-TWO

WHEN JUDGE ADAMS CALLED AN END TO THE DAY A couple of witnesses later, I waited until Corinne had been escorted from the courtroom before making my own exit.

"Think I'll head home," I told Grace as we walked out together. "Been a long day."

"I'll meet you back here in the morning?"

"Sounds like a plan," I said, and once we reached the parking lot, we each went our separate ways.

I didn't start the car immediately, instead sitting in the driver's seat with my finger hovering above the Start button. My attention had been drawn to a place literally just a couple of hundred yards away, a place I probably should have visited a lot earlier than that moment. Intrigue was what finally pulled my hand away and opened the driver's side door, more so than just plain curiosity.

I walked back out onto the sidewalk, turned north, and crossed Sixth, where I turned west. Half a block down, I entered the narrow alleyway, Garland Way looking ominous in the diminishing light. I slowed to a casual walk as I listened to the traffic noise fall away behind me. Tall buildings reached skyward on either side, each shielding the ground from whatever light remained in the sky. The farther I walked, the stronger was the scent of piss, each step bringing with it a more defined experience.

A hundred yards along the alley, a shudder of dread rolled down my spine when I found the driveway spoken about earlier in the day. I could still hear Margaret Pierce describing the length of the narrow driveway when I stopped to look down the very same spot. She was right. The bend in the narrow way hid one end from the other and was probably the reason nobody could have spotted the body of Dale Rich unless they had specifically walked away from the building at the other end.

Nothing remained of the crime that had been committed in the place, not even the faintest trace of blood that I had only seen in photographs. I stopped at the very spot where the bellboy had found Dale Rich. I imagined him lying there on his back, the pool of blood slowly building as the man bled out from the multiple holes punched into him. I knelt down, touched the concrete, and ran my finger along the rough surface until a divot highlighted another aspect of the crime. It wasn't exactly deep, but there was no denying the distinctive shape of a blade's point chipping away a piece of it.

"Sad place to die," a voice suddenly said from behind, close enough to catch me completely off guard. I jumped at the sound and almost lost my balance as I tried to push myself upright again. "Sorry, I didn't mean to startle you," Morris said from half a dozen yards back.

"Damn it," I said, trying to slow the beating in my chest with controlled breathing. "You scared the crap out of me." He held up a hand apologetically. "Did you follow me here?"

"No, I promise. I was actually just curious after listening to the testimony today and knowing how close it was to the courthouse..." He walked a little closer and looked around, particularly up both flanking buildings. "Such an eerie place."

"Only in the fading light," I said, although I agreed with his sentiment.

"You know, I have a thing for true crime shows. I tend to stream them most nights. It's almost surreal to be standing in the place where someone's life was so brutally taken." He turned his attention to something behind me. "That's where they found him, huh?" He pointed to the spot where I had knelt just moments before, and I nodded.

"That's the spot."

"I can't imagine what he must have thought during those final moments."

"I'm guessing he wouldn't have thought much after the attacker stabbed him in the heart."

"No, of course, but still. It's a terrible way to go," Morris said.

Before I could answer, headlights suddenly lit up the main alley, and a few seconds later, a truck rolled to a stop after passing by the mouth of the driveway. At first, I thought it might attempt to reverse into the driveway where we remained standing, but then it suddenly sped up again before stopping farther down Garland. The light coming from between buildings reminded me of the restaurant Corinne had mentioned. A figure suddenly appeared to emerge from behind a wall, and the driver shook hands with them before opening the back of the truck. Behind me, my would-be stalker continued to study the place, and I watched him for a moment or two before needing some answers of my own.

"What's your end game here, Morris?"

He stopped to look at me with surprise. "My end game? I'm not following."

"You hire me in secret to defend Corinne, then show up at the courthouse and don't seem bothered to be seen by her. Now I find you following me here to what? Sightsee?" I shook my head in confusion. "Where do you see this going?"

"Well, hopefully, you'll weave your magic and manage to convince the jury of your client's innocence. Once she's free again, I might try to rekindle some sort of friendship with her and see where it leads."

"You really think you have a shot with her?" I tried to recall our initial conversation. "Especially after she lost her husband to your wife?"

"If there's one thing I know about Corinne's ex-husband, it's that she should have been glad to see the back of him. Eric wasn't exactly a devoted partner, if you catch my drift."

"That much I gathered from the fact that he ran away with someone else's wife," I said.

"I mean, he wasn't exactly husband of the year long before that moment. The guy made it his living duty to be an asshole."

"And you're hoping she'll just open her doors and invite you in?"

"Who knows?" he said with a shrug of the shoulders. "I'm not holding my breath, but if it happens, it happens."

"And the part about starting a relationship with a lie? Isn't that kind of the same thing as her ex?"

He chuckled once and nodded. "I guess so, but a white lie pales in comparison to what he did."

"A lie is a lie," I said, but he ignored it.

"I'd better get going. I have a cat who gets mighty anxious when left alone for too long."

When Morris waved me goodbye and headed back down the alley, I didn't follow him, not until I was sure he was gone. I spent a few extra minutes at the crime scene, trying to sense the energy of the place. Morris was right about the place feeling creepy. The darkening shadows and the distant sounds of the city in general gave it a definite vibe I didn't care for. I walked back out into the main alley and waited a few extra minutes to see just how many people used it as a shortcut. I still believed it to be the perfect place to ambush an unsuspecting victim, and if Marco De Baun really had set a trap for an unsuspecting victim, then I was standing in the very spot where he would have been on the night of the murder.

I waited a good ten minutes and saw exactly one person trudge through the back alley. The person did slow when they spotted me in the distance, and I realized I must have been giving off similar vibes to a mugger. When the businessman got near enough, I waved a friendly hello to assure him I wasn't going to attack.

What's funny is that I chose that moment to head back to my car, and I ended up following the unfortunate soul to the end of the alley. He took several glances over his shoulder for a few nervous minutes, and I breathed a sigh of relief when he turned the opposite way to where I needed to go. Once back at the Mustang, I didn't hesitate to fire it up and head home. I'd barely gotten half a block down the road before my cell phone began to ring.

"Linda, how are you?" I said after hitting the answer button on the steering wheel.

"I'm good. How was your first day in court?" I could hear voices in the background, and it took me a moment to realize it was Brittany Munro, the news anchor on Channel 11.

"Not too bad. Not exactly kicking goals, but I don't think

the witnesses really offered much chance of that. How are things on your end?"

"I actually just had a very interesting phone call from a nervous receptionist who isn't sure whether she should be bothering you with trivial things."

"Dale Rich's secretary?"

"No, Bryce Lloyd's." It took me a second to picture the woman from the previous visit.

"Trudy?"

"That's her. She told me she wasn't sure whether to bother you, but when she told me what she knew, I organized for her to meet with you tomorrow after court."

"She's got information to blow this case wide open?" I tried to sound hopeful, but I think it came out sounding more facetious than anything else.

"She actually might have," Linda said, ignoring my attempted humor. "She says she has information regarding her boss emailing Dale Rich. I'm not sure about the details. She didn't want to share them over the phone."

"Lloyd conversing with Rich?" I couldn't believe what I was hearing and had to stop everything else to focus on the words again. Thankfully, the red light helped my cause.

"Sounds to me like you might finally find out what had gone on between them."

"Damn it, Linda, this could change everything," I said, hoping that it was the smoking gun I so badly needed. "If this shows Lloyd accepting Rich's offer, then..."

"Let's wait until we see what she has first," Linda said. "Better not to jump the gun. It could just be Lloyd trying to cover his butt."

"Could be, but I don't have a good feeling about this. What time is she coming to see me?"

"Five-thirty at your office."

"OK, thanks," I said, and hearing a pause at the other end, asked whether she had anything else for me.

"I do, actually. Those voice samples just came in. I compared Van Hess to the caller of the anonymous tip, and they don't match, Ben."

"Damn it," I said. "Would have been a nice, easy slam dunk if they had."

"Let me poke around a bit and see if I can find samples from some associates. Maybe we'll get lucky. I'll email these so you can have a listen."

"OK, thanks," I said and ended the call.

I drove the rest of the way home in silence, positive that what Linda had told me would be the actual revelation. To be honest, I thought about nothing else that night, and when I finally managed to get myself to bed, I lay on top of my mattress with one arm under the back of my head, staring up at the ceiling. Sleep felt a million miles away, and the fatigue that had briefly appeared after my shower also disappeared the second I lay down. It felt like an actual nightmare haunting me night and day, the same four people constantly shuffling positions in a case I still struggled to get my head around. Who knew the eventual outcome if I didn't start making sense of it all?

TWENTY-THREE

I woke the following morning to the same thought that I had gone to sleep with: Who among the three main players of the case was telling the truth? I thought about my meeting with Bryce Lloyd during my shower, remembering how charming he made himself out to be. In a way, I couldn't wait to speak with his receptionist, if only to ask her whether he really was like that when nobody was watching.

Thanks to falling asleep late and then hitting the snooze button on my alarm multiple times, I ended up jumping out of bed almost half an hour late, and it put me behind enough that I had to skip making myself coffee. Thankfully, my assistant had an out-of-the-ordinary ability to sense whenever I lacked something, and when she messaged me asking if I needed anything on her way to the courthouse, I asked for a coffee.

Grace ended up meeting me in the parking lot instead of inside the foyer, the way she normally did, and let me tell you, that first taste of double espresso reached all the way down to my toes. A shiver, the kind some people referred to as someone walking over your grave, followed close behind, the uncontrollable spasm almost causing me to spill some.

"You OK?" Grace looked at me oddly as we turned for the courthouse.

"Didn't sleep well last night," I said and took another sip to ensure the caffeine hit me in time for the first witness. "Linda called last night to say that we're having a visitor drop by this afternoon."

"Oh? Who?"

"Bryce Lloyd's receptionist. Or should I say Corinne's receptionist?"

"I'll make sure to be there after the hospital appointment." I looked at Grace and saw something change in her demeanor.

"Hospital? Is everything OK?" The smile she pushed out looked forced, but I left it alone.

"Yes, it's just Dwight having a routine check-up, that's all. It's set for two, so I should be back in time."

The media pack waiting in front of the courthouse robbed me of the chance to follow up on my original question. I stopped to answer several of their questions before continuing on. Grace waited for me just inside the foyer, and together, we made our way through to the courtroom, where the prosecutor already sat at her desk discussing something with the DA. She did spot me and flash that eye-catching smile of hers, but she made sure Clements's attention was elsewhere before risking such a bold maneuver.

In case you've been wondering, I think Elsa Schwarz continued her pursuit of me because she could sense a certain amount of interest from my end. Yes, I found her incredibly attractive, and the fact that we were both lawyers also made the prospect of a relationship with her extremely appealing. I know that if I had walked over and asked her out on a date, she would have accepted in a heartbeat, but my problem was and always had been my ongoing commitment to Naomi.

Oh, I can hear you groaning at the mere mention of her name, but the truth is, I couldn't let go. I'd heard people tell me plenty of times that it was time to move on, that it wasn't a betrayal to move on after the death of a partner. It was Linda who once told me that it was actually a sign of respect to move on. How did she put it?

"Do you really think she would have wanted you to go through life alone and always grieving her?"

The thing is, it wasn't betrayal I felt. I hadn't moved on to someone else because I thought it was me cheating on the memory of my wife and child. What I felt was unfinished business. To me, the chapter remained wide open, and until I found the person responsible for her death, I didn't think I could ever move on. I wasn't looking for closure in the arms of another woman. I needed the closure to be me finding the reason behind her accident.

When I turned to my chair, I found Grace watching me from her seat, and the grin on her face was enough to tell me what she was thinking. No words needed. I pursed my lips and shook my head, pretending to look annoyed, but Grace's snicker signified my failed attempt. It took the bailiff bringing the court to order for me to escape my assistant's amusement.

When Adams retook his seat on the bench, the judge didn't waste time bringing out the rest of the parties, and only when the jury members were seated did he hand the prosecutor the floor. Elsa gave me a brief sideways glance before calling her next witness. That brief look stirred something inside me, and not in a good way.

"We call Wen Yu to the stand, Your Honor."

The woman who walked into the courtroom would have

struggled to reach the five-foot mark, but whatever she might have lacked in height, she more than made up for with confidence. You could see it in her stride, the woman walking with purpose, and when she glared at the defendant on her way to the witness stand, I knew that things were about to get serious.

"Please raise your right hand and state your name for the record," the bailiff asked her once she took her seat.

"Wen Yu."

"Do you swear that the testimony you are about to give will be the truth, the whole truth, and nothing but the truth, so help you God?"

"I do," the woman said and immediately turned to face the court.

Knowing that this was the kind of witness to make a case, the prosecutor first rose from her chair and walked almost the entire distance to the witness stand before speaking. Behind us, the rest of the courtroom sat in silent anticipation of what would come next, including me.

"Ms. Yu, could you share with the court what you do for work?" Elsa took up the perfect position to maintain eye contact with both the witness and the jury.

"I run a small restaurant."

"And where is this place of business located?"

"615 Grant Street," the woman said without hesitation.

"That's the Lutheran church, is it not?" The prosecutor knew her city.

"We lease a small building from the church, yes."

"And I understand this building has two entrances, is that correct?"

"Yes, that's right. Our main entrance faces Grant Street, while the other opens onto Garland Way. We keep the door to the kitchen open for patrons to walk through and see the food cooked for themselves."

"Ms. Yu, do you recognize the defendant as ever having frequented your restaurant?"

"I do, yes. A couple of times, I believe." She looked from the prosecutor to Corinne and held her gaze when Elsa asked her next question.

"And you contacted the police regarding an interaction you say you witnessed between the defendant and the victim, Dale Rich, is that correct?"

"I did." Her eyes never shifted.

"Can you tell the court what you saw?"

"I was out the back emptying some bags of trash when the defendant first walked past me. She spoke so loudly into her phone."

"Would you describe Ms. Lucas as being agitated?"

"Yes, definitely. She wasn't happy, that's for sure. I watched her for a few seconds and then continued with the trash."

"Objection, Your Honor," I interrupted. "Speculation. How could the witness know my client's emotional state?"

"Sustained." The prosecutor didn't miss a beat, anxious to get to the point of the testimony.

"How long would you say you noticed the defendant talking on her phone for?"

"I watched for maybe a minute before turning my attention away, and then another minute when I finished with the trash."

"Was there anybody else in the alley at that time?"

"Yes," the witness said. "A man walked into it a few minutes after Ms. Lucas."

"Did you happen to get a good look at him?"

"I did, yes. It was the victim, Dale Rich."

The prosecutor took a few steps away from the witness stand to give herself time to spread out the testimony. The jury followed her, watching and waiting for the next question while the witness continued staring at the defendant.

"Did you ever see any interaction between the victim and the defendant?" Elsa asked but didn't turn to face the witness. Instead, she also watched my client from a distance as if to try to amplify the question's relevance.

"Yes, I did. I had to go back into the restaurant, but when I came out again a couple of minutes later, I heard the defendant arguing with Mr. Rich."

"Were you able to hear what they were arguing about?" Elsa sounded hopeful, but of course, she already knew the answer.

"No, I couldn't."

"How would you describe their conversation?"

"Mr. Rich appeared quite calm despite Ms. Lucas getting right into his face. She did look quite angry, but like I said, I couldn't hear what they were arguing about."

"Did you ever see the defendant strike Mr. Rich?"

"No, I did not."

I listened intently to the questions as the prosecutor continued extracting as much detail from the witness as possible. Despite doing my best to look for a chance to interrupt the flow, the prosecutor kept a fairly tight rein on the witness, effectively denying me the opportunity to interject with objections.

My chance for redemption came when the judge handed the witness over to me for cross-examination, and I didn't waste time getting to my feet.

"Ms. Yu, I'm curious to know how long it took you after

that night to contact police about what you saw." It was the first time I watched her hesitate to answer.

"Three days," she eventually said.

"Why did you wait so long before contacting the police?"

"I was busy."

Feeling a need to play the game as much as the prosecutor, I looked at the jury and amplified my confusion.

"Too busy to report witnessing a murder victim arguing with a potential suspect? Did you not see the first responders on the scene? The emergency services eventually flood the alley?"

"No, I didn't. I ended up heading home soon after watching the argument."

"May I ask why?"

"My daughter phoned me to say that she needed help with a school project, and I obliged." I wasn't buying it and felt the need to go fishing.

"You didn't hear about the murder from your colleagues the next day? No news bulletins?" Again, I saw her hesitate, this time briefly looking over to the jury before turning back to me.

"I read something in the newspaper the following day, but I honestly didn't make the connection until I saw Ms. Lucas on the front page of the *Post*."

Rather than let it go, I knew I needed more, especially if I was going to try to change the course of the testimony.

"Ms. Yu, did you happen to see the defendant again that night?"

"Yes, I did. It was about five minutes after I came back into the shop that she walked through."

"Did she say anything?"

"Yes, she canceled a reservation for that night."

"And who took this cancellation?"

"I did." Needing to put on a show and amplify every possible positive answer, I turned again to the jury and directed my next question in their direction to ensure maximum engagement.

"So you spoke directly with the defendant?"

"Yes, I did."

"And how did Ms. Lucas sound? You described her as highly agitated just moments before. How did she look when she stood in front of you, canceling her reservation?"

"OK, I guess."

"OK? OK, as in calm?" The witness looked from the jury back to me again as if needing some reassurance.

"She was calm, yes."

"And did she appear nervous at all?" I took a couple of steps closer to the witness stand and held my hands clasped in front of me as if ready to welcome her answer.

"Nervous? I don't understand."

"The prosecution would have us believe that the defendant had just murdered Dale Rich during a heated argument, and I'm asking you how the defendant appeared when she stood in front of you just a few minutes later. Did she appear nervous to you?"

"No, she wasn't nervous."

"Not agitated? Not distraught in any way?"

"Objection, Your Honor. Asked and answered."

"Sustained."

"I withdraw the question, Your Honor," I said and moved things along.

"Ms. Yu, in your own opinion, would you say that the defendant resembled someone who had just committed a murder?"

"No, she did not."

"Thank you. No further questions, Your Honor."

While I don't think I completely destroyed the prosecution's witness, I do think I managed to introduce enough doubt into the minds of the jury as to the mental state of my client in the moments immediately after the murder. It was obvious Corinne Lucas wasn't a serial killer, and if she had committed the murder of Dale Rich, then it was highly probable that she would have displayed some sort of visible trauma. A woman like her doesn't go and stab someone fourteen times and then walk away, concerned about an unnecessary restaurant reservation, and I think the jury could see that.

The prosecutor ended up calling a further four witnesses that day, although none of them compared to the first. Three of the witnesses turned out to be experts in various fields who took the jury through several forensic pieces of evidence, one a clinical psychologist who tried to draw comparisons between the defendant's mental state and that of a number of previously convicted killers. It definitely felt like the prosecution was grasping at straws.

When I walked out of the courthouse later that afternoon, I almost groaned when I remembered that I still had an appointment back at the office. Fatigue had begun tormenting me during the previous hour, and I had struggled to suppress the urge to yawn again and again while listening to the prosecutor question the last witness of the day. All I wanted to do was head home and crash on my bed, but it wasn't to be. Grace also reminded me of the appointment via text, having left the courthouse for the hospital appointment with Dwight. It appeared as if she wasn't going to make it back in time after all.

Trudy, on the other hand, turned up a lot earlier than expected. I found her already sitting in the waiting room near our reception when I walked back into the building. Dawn, our new receptionist, led her into my office after giving me a moment to prepare myself. It had been a long and hectic day, and sometimes, nature just needs to be given a little bit of attention to bring things back to a comfortable state.

"Ben, I have Trudy Wallis for you."

"Thank you, Dawn," I said, rising from my chair to welcome my visitor.

Dawn stepped aside and waited for the guest to walk in before offering us a drink. When we both declined, she quietly made her exit and closed the door.

"Please, Miss Wallis, take a seat," I said once we got the initial greetings out of the way. I did note her looking quite nervous and immediately set her mind at ease. "You know I will keep this meeting in strictest confidence."

"I don't see how you can once you see what I have for you." As if needing to explain her words, she leaned forward and placed a folded sheet of paper on the desk. "If Lloyd finds out I have this, he's not going to be very happy."

I picked up the paper and unfolded it to reveal print on both sides. It appeared to be an email exchange between two parties I was well aware of. The first, Dale Rich, appeared to be the aggressor, demanding that the second party, Bryce Lloyd, accept his terms.

Dale Rich— *"I've been more than generous with you, Bryce, and after giving you the Hanscom account for free, I think it's only fair that you accept my terms."*

Bryce Lloyd— *"Damn it, Dale, how many different ways can I possibly tell you to beat it before you accept my decision? I'm not interested."*

I continued reading the exchange until it abruptly ended with Lloyd threatening legal action if Rich didn't stop harassing him. The one part of the exchange that raised eyebrows for me was when Rich threatened to expose a secret about Lloyd that had the potential to ruin him for life. Only when I finished did I look over at Trudy, who had taken an interest in the photo hanging on the wall behind me.

"What's this secret that Rich threatened to expose?" Trudy looked at me but didn't answer on account of her boss finding out, and so I had to try to convince her. "Trudy, if I'm going to use this to try and clear Corinne's name, then I need to know everything. That is why you're here, isn't it? Because you want to see your employer walk free?"

She nodded, rolled her hands into fists, and held them in her lap while looking at the photo again. It showed a much younger version of me receiving my degree during a long-ago graduation ceremony.

"I always dreamed of becoming a lawyer," she finally managed. "My father was one, and he often spoke about his daughter following in his footsteps."

"It's never too late," I said.

"My father was an abusive drunk who used to beat my mom. I wanted to be a lawyer to help people like her."

I immediately understood her dilemma. "And you didn't want to become a lawyer because he would have thought you were fulfilling his dream." She nodded.

"Maybe now that he's gone and no longer hurting anyone, I might give it a shot." When she looked back at me, I could see a strong sense of loyalty to her mother. "He died from cancer last year."

"I'm sorry for your loss."

"Don't be," she said. "I'm certainly not."

Trudy shifted her weight, straightened, and rubbed both of

her hands along the top of her pants as if wiping away some unseen lint. It was her way of refocusing herself.

"Ms. Lucas doesn't deserve to be sitting in that jail cell, Mr. Carter. She's a kind woman and definitely not capable of killing anyone. Whatever grievances she had with Mr. Rich, she would have sorted them out another way."

"I believe you, Trudy," I said and waited for her to remember my original question, which she did without another prompt. "Mr. Lloyd is a very private man, Mr. Carter, and prefers to keep to himself when away from his work." She took a deep breath before continuing. "He's also very private about who he sees away from the office, namely his partner."

That was when I understood, the questions in my head finding their own answers from the information I had already put together. Trudy didn't need me to confirm that I knew; the look on my face was confirmation enough.

"He and Matthew have been seeing each other for more than a year now, but given his own situation, neither of them wanted to make it public."

"Now I'm starting to see the whole picture."

"Dale Rich tried to blackmail Mr. Lloyd into a deal by using his sexuality," Trudy confirmed with another nod. "Matthew is the principal at St. Augustine's, a private school in Morgantown."

"I'm guessing even with today's understanding, Matthew wouldn't feel secure in his role if the school board found out about his relationship."

"The school is Catholic, and from what I understand, extremely strict," Trudy said.

"And Bryce didn't want to risk his partner's career," I finished, now able to see the whole story.

I looked at the piece of paper still in my hands and considered my options. Introducing it into evidence would mean bringing up the blackmailing, and that in turn would force me to reveal the reason behind it. Revealing such a secret in open court would undoubtedly cost a man his career, the woman in my office her job, and still not clear my client's name. If anything, it might actually benefit the prosecution by proving yet more intent on the part of my client or even her business partner.

Instead of using the information, I decided that I needed to find another way. I refolded the sheet of paper and held it out to Trudy, who looked at it with surprise.

"You keep this," I said.

"But it will help the court case against Ms. Lucas."

"No, it won't," I said. "It will end up costing Matthew his job and probably yours as well. Keep it, Trudy. I'll find another way."

TWENTY-FOUR

IF YOU EVER WANTED TO FIND OUT HOW MUCH manipulation was going on behind the scenes of a murder trial, just check out the list of witnesses assigned to testify against the defendant. Sometimes, it will look obvious, but other times, certain witnesses make it onto the list completely undetected. Or so I thought.

When the prosecutor called Hayden Gunn to the stand to open the next day's proceedings, the morning began with quite a bang. The first indication I got of the subsequent furor was when my client visibly flinched at the sound of the name.

"You know him?" I asked while watching the witness walk down the aisle on his way to the main floor.

"I do," Corinne said. "He helped Dale open his business back in the beginning. Not someone I've been looking forward to seeing here."

"So a competitor?"

"You could say that."

Gunn took the stand, and after being sworn in by the bailiff, he turned to face the approaching prosecutor.

"Mr. Gunn, could you tell the court how you came to know the deceased, Dale Rich?"

"I met Dale during a fundraising event in New York back in 2021. He told me about a business plan he had and said that I would make the perfect partner."

"And what did you tell him about his offer?"

"I told him I wasn't interested. I was happy where I was, and it would only inflame the relationship with my current business partner."

"But you did in fact end up working with Mr. Rich, did you not?" The prosecutor took up a position in the middle of the floor facing the witness.

"I did eventually, yes."

"What changed?"

"I found out my business partner was cheating me, and Dale's subsequent offer turned out to be too good to turn down."

"Care to share with the court the details of his offer?"

"Yes, of course. A hundred thousand sign-on bonus, two hundred thousand annual salary, and five percent commission of all sales the business generated."

"That's quite a package," Elsa said as she remained fixed to her spot.

"Yes, it was."

"And when did you meet Ms. Lucas?"

"I'd known Corinne for a few years prior to signing up with Dale. It's a rather niche industry, and we know most people within it."

"What was your opinion of Ms. Lucas when you first met her?"

"She seemed very professional. We crossed each other's

paths on a few occasions, and she always treated me with the utmost courtesy."

"Did everyone else feel the same way about her?"

"Objection, Your Honor, speculation."

"Sustained," the judge said without delay. Rather than react, the prosecutor simply sidestepped the question.

"Mr. Gunn, do you know the defendant's business partner, Bryce Lloyd?"

"Yes, I do."

"Could you describe your relationship with Mr. Lloyd?"

"Again, we kept our interactions mostly professional."

"Mostly?" The prosecutor took a couple of slow steps forward.

"There was one time recently where I found Mr. Lloyd drinking alone in a bar in LA, and since we both hailed from the same city, I decided to strike up a conversation with him."

"Could you tell us about that conversation?"

"Bryce appeared frustrated, angry almost, and I asked him if he was OK," the witness said, looking directly at the jury as if speaking to them.

"Did he tell you why he was angry?"

"Yes, he did. He said that he had been approached on several occasions by Dale Rich to join the firm."

"Why would your business partner approach another competitor?"

"I wasn't his partner by then. When I signed up with Dale, I made it clear I would only stay for two years, just enough time to establish his business."

"I'm sorry, I thought you approved of the package he offered you?"

"I did, but I had already made up my mind to leave the

industry before Dale ever approached me. I think he wanted Mr. Lloyd to take my place."

"And did Mr. Lloyd consider your former partner's offer?"

"He said he was considering it, yes, but hadn't yet made up his mind."

"That's a lie," Corinne suddenly snapped loud enough for the judge to look over at her. I felt her tense up and reached over to give her forearm a squeeze. Not wanting to miss an opportunity, the prosecutor turned to also look in our direction before turning back to the witness.

"Please don't," I whispered to Corinne, but she didn't answer.

"Mr. Gunn, please continue."

"I asked why he would consider leaving his current business partner, and he said that he was tired of constantly dealing with the financial woes."

"His business had financial issues?"

"Objection, Your Honor, the witness can't testify as to the financial situation of a business he has no involvement in."

"Sustained," Adams ruled as I retook my seat.

"Let me rephrase," Elsa said. "Mr. Gunn, did Bryce Lloyd elaborate on his statement?"

"He said that he saw repeated overdue invoices that were supposed to have been paid by his business partner. According to him, she handled the banking side of the business."

"That's a lie," Corinne repeated, this time with slightly more volume than the judge cared for.

"The defendant will remain silent during these proceedings, or I will have her removed from the courtroom." Adams looked at me as he spoke and, knowing he meant it, I leaned closer to my client.

"Corinne, you need to keep quiet," I whispered, and again,

she didn't respond, although she did glance ever so briefly in my direction. The judge continued staring at me for another few seconds before giving the prosecutor the nod to continue.

"Mr. Gunn, I apologize. Please go on."

"Mr. Lloyd said that if things didn't improve with his partner, then he would be forced to relocate his interests to a new partner."

"Did he say why he thought the issues were happening?"

"He said he had a suspicion that she was going broke and—"

"THAT'S A LIE!" Corinne suddenly screamed, this time rising to her feet and slamming both fists down onto the table hard enough for me to jump. She caught me completely by surprise, and it took me a second to realize what was going on. The judge, however, didn't miss a beat.

"Remove the defendant from the courtroom," he yelled to one of his officers before calling a brief recess.

What followed was a scene worthy of any front-page headline as three court security officers wrestled with the defendant as she continued screaming at the witness. Unperturbed, Gunn remained sitting on the stand with a blank expression while Corinne unleashed. I tried to calm her down as much as possible, but she wasn't listening to a single word I was saying. It ended up taking almost three full minutes before the officers managed to drag her through the door and out into the holding cells.

"That's a wild one," the prosecutor whispered to me when she walked past on her way back to her side of the courtroom, but I didn't respond. Instead, I headed around to where I knew Corinne would be held until she calmed herself. The second she saw me, she unleashed a second time.

"He's lying, that son of a bitch is lying."

"OK, but this isn't—"

"HE'S GOING TO BURN ME DOWN, BEN."

I stood on the other side of the bars in silence as her screaming brought one of the officers back around. He gave me a look of frustration, and I waved an acknowledgement in return, the kind that said I would take care of it. He eventually agreed to leave it to me, and I think Corinne finally realized that she'd screwed up when she dropped to the metal bench and began to sob.

"I've screwed everything up," I heard her whisper into her hands. "And now they all think I'm guilty."

"Nobody thinks you're guilty," I said, an exaggeration, but one I needed to try and calm her. "Not that it matters what everyone thinks. The jury needs to be convinced beyond a reasonable doubt, and this outburst doesn't prove anything except that you are someone under extreme pressure." I knelt down to get on Corinne's eye level. "Do you know who wouldn't lose control? Someone who knows their guilt."

After spending a few minutes with her, I left Corinne to gather herself while I headed back to the courtroom. The bailiff greeted me at the door and asked me to join the judge in his chambers. I found the prosecutor waiting for me at his closed door.

"I hope she calmed down for you."

"She did," I said. "Let's go inside, shall we?"

The meeting wasn't anything significant other than the judge telling me that he was considering blocking the defendant's return for the rest of the day. It didn't surprise me, given his reputation, but after assuring him that my client would control herself, Adams gave in.

"This will be her only warning, counselor," he said before asking us to leave him.

"Think she'll control herself?" Elsa asked once we were back out in the hallway.

"I certainly hope so."

"I haven't seen you at the gym lately. Didn't scare you off, did I?"

She sounded so genuine, and I could feel her interest in me. While our current case meant a direct conflict of interest, I knew it would be short-lived. When she smiled at me, it just hit me in all the wrong places, or right places depending on your point of view.

"Elsa, listen to me," I said, briefly pausing as a couple of lawyers walked past. I waited until they were out of earshot before continuing to speak. "I don't want you to think that I'm trying to ignore your advances. I like you, I really do."

"Then what's the problem, Ben? We're both adults."

I felt bad, I really did. "It's just that I have a lot going on right now with work and with home. I don't want to commit to something I might not be able to devote enough time to."

"You know, I found out from a friend that you haven't really dated anybody since your wife died." She smiled empathetically at me. "I understand, I really do. But I'm not asking for a marriage proposal, Ben. Just dinner, a movie, a drink, something informal between friends."

I wanted to say yes, I really did, but something kept me from doing so. A continuing nagging in the back of my head about needing to do...what? I couldn't put my finger on it, but I could feel Elsa's frustration despite the smile remaining.

"Ask me again when this case is over," I said.

"Promise?"

"Yes," I said and followed her back to the courtroom.

When the judge retook his seat a few minutes later, the first thing he did after calling for the defendant to be brought back out was to give her a stern talking to. Fierce color filled Corinne's cheeks, rising all the way to her ears as the courtroom sat silently listening. Once Corinne promised to keep quiet and not interrupt again, Adams resumed proceedings by reminding the witness that he remained sworn in.

The prosecutor only asked a couple more questions of Gunn, and neither of his answers held any kind of explosive revelations. Elsa thanked the witness, and the judge handed Gunn over to me for cross-examination.

"Mr. Gunn, you stated that Bryce Lloyd told you he was considering joining Dale Rich's business. Did he?"

"No, I don't believe he did."

"Why do you think that is?" I asked while still standing behind my desk.

"I'm not sure. You'd have to ask him."

"Could it be that perhaps there was no issue between him and his business partner, and he was simply messing with you?"

"Why would he do such a thing?" Gunn looked amused by the question.

"Maybe because he knew you still talked with your former colleague, and he wanted to make him think that there might have been an issue."

"Again, I don't know."

"Mr. Gunn, are you aware of a man named Otto Van Hess?"

"Yes, I know Otto very well."

"Well enough to know that your former colleague stole an expensive piece from Mr. Van Hess and made a considerable sum of money from its subsequent sale?"

I expected the prosecutor to jump in with an objection since there had been no official proof of such a theft or sale, but Elsa never made a sound. I guess her intrigue matched my own.

"I heard a rumor about such a sale, yes, but Dale never discussed it with me."

"Do you recall the value of the sale?"

"North of a million dollars," Gunn said, and several people reacted to the sum, including a couple of jurors.

"What about Otto Van Hess? Did he ever mention it?"

"He did."

"And how did he feel about it?" That was when I slowly stepped around the table and walked out onto the floor.

"He wasn't happy about it."

"Did he ever threaten to retaliate?" I stopped in the middle of the floor and looked at the jury.

"Retaliate?"

"Retaliate for the theft."

"Not that I recall, no."

I turned back to the witness and closed the distance between us while asking the next question.

"Mr. Gunn, have you ever known Otto Van Hess to take action against anybody who might have wronged him?"

"Not that I know of, no."

"Never?" I went back to my table and picked up a piece of paper. When I turned back to him, I repeated the question. "Mr. Gunn, never? I remind you that you're under oath."

"OK, maybe once."

"Could you share the details with the court?" I stopped halfway across the floor.

"He paid someone to beat up a competitor who double-crossed him."

"Double-crossed him how?" I tried to sound intrigued and looked at the jury to make sure I had their attention. Gunn hesitated to answer, and I had to hold my hands out to encourage him.

"OK, so I found out how much he bid for a piece and ended up winning a piece I maybe shouldn't have."

"You?"

"Yes, me. I betrayed his trust, and he sent some boys around to make sure I didn't betray him a second time."

"He had you beaten?" I sounded surprised, continuing to act my part.

"Yes, he did."

"How badly?"

"I ended up in the hospital for a couple of days, but no permanent damage."

"That's good to hear," I said, and then to the judge, "No further questions, Your Honor."

When I got back to the table, I took my seat next to Corinne, who looked at me curiously. When I unfolded the sheet of paper and set it back on the pile, she leaned in and asked, "You had someone investigate Gunn?"

"No," I whispered back before showing her the contents of the page. When she saw the doodle of the horse I'd drawn earlier, she eyed me questioningly.

"Sometimes, you just have to know how to play the game," I said with a grin.

TWENTY-FIVE

THE PROSECUTOR ENDED UP CALLING THE BELLBOY to the witness stand after lunchtime recess. Toby Walker looked like a kid caught in a riptide when he walked into the courtroom, his eyes wide with nerves as he was required to be directed to where he needed to be. The bailiff had to repeat himself twice before the witness confirmed his oath while the rest of the courtroom looked on with amused silence. I did hear a couple of snickers that immediately turned the poor lad's cheeks several shades darker, but one look from the judge shut them off just as fast.

The questions asked of him weren't anything out of the ordinary, his answers almost as straightforward as the facts of the case...with one minor exception. It wasn't the first time he'd seen the defendant at the location.

"Can you describe the other time you saw Ms. Lucas in that loading dock, Mr. Walker?" the prosecutor asked after ascertaining the fact, a fact which again made me question the openness of my client.

"It was a couple of days prior."

"And what was the defendant doing exactly?"

"She wasn't really doing anything. At first, she was standing there looking around as if waiting for something. Then she dialed a number and was just talking on her phone." His face scrunched up whenever he thought hard about an answer, and I could imagine some of his so-called friends ribbing him over it.

"And for how long would you say she was there?"

"At least a cigarette's worth," Walker said and then looked surprised when a few chuckles rose from the crowd. "That's how long I was out there for."

"Would you say more than five minutes?"

The prosecutor kept taking a very slow step back each time she asked a question, and then another two forward when waiting for an answer.

"Nah, maybe five. It was just after four, because the second I walked back inside, Mr. Cables, my boss, asked me to take some envelopes up to one of the suites."

"And was the defendant still there when you went back inside?"

"No, she left by then. I'm pretty sure she headed in the direction of the Jade Dragon."

"The restaurant?"

"Yes."

While the prosecutor continued questioning the witness, I needed to catch up on the revelation myself by leaning lightly closer to my client and whispering the question she would have been expecting.

"Another point you didn't think to mention to your lawyer?"

"I actually completely forgot about it. That was the afternoon I went and made the reservation for my friend and me. I was already in the area and figured it would be easier to go and check it out for myself. I hadn't been there before, and while walking through the kitchen, I got a call from a friend. There's really nothing sinister about it, Ben."

It made sense to me how such an off-the-cuff detour might slip one's mind, especially when then caught up in an absolute nightmare that would have drowned out everything else.

"Let me get up on the stand and explain it," she followed up, but that was where I drew the line.

"Absolutely not," I whispered back, although it might have sounded more like a hiss, the words pushed through clenched teeth.

"Then you tell them," she hissed back, but the judge interrupted before I could respond.

"Your witness, Mr. Carter," Adams called out.

"Thank you, Your Honor." I rose to my feet. "Mr. Walker, how many times a day would you say you go out to that part of the hotel for a cigarette?"

The kid looked like he didn't want to answer at first, scanning the public gallery for any faces he might know. That was when I understood.

"It's OK, I don't think your boss is here listening," I said with amusement, looking at the jury. While the subsequent laughter came mostly from the public gallery, I did get a couple of laughs from several of the jury members.

"Maybe half a dozen times?"

"And would you say these half a dozen times are spread out throughout the day?" he nodded. "I need a verbal yes or no answer, Mr. Walker."

"Yes, spread throughout whatever shift I'm on."

"So you work shifts at different times?" I took a few steps closer to the witness stand to keep the jury engaged.

"Mostly day shifts, starting at eight and finishing around six, but sometimes, I also work night shifts, which start at ten and finish at eight in the morning."

"I see," I said. "And during these smoke breaks, do you ever see other random people in that part of the alley where you saw Ms. Lucas?" He didn't hesitate to answer, his tone turning almost proud as he delivered a convincing answer.

"Oh yeah, loads. Even have conversations with some."

"And what sort of people do you find? Where do they come from?"

"All sorts. Sometimes a delivery driver will come and walk around while waiting, especially down at the restaurant, but I also see the occasional diner from there as well, although they usually tend to be on the phone."

"You mean like Ms. Lucas?"

"Yeah, like her."

"Thank you, Mr. Walker," I told the witness and then handed him back to the judge.

I felt rather impressed with myself for managing to deflect what could have ended up as a potential landmine. Thanks to the kid who probably didn't realize the true power of his observations, I managed to tone down what the prosecutor would have hoped to be a bombshell into nothing more than hearsay. Elsa did give me a sideways glance when I walked back to my table, and the look on her face didn't need words.

"Please call your next witness," the judge said the second I retook my seat, and the prosecutor obliged by calling one Emmet Mulroney, a forensic pathologist I was more than a little familiar with.

Mulroney had an almost cult-following on social media thanks to his fourteen-year-old granddaughter, who had taken the man's thirty-eight years of experience and turned it into a kind of podcast. I'd personally seen him approached by random strangers in a supermarket asking for autographs, something he always obliged them with. He had this warm demeanor that drew people in, making him feel more like a friend than a stranger.

Mulroney greeted Samson McDeere with a heartfelt good afternoon, and the smile on the bailiff's face proved my point. He'd built a connection within a matter of seconds, far outperforming any salesman I'd ever come across. Like me, Elsa Schwarz had a history with the man herself, and the prosecutor wasted little time reminding him of it.

"It's good to see you again, Dr. Mulroney. Thank you for appearing today."

"Good to see you too, Madam Prosecutor," Mulroney said with a grin that almost gleamed under the fluorescent lights.

"Could you describe the injuries you found on the victim, Dale Rich?"

"Yes, of course. Including a number of smaller bruises on the victim's forearms, Mr. Rich sustained fourteen stab wounds spread across his front and back. Six to the back, eight to the front, including two directly into the heart."

Instead of positioning herself on the far side of the witness stand where she could still maintain frontal contact with the jury, the prosecutor instead stood closer to the jury, the reason being the large projector screen the witness used to display his evidence. Each time he spoke, he would use his green laser pointer to highlight a specific area. Some people in the public gallery actually moved seats so as to follow the proceedings.

"Since the murder weapon hasn't been found," Elsa continued, "could you describe the size of the blade used?"

"Seven and a half inches is my best estimate," Mulroney said.

"How can you be so precise?"

The doctor used his laser to point to a specific wound on the front, the photo displaying enough detail to show a slight bruise. "Given that this specific area shows the underlying bruise made from the weapon's guard, I was able to measure the depth of the wound to ascertain the weapon's length." He lowered the laser and looked back at the prosecutor. "Seven and a half inches exactly."

"Thank you for being so precise, Doctor," Elsa said. "How quickly would you say the victim died from his injuries?"

"Mere seconds," Mulroney said with a shake of the head. He raised the pointer again and began to wave it between two specific knife wounds. "Both of these proved to be fatal blows, each puncturing the heart."

"And would you say these two wounds would have been the final blows?"

"Not necessarily, although I imagine the perpetrator attacked Mr. Rich from the back and when he fell continued the assault on the ground." He highlighted a cut on the body's left side. "This here is where the attacker almost missed the victim completely, probably caught up in their frenzied state."

The prosecutor walked a little closer to the witness stand while gazing at the floor, a common bit of theater to make it appear as if she was deep in thought. I can assure you that she knew exactly which question to ask next, having studied each carefully during the preceding days.

"I'm curious to know if there's any way to ascertain the size of the person inflicting these wounds, Dr. Mulroney? From what I can tell, some of these wounds must have taken considerable strength to inflict." The pathologist didn't blink before answering, his response rolling out just as smoothly as if he'd been sharing his latest weekend away.

"If the victim had been standing at the time, I would have said it must have been someone of considerable size and strength, but not with the victim sustaining most of the wounds on the ground. The attacker would have had gravity on their side, and that can make all the difference." That was when the prosecutor dropped the one question she had been heading toward since bringing the witness to the stand, the one question needed to implicate my client.

"So you would say that someone of the defendant's size would be more than capable of inflicting the injuries seen on Dale Rich?"

"Yes, definitely."

"Thank you, Dr. Mulroney. No further questions."

"Your witness, Mr. Carter."

The problem with a forensic pathologist is that they generally speak in facts, rarely offering opinions on their findings. Dale Rich had a specific number of wounds, each wound displayed their own unique characteristics, and those characteristics could tell a story about the weapon and possibly the person wielding it. The one thing those wounds couldn't share was the specific person who caused them.

"Thank you, Your Honor," I said before turning my attention to the witness for just a single question. "Dr. Mulroney, would it be possible that someone of my size and stature could have caused the injuries to Dale Rich?"

"Yes, I would think so. Like I told the prosecutor, gravity changes things. A larger and stronger person would need less strength to inflict the same damage as a smaller and weaker person. So yes, someone of your stature could have also inflicted those injuries."

"Thank you, sir. No further questions."

TWENTY-SIX

THE PROSECUTOR ENDED UP RESTING HER CASE AFTER just one more witness, a friend of Dale Rich who detailed the relationship Rich had had with the defendant, the *private* relationship meant to remain behind closed doors. While it did add another potential nail in the coffin, I managed to deflect potential harm by highlighting that the relationship had been over for quite some time, and it had been the victim playing the aggressor.

Rather than have me start with just enough time for perhaps one witness, Judge Adams instead adjourned the matter until the following morning. The end of the day couldn't come quickly enough, and when Linda sent me a message asking if I was up for a drink at the Hose and Ladder, I took her up on the offer. While not exactly exhausted, I needed a distraction, even if just a temporary one. The thing is, I still hadn't completely gotten over the whole Riccardo Costa thing. Throw in the recent anniversary of Naomi's death, and it hadn't been easy trying to move past it. The court case should have been enough of a distraction, but instead, it felt more like a hindrance.

Linda was sitting up at the bar, appearing to be in deep conversation with a man I didn't recognize. When she saw me stroll up, she waved me over and quickly introduced me.

"Hank, this is Ben Carter, the lawyer I was telling you about. Ben, this is Hank Mason. You remember the guy who tried to break into SpaceX last year and hoped to hitch a ride to the International Space Station?" She grinned and pointed to her new friend. "Hank here defended him in court."

"Ah, a fellow defense attorney," I said and shook the man's hand. "That was one hell of a case to work."

"Nothing but an inflated bunch of exposure," Hank said with a grin before checking his watch. While he tried to make out that he was running late for something, to me, it looked like he'd struck out with the attractive investigator and needed to retreat with his dignity intact.

"Nice guy," Linda said once he was gone and made a revelation old Hank should have probably hung around for. "Could have definitely listened to him until breakfast time."

"Oh really? Hoping for a bit of attention from the Hankster, huh?"

She slapped me playfully on the shoulder as I ordered a beer, and once the bartender set it down in front of me, Linda led me over to one of the booths.

"How is the case going?" she asked once we'd sat down. "The media seems to think your client is going to sink any day now."

"I'm sure they do," I said, and unfortunately, I didn't have the confidence to say otherwise.

We still hadn't managed to find the smoking gun, so to speak, the one piece of evidence I needed to prove my client's innocence. The prosecutor, on the other hand, had managed to link my client to multiple aspects of the case, having proven both opportunity and motive. I felt like my end was sinking and sinking fast.

"I want you to refocus your efforts on Van Hess. Now that we know he paid someone to beat up Gunn, I wouldn't put it past him to hire a hitman over a million-dollar theft."

"You no longer think it was Lloyd?"

"I don't, no, not even after that email exchange Trudy shared with me. Yes, Bryce Lloyd would have done everything in his power to protect himself and his partner, but I highly doubt he'd resort to murder." I shook my head absently. "I'm willing to put money on Van Hess paying someone. If only we could find a way to lure him back into the country and force him to testify."

"Let me look into it. I'm waiting for one of his ex-partners to get back to me. She was the one who came to the States with him when he saw Rich that final time and pressed domestic abuse charges against him, not long after their return. If she *was* here with him, maybe she could tell us something about that visit."

"That would be super helpful. God knows we need something because right now, Corinne Lucas is the sole suspect in this matter, and we haven't been able to identify another."

We fell into a moment of silence while taking several sips of our beers and listening to a rather animated conversation between two slightly intoxicated off-duty cops at the bar. It's funny just how often the same argument about Bruce Lee versus Muhammad Ali comes up within drinking establishments. The argument ended up stretching out to four others sitting nearby before finally dying out. When it did, I said something I had no idea I was going to until the words fell out of my mouth.

"I've been thinking about paying Brian a visit," I said.

For a moment, Linda looked at me with the kind of face indicating that she was searching her brain for the corresponding face that went along with the name. I had no doubt she began with colleagues, associates, witnesses, and even friends. Only when none of them seemed to jump out did she finally make the connection, and when she did, her jaw dropped just like I had envisioned it would the second I told her my plan.

"Brian? What? Are you serious?"

The reason for her shock didn't come as a surprise to me. Brian wasn't exactly someone holding a place in my life, not since the argument we'd had on the day of his daughter's funeral some years earlier. At the time, I swore the man was dead to me and that I wouldn't spend another waking minute in my life thinking about him. If it hadn't been for Riccardo Costa sending me that stupid card trying to mess with me, perhaps I could have continued ignoring him for the rest of my life.

"I think Brian might be one of the reasons I can't move on with my life," I said when Linda managed to close her mouth again. "Maybe it's him I need to reconcile with if I'm ever going to feel some closure around this."

"But you've always been so adamant about not wanting him in your life," Linda said. "What's changed?"

I didn't answer immediately, although it wasn't the first time I'd thought about the answer, one that had reared its ugly head on more than a few occasions over the years, more recently in the hallway outside of a judge's chambers while in the company of a certain prosecutor. Before answering, I took a large swallow of beer, holding it in my mouth for a long time before finally swallowing it and revealing the truth.

"I want to move on, Lin," I said when I looked over at her again. "I don't want to feel alone anymore. I know I could never lose the love I have for Naomi, but like you said, I can't live the rest of my life grieving for her."

"It's Elsa Schwarz, isn't it?"

"In part, yes," I said, no longer feeling a need to deny it. "I'm just not sure how many more perfectly good possible relationships will come my way. How many times can you keep turning sincere people away before they quit coming altogether?"

Linda didn't answer. Instead, she took our glasses back to the bar and got us a couple of fresh drinks. After setting them down on the table, she disappeared to the bathroom for a few minutes, giving me more time to contemplate my decision. It should be evident to you how little the man means to me, given this is the first time I'm mentioning him. Brian didn't exactly have the best relationship with his daughter when I first met her, and it certainly didn't improve. It wasn't exactly strained during those early years, but let's just say that Brian never got a dinner invitation.

When Linda finally returned, I had pretty much made up my mind to visit Naomi's father, although I still didn't have a timeline in mind. It wasn't as if I had a great urgency to meet the man who'd caused so much of my deceased wife's misery during her living years. I'm sure he wasn't watching his door waiting for my grand return either. I doubt he would have spared a single thought on me anyway, no surprise given how we ended things.

To understand how things ended, you have to see the situation from my point of view, the point of view of a grieving husband still struggling to understand the raw emotion running through him. Brian took it upon himself to organize the funeral and everything associated with it and then didn't follow through when the time came. The one service he actually hired someone for, the caterers for the wake, ended up canceling for nonpayment, leaving me to run around like an idiot at the last minute. Imagine then my reaction when he showed up at the actual funeral, trying to take credit for the entire event.

The tension had simmered throughout the church service and then completely boiled over at the burial. It didn't exactly get to the punch-throwing stage, but there was certainly some pushing and shoving, enough for a few others to step in and separate us. It probably didn't help that both of us had been drinking. It definitely wasn't my finest moment, but unable to change the past, I accept that I screwed up. Pushing Naomi's father onto his ass, however, is not something I consider as part of that screw-up.

"So when do you plan on going to see him?" Linda asked once she retook her seat.

"I haven't thought that far ahead," I said. "I'll probably wait until the case is over. I don't think I need two headaches to deal with."

"Well, good luck is all I can say," she said and held up her glass. "You're going to need it."

We clinked glasses and drank. In my mind, I pictured the moment, trying to imagine how each of us would react after such a long time. But despite my knowing that I would imagine a thousand different ways the meeting would play out until the day actually came, one thing remained the same. He would always be Naomi's father, and that was something I could never change.

TWENTY-SEVEN

IF THERE'S ONE THING I KNOW ABOUT COURT CASES, or more particularly murder trials, it's that nobody ever has complete control. Not the judge, not the jury, and certainly not the prosecutor. All it takes is time and patience, sometimes more of one, sometimes more of the other. When I walked into the courthouse the following morning, I knew my time had come, the moment when I would move from a defensive position to an attacking one. It was time for me to start fighting for our side of the case. The only problem I still faced was having the witnesses needed to prove Corinne Lucas's innocence.

Grace met me in the foyer of the courthouse, handed me a coffee, and told me about a file she had added to our Dropbox earlier that morning containing everything she could find on Otto Van Hess. While I had Linda busy looking for evidence linking him to the Dale Rich murder, Grace had been in the background gathering everything she could find on the man's history. I still didn't have any way of bringing him into the country, especially with no legitimate proof of his involvement, which meant I had zero opportunity even to raise his name in court.

The weird thing is, I was more nervous that morning than I had been on any previous day since the start of the trial. Maybe it had something to do with the fact that I didn't feel like I had any case to present. Sure, I had witnesses lined up, some of them capable of throwing the case wide open, but I just lacked that slam-dunk moment. I still didn't have conclusive evidence needed to clear my client's name.

"All rise," the bailiff called shortly after Grace and I took our seats. A phantom hand reached inside me and squeezed when the words echoed across the room.

The next few minutes went by as if on a movie screen. I barely felt a part of the moment, somehow watching things unfold from an entirely detached position. As each piece of the usual routine played out, I tried to remind myself that now was the moment I would have that lightbulb event, that spark flash alive in my brain. The only time I did feel a part of the landscape was when my client came and sat next to me.

"I guess today it begins," Corinne said under her breath, careful not to let the judge hear her.

"Today it begins," I said and smiled.

"Mr. Carter, you may call your first witness," the judge said once the last of the jury had taken their seats.

"Thank you, Your Honor," I said and rose to my feet. Just before I called the name, I looked down at Corinne. She looked back up at me, aware of the decision regarding the witness, and nodded, a final OK for me to proceed. "Defense calls Bryce Lloyd to the stand."

When the business partner of Corinne Lucas walked into the courtroom, I expected to see a man brimming with confidence and ready to help clear his partner's name. Instead, Lloyd walked in looking more confused than anything else. He took a couple of steps inside the doorway and actually stopped to turn and look back over his shoulder. It was only when a second person walked in directly behind him that the confusion hit me as well.

I recognized this second person as an associate of the prosecutor, and it was Elsa Schwarz that they immediately went to. A subdued kind of murmur rolled over the room as this new arrival whispered something into the prosecutor's ear, and with Lloyd still not at the witness stand, the judge finally caught on to the interruption.

"Ms. Schwarz, what is the meaning of this?" he asked with an annoyed tone.

"I apologize, Your Honor, but it appears that there has been a significant development in the case."

"What sort of development?" Adams asked, a question I felt like asking myself.

When the prosecutor gave me a brief glance while listening to her colleague continue to share the details, I sensed something significant was about to happen. All across the courtroom, I could see people exchanging puzzled looks with each other, including me and my client. The problem was that nobody other than the prosecutor and her colleague knew the answer.

"Well, Ms. Schwarz? Are you going to enlighten the rest of us?" Adams sounded more than annoyed, a man who took his position seriously. He wasn't someone to accept letting someone else direct his courtroom.

"Your Honor, I request a brief adjournment and a meeting in your chambers with my co-counsel." Adams didn't look to be in an approving kind of mood.

"And the reason being?"

"There's been a significant development in this matter, and it needs to be discussed in Your Honor's chambers as soon as possible."

"Very well, Ms. Schwarz, but this had better be eye-opening."

"It is, Your Honor," Elsa said and shot me another glance.

"Let's call it thirty minutes," the judge said and slammed his hammer down a single time after giving the prosecutor a questionable look.

"Ben, what is going on?" Corinne whispered to me.

"I'm about to go and find out," I said and followed the prosecutor out of the courtroom.

I hoped Elsa would have given me an indication of what she had found out during our short walk to the judge's chambers, but instead, she held her silence. Not that I asked, of course. This was one of those moments where a lawyer needed more patience than time, the latter not really being an issue. When we reached the door leading into the chambers of our judge, Elsa exchanged another look with me, and that was the first time I had ever seen the woman without her smile.

"Come," Adams called out when I knocked on the door, and after holding it open, I followed the prosecutor inside.

"I apologize for the disruption, Your Honor," Elsa said once we were inside.

"Save your apologies and let's have it, Ms. Schwarz. The suspense is killing me here." I didn't know whether he was joking or just being sarcastic, but I remained silent.

"Your Honor, I've just been informed that the police have located what's believed to be the weapon used in the murder of Dale Rich."

I barely heard the words. I'm pretty sure my brain played them again just to be sure it had heard them correctly. Adams didn't bother waiting for his brain to decipher the words on its own.

"I beg your pardon?"

"The landlord of Marco De Baun, a drug addict who was killed by police while in possession of Dale Rich's property, has been renovating the apartment where the deceased lived. He came across the weapon hidden inside an old bathroom cabinet. The landlord contacted police, who have taken the weapon into evidence and are currently running multiple tests on it."

"Well, I'll be," Adams said as he leaned back in his chair. He sat in silence for a few seconds before looking up at me. "Looks like someone might have been saved the rigors of a trial, Mr. Carter. I propose we temporarily halt these proceedings until we can get the results from these tests. Does each counselor concur?"

Both Elsa and I agreed in unison, our voices almost an echo of each other. When we walked out of the chambers again, I swear I felt like I had just won the lottery. Imagine spending weeks trying to defend a case only to find that the one theory nagging you since the very beginning might just turn out to be the game changer. Yes, I thought that Marco De Baun might have been the one responsible for Dale Rich's murder, but how often is the simplest thing the truth?

People needed weight behind a heinous crime in order to accept it as fact. Think about how many people would prefer to believe some wild conspiracy theory about the assassination of JFK rather than accept that a lone gunman might have been responsible. Lee Harvey Oswald didn't sound like he could have pulled it off alone, and thus didn't hold the weight needed to break through all of the different lines of defense that National Security put up.

I'm not comparing Dale Rich to JFK, but to me, Marco De Baun felt the same. The prosecution needed more than just some random mugger who lost control. If the tests on the weapon proved De Baun as the killer, imagine the DA needing to completely exonerate Corinne Lucas. Imagine the amount of time and effort they put into building a case against my client only to have it all washed away by some junkie.

All Corinne could do was stare at me when I told her the development. She didn't quite have tears in her eyes, but I could tell they weren't far from appearing. At first, she sat there with her mouth hanging open in complete disbelief, and only when I repeated the revelation a second time did the grin break through.

"How long will it take for the tests to come back?" was the first thing she asked.

"Maybe a day at the most. I'm going to petition the court to release you into my custody pending the results, but don't get your hopes up. I'll have you transferred into a holding cell at the very least."

"So I won't be going back to jail?"

"Not if I can help it," I said, and that was when the judge came back into the room to adjourn the matter pending the test results.

Just as I'd promised, I requested Corinne to be released into my custody, but unfortunately, the prosecutor rigorously opposed such a move. While disappointing, it wasn't the end of the world, and after a little more negotiation, I managed to confirm her transfer to a holding cell outside the jail. It meant she would spend the night within the courthouse, but it wasn't unheard of. It just meant she might struggle to sleep in a place where the lights stayed on throughout the night.

I was still pinching myself an hour later when I walked out

of the courthouse into the waiting arms of the media pack. It appeared as if the news of the find had spread quickly throughout their ranks, and I felt ambushed as dozens of questions came flying my way. Most of them asked about how Corinne had taken the news of the find, while others wanted to know how we would move forward if the tests came back inconclusive. I actually shuddered at the thought, unsure of whether the case could survive such a hit. Imagine thinking you stood on the very brink of victory, only to have it snatched away again just as fast.

It was right before I planned to answer the final question when someone threw me an absolute curveball from somewhere near the back of the pack. In fact, I had to ask the reporter to repeat the question to make sure I heard it correctly.

"I'm sorry," the reporter said as he elevated his voice. "I asked whether you had any comment about the death of Riccardo Costa?"

If you've ever been standing in front of a media pack and asked a question everybody wants to know the answer to, then you'll know what I mean when I say the tension intensified exponentially at that moment. It's hard to imagine complete silence in the middle of a huge city, but that is exactly what I heard while standing in the middle of a crowd at that moment. The only sound I remember hearing was some overzealous seagull squawking for food somewhere above me.

"Riccardo Costa is dead?"

"Yes, he was found dead in his cell just a couple of hours ago," the reporter confirmed. The rest of his colleagues continued staring at me, some with their cell phones held out, ready to record my response.

What did they expect a man in my position to say about

the death of someone as well-known as Riccardo Costa? Yes, the man was a stain on the city's image, a diseased lump it would have been glad to get rid of, but could I say it out loud?

"My condolences go out to his family" was all I said and effectively cut off the rest of the questions.

When I walked through the path made by the reporters abandoning their attempts for further answers, I saw my investigator leaning against her Jeep farther up the street, and the head nod she gave me when I approached her confirmed the news I'd just been delivered.

"He's dead?"

"As a doornail," Linda said. "Stabbed to death in his cell."

"Geez, do they know who did it?"

"Hasn't been confirmed yet, but..." She paused and looked down at her feet uncomfortably.

"What is it?" When she still didn't answer, I took a couple of steps closer. "Linda?"

"Costa wrote something on his cell wall in blood before he died." She shook her head in disgust. "The guy had just been stabbed multiple times, and he used his own body as an inkwell, can you believe it?"

"What did he write?" I asked and again felt her tense up. "Just tell me."

"How about I show you?" Linda said and held out her cell phone.

On the screen was a picture of a dirty wall, one corner of the image a sliver of a thin mattress atop a metal bed soaked in blood. I could make out the left arm of what I assumed to be Costa himself, but it was the words he'd inscribed on the wall that I couldn't take my eyes off.

BC was right.

TWENTY-EIGHT

No matter how many times people told me to keep an open mind about the words Costa had written on his cell wall, I couldn't stop thinking about them. For one, not everyone was sure he meant them for me.

"There are plenty of people with those initials, Ben," Linda told me when I handed her the phone back, something Grace echoed an hour later when I walked into the office. Even Dwight added his two cents, telling me that I took the words personally because of what he had done.

"There has never been any connection between that man and your wife," Dwight added when it looked like I wasn't going to accept his initial advice. "If you keep chasing this, son, you're going to end up a miserable and lonely old man."

His words frightened me, especially after the recent conversation I'd had with my investigator about visiting my ex-father-in-law. I already knew I was on the verge of lifelong loneliness, and his words only further proved that. And yet the emotions I felt upon reading the words on that wall just about knocked me over. Who could blame me, right?

Sitting in my office that afternoon felt like torture as two sides of my life felt like they were playing out in my absence with me having no control over either. I imagined Costa getting dragged from his cell in a body bag, thrown into the back of a van, and driven to the nearest morgue. While he might have had the presence of mind to reveal one last secret to the world, the rest of those secrets died with him.

I also imagined a knife sitting in a scientist's tray in an unknown lab, waiting to be tested. Closing my eyes, I could see it glinting under the fluorescent lights, people in lab coats walking back and forth, none of them hurrying to solve our case. I pictured myself standing behind the desk and screaming for someone to pick it up, but none of them heard me.

When my phone rang just after three, my fingers closed a split second before actually grabbing the phone off the desk. It went skittering across the stained timber and slid off the edge, landing with a dull thud onto the carpet.

"Shit," I whispered to myself and hurried to retrieve it. A part of me panicked when I picked it up, positive that the caller would tire and hang up, but thankfully, it continued ringing. "Yes?" I managed to ask when I finally answered the call.

According to the caller, the judge had requested all parties to return to the courthouse at 4 p.m. sharp. The weapon had been tested and the results delivered to the prosecutor. It looked like we would have our answers the very same day.

"Grace, we need to go back," I told my assistant when I emerged from my office.

"That was quick," she said while grabbing her things.

"Looks like they really wanted the answers," I said, remembering Dale Rich's connections. "Amazing what can be achieved when you know people."

When I walked into the courthouse for the second time

that day, I felt a very different energy hanging over the place. A kind of unseen buzz filled the air, a silent energy rippling through every person in the place, in particular those heading to Courtroom 3. The prosecutor was already sitting at her table, as was the district attorney himself.

It appeared as if our courtroom was the place to be, with every seat filled by an enthusiastic onlooker. It looked like the kind of event where ticket scalpers could have been standing near the doors, ready to take advantage of those wanting to be inside. The only person who appeared completely separated from the energy was the one who called the room to order, which he did the second the last of the official parties entered.

"All rise," the bailiff called, and Judge Adams appeared almost immediately while people were still getting to their feet.

When court security brought Corinne out from the holding area, I could tell she had her hopes up. Even her walk had an extra bounce in it, and when she sat, she gave me the kind of smile fueled by hope.

"Please tell me this is it," she whispered, again mindful of the judge hearing.

"We'll know soon enough," I whispered back.

"Well, Ms. Schwarz? Did you get the results you'd been waiting for?"

"Yes, Your Honor, we have," Elsa said as she rose to her feet. She took a quick look in my direction. "Test results handed to me just an hour ago prove conclusively that Marco De Baun used the weapon to murder Dale Rich. His fingerprints match those found on the handle, the blood found on the handle and blade match those of the victim, Dale Rich, and the injuries found on the body match the dimensions of the weapon. The prosecution hereby drops all charges against Corinne Lucas."

I don't remember the cheering from the gallery, but what I do remember is seeing my client close her eyes and begin weeping tears of relief. She also squeezed my hand when I reached over to congratulate her. Once the judge made it official and closed the proceedings, the district attorney led the prosecutor out of the courtroom, leaving me behind to take care of my client.

The pack of reporters who'd swarmed me earlier in the day repeated the process a second time, and it felt great to watch Corinne answer several questions on her own. She looked like a woman reborn, the color already back in her face as she spoke about getting on with her life now that her worst nightmare had come to an end.

This time, I didn't cut the questions short and remained standing by my client until the very last question was asked. Once Corinne answered it, I led her to my car and subsequently drove her home. Along the way, we stopped at a supermarket so she could pick up a couple of items, namely a pizza, which she intended to eat out on her deck underneath the setting sun.

"I haven't seen a sunset in too long," she told me while we were waiting for the pizza to cook.

I dropped her off just after six, and after giving me a final hug, she thanked me for my support, and I headed home myself. I was beat, genuinely exhausted, both physically and emotionally. The day had been one of the craziest in a very long time, and I was ready to close the door on it with a couple of drinks and an early night. Unfortunately, for me, my investigator had other ideas.

"Didn't think I was going to let you celebrate alone, did you?" she told me when I found her sitting at the front door of my apartment. I couldn't help but laugh.

"No, I guess I shouldn't have expected as much," I said and led her inside. "There are some beers in the fridge," I added on my way past the kitchen after setting my briefcase down on the table. "Going to get changed."

After replacing the suit and shirt with a T-shirt and sweatpants, I went back into the living room, where I found Linda waiting for me with a couple of open bottles. She held one out to me as I sat down.

"The first after a win is always the best," I said, clinking the necks of our bottles together and taking a huge swallow.

We chatted for almost an hour before I grabbed my laptop out of the briefcase. I had the habit of needing to clean up the desktop section of my home screen, which I normally filled with all manner of folders and files during an active case. The bigger the case, the more real estate it took up on the screen. Once a case was finished and I had no more reason to keep the files close at hand, I liked dropping them into an archive folder.

While I worked on the computer, Linda grabbed us another beer and began telling me about her new friend, Hank Mason. I almost fell out of my chair upon hearing the name.

"You actually chased him down?" I swear I could see heat rising in her cheeks as I ribbed her. "You? Chased him?"

"OK, so I have an interest in a guy," she said defensively. "Sue me."

"I think it's great that you've found someone."

"Yeah, well, maybe it's your turn," she said.

I had cleared about half the folders when my eyes fell on one in particular, one I hadn't actually accessed since creating it. Seeing it raised a question in my mind.

"You know, we never did find out if it was Otto Van Hess who hired De Baun to murder Dale Rich," I said while opening up the folder.

"Do you really think he did?"

"Not sure, but the first rule of assassination is to assassinate the assassin, is it not?"

"Yes, but the anonymous caller didn't match Van Hess. Unless, of course, he had someone else make the call for him."

Feeling intrigued, and having not listened to the voice samples myself, I clicked on the file marked *Anonymous Caller* and turned the volume up. Linda sat silently by while a voice suddenly filled the room. The call didn't last long, just a couple of sentences, and Linda drank her beer while listening. When it finished, she held up her bottle.

"See? Not Otto Van Hess."

That was when she must have seen the look on my face because I could feel the beating in my chest kick up a gear.

"Ben? What is it?" Instead of answering, I restarted the recording, feeling a need to confirm what I already knew to be true. "Ben?" I held up a finger and pressed Play.

Dread washed over me when I heard the voice a second time, a voice I immediately recognized from several meetings and phone calls.

"You know who it is, don't you?" Linda said when she recognized the look on my face.

"I do," I said, the sinking feeling in my gut robbing my words of all strength. "That's Walter Morris."

"Morris?" Linda sounded as shocked as I was. "Why would Morris make an anonymous call to..."

She didn't need to finish the question, a question I already knew the answer to or had already answered.

"Assassinate the assassins," I repeated while staring at the remaining folders on my desktop.

"What the hell is going on, Ben?" Linda asked, but this time, I had no answers to give.

A million thoughts ran through my mind, none of them connected, and yet all of them surrounding the same thing. I wasn't sure who had played me, but one thing was for certain... I had been manipulated in a way I still couldn't get my head around.

"Give me a sec," I said as a thought suddenly struck me.

I went into the Archive folder and retrieved one of the recent additions. Once opened, I sorted through several files until I found one in particular.

"I need to check this phone record," I told Linda as she climbed off the couch and walked behind me to watch what I was doing on the screen.

"That's Corinne's," she said when she saw me open it and begin running through the individual calls.

At first, nothing out of the ordinary stood out. The previous phone calls I'd checked for remained just where they were supposed to be, mainly the one Corinne had been on in the minutes leading up to Dale Rich's murder. I even pointed it out to Linda, who confirmed the entry.

"I'm not sure what you're looking for," she said. "A call from Morris, maybe? Think they were working together?"

"I don't know," I absently said, and that's when I saw it, or rather, didn't see it.

"It's not here," I said, physically running my finger down the screen.

"What isn't?"

"The call Toby Walker told the court Corinne was on when he saw her a couple of days earlier. He said it had been just after four." I rechecked the date and pointed to the specific section. "See? No call."

"What if she didn't make it, though?"

"But the kid said he saw her dial the number."

"Second cell phone? It's not unheard of," Linda said, and she had a point. The thing was, I could sense something was wrong.

"We have to get to her house," I said. "Maybe Morris wanted her out so he could, I don't know, abduct her?" I closed the laptop and looked at my investigator. "You got your piece on you?"

She chuckled, amused by the question. "Uhm, yeah."

"Let me grab mine. We'll take your car, if that's OK."

Linda swung the Jeep onto the road while I tried to phone Corinne. I wasn't sure what I was going to tell her when she answered, but as it turned out, I didn't need to worry about that as each call I made went directly to voicemail.

"Step on it," I said when I spotted a huge gap in front of us. My concern for my client grew with each passing mile, and I wondered just how much I had screwed up by taking on Morris's proposition to begin with.

We reached Corinne's house just after eight, and from the outside, things looked exactly as they had when I'd dropped her off a couple of hours earlier, save for one thing...the extra car now parked in the driveway. With her house at the very end of a lane running alongside the Ohio River, it kept neighbors down to a minimum. She'd told me how much she enjoyed the isolation when I dropped her off, and I guessed it could have been someone visiting to congratulate her on her release. That opinion changed the second we stepped out of the car and heard the arguing.

Linda and I exchanged a look as we approached. Two voices, one male and one female, came from somewhere at the back of the house. Linda checked the front door and, upon finding it unlocked, entered, while I continued along the driveway and followed it around the side.

It wasn't until I reached the corner of the house that the argument became fully audible. Corinne was the only one talking, and what she was saying made absolutely no sense to me.

"You had one job to do, and you did it. No use begging now."

"I'm not begging, lady," Morris said, his voice sounding panicked. "I did what you asked. Now pay me."

"Oh, nobody is getting paid, you fool. Just how dumb are you?"

When I reached a part of the driveway where I got a clear view of the backyard, I saw my former client standing with her back to me, a gun pointed at the man responsible for hiring me in the first place. Seeing them like that shocked me enough to temporarily freeze my reaction time, but I still had the presence of mind to pull out my own handgun. It was all the time Corinne needed to finish her plan.

"You served your purpose, Walter. Now die," she said, the words sounding as calm as ever before a gunshot punched through the air and cut off the rest of whatever she said. I remember calling out her name, but the bullet's echo far outweighed my voice, and the name simply faded out the second it left my lips.

Walter Morris hit the ground with a bullet to the chest. The way his eyes stared in my direction told me the soul behind them no longer existed. When Corinne turned to walk back into the house, seeing me was enough for her to raise the gun a second time.

"What the hell are you doing here?" she snapped. The question actually sounded more frustrated than surprised.

"I came to save you from a potential stalker," I said, still unsure of what I had walked in on.

"You think Morris stalked me?" She shook her head in disgust. "You really are clueless, aren't you?"

"But you're innocent of Dale Rich's murder. Why would you need to..." I didn't know how to finish the question and so held the gun a little higher. "Put it down and let's talk about it."

"Talk about it? There's nothing to talk about. I kill you, throw you in the same hole I plan to throw this idiot into, and then I'll get on with my life."

With my back to the house, I wasn't sure where Linda was, but I didn't think Corinne knew of her presence, which gave me a hope of someone covering my back.

"Then what's the harm in telling me the truth if you plan to kill me anyway?" She considered my request while continuing to aim her pistol at me. A stand-off was not how I'd imagined the rest of the day playing out.

"Do you have any idea just how close Hayden Gunn was to the truth, Carter? I mean, geez, that guy knows how to send a woman into early menopause." I tried to talk, but despite the lips forming in preparation for the words, none came. "What's the matter?" Corinne asked with a bemused grin. "You look like you're having a stroke."

"Just trying to absorb this."

"This idiot is the one who actually killed Dale. *I* hired him. Offered him a hundred grand."

"What do you mean, hired him? I thought he was your neighbor."

"Nope, got him off the dark web. You'd be surprised what you can find on there." She laughed at the revelation, amused by my complete ignorance. "The only problem was, I didn't have a hundred grand, and so I had to blackmail him into helping me get released. I filmed him murdering Dale."

"You filmed him?"

"How else was I going to blackmail him out of needing to pay him?" She laughed, the sound both grotesque and irritating.

"You put yourself at risk of getting arrested all because you wanted to film him? Why? You want to call others clueless?" I shook my head in disgust. "What about Marco? His fingerprints are on the weapon."

"Put there by Morris. He even gave the guy the clothes he wore during the killing." She laughed again, amused by her own genius. "The only thing Marco thought he had was the Rolex and wallet, and even that came from Morris."

"But why, Corinne? Why go through all this in the first place? What warranted killing Dale?" She grew serious then, the smile fading out completely.

"He was going to steal Bryce from me. Even with all of his loyalty, I knew I couldn't keep him. Gunn was right. I'm broke. Gambling really does suck, you know?" She shook her head in disgust but lacked any real conviction.

"Gambling? That's it? You ruin your business because of gambling and end up murdering a father?"

"Oh, don't give me the sob story, Carter," Corinne jeered. "Dale Rich was far from the man people thought he was. He deserved what he got." She thrust the gun forward a few inches and grinned. It was the first time I saw an evil within those eyes, an evil capable of murder. "Just like you deserve what you've got coming. Goodbye."

"Hey," Linda suddenly called from the back porch, and the distraction was enough to grab Corinne's attention. She turned the gun toward my investigator, the intention to shoot written on her face. I don't know who fired first, but what I do know is that my bullet hit its mark, cutting the woman down in an instant and ending her life as a villain. What I didn't know was the consequences of my actions.

The fallout from Corinne Lucas's death stretched in multiple directions, the biggest winners of all being the media. The reporters arrived at the home just minutes after first responders and immediately began trying to interview anybody who would talk to them. Linda and I spent time being interviewed by police and ended up being taken downtown.

When the sun broke over the city the next morning, I hadn't slept a wink. In fact, both Linda and I had spent the entire night telling our stories to detectives who took quite a bit of convincing as to the details of Lucas's confession. I think the craziest revelation I learned during those hours was that Walter Morris turned out to be an actual hitman, although the numbers surrounding his victims couldn't be verified. The other thing I found out was the identity of a certain individual who hired a number of thugs to beat the crap out of me. Winston Parker? None other than Walter Morris's alias. It turned out that the hitman/slash public defender of Corinne Lucas was running two operations, each in direct opposition to the other. On the one hand, he wanted his employer to remain behind bars and was actively trying to throw her defense into disarray, while on the other hand, he tried to free her by following her instructions and hiring me. Talk about a complete mind...you know what I mean.

Defending Corinne Lucas turned out to be one of the strangest cases of my career. The fact that I didn't need to call a single witness and still effectively ended up with a free client became front-page news. Actually, Corinne ended up on the front page of most Pittsburgh newspapers for three days straight as the media frenzy continued. And me? They called me the Hitman's Lawyer, the tiny headline sitting just above my photo on Page 3.

It's funny how things play out sometimes. I never expected to go into a murder trial fighting for the freedom of a client whose life I would end up taking after she beat the system. Corinne could have walked away but instead ended up lying in a bloody mess right beside the man she had killed just moments earlier.

After getting released from the police station, Linda and I took a cab back to the house to pick up her Jeep. Our intention was for her to drop me at my apartment and then head home herself for a well-deserved sleep. Unfortunately, that's not what happened. Call it a fatigued state of mind, if you will, but halfway back to my apartment, I asked Linda if she wouldn't mind making a quick detour.

"Sure, where are we going?" Linda asked without hesitation. We did make a nearby coffee shop our first stop and grabbed a couple of double-shot espressos for the road.

I gave her the address, and recognizing it immediately, she looked at me across the seats.

"You sure that's where you want to go?"

"I'm sure," I said and nodded my confirmation.

Ten minutes later, my investigator parked her Jeep across the road from a building I hadn't been inside of for the better part of five years. My insides churned with both dread and fear, although I couldn't decide which was worse. Brian Watson's business didn't appear to have changed a single bit since I'd last seen it, the sign hanging in the middle of the building looking just as worn as it had back then.

"Well," I said after finishing the last of my coffee, "may as well get this over and done with."

I was about to grab the door handle and let myself out, my

mind made up to go through with the reunion, but that was when I felt a hand grab my other arm.

"Wait," Linda hissed, her fingers digging into my skin.

"Linda, what the hell?" I cried out, but when I looked at her, the expression on her face immediately silenced me. She was pointing through the windshield to a car parked halfway up the block. The two men who had just climbed out were walking along the sidewalk, headed for the only open business on the block. When they reached the steps of Brian Watson's building, one of them paused to drop a cigarette butt to the ground. As he stomped on it, he looked around at his friend and gave him a nod. I didn't need Linda to tell me who they were: Riccardo Costa's former bodyguard, already known to me.

Don't miss FINAL DEFENSE. The riveting sequel in the Ben Carter Legal Thriller series.

Scan the QR code below to purchase FINAL DEFENSE.
Or go to: righthouse.com/final-defense

DON'T MISS ANYTHING!

If you want to stay up to date on all new releases in this series, with these authors, or with any of our new deals, you can do so by joining our newsletters below.

In addition, you will immediately gain access to our entire *Right House VIP Library,* which currently includes six original novels!

righthouse.com/email

(Easy to unsubscribe. No spam. Ever.)

ALSO BY DAVID ARCHER

Up to date books can be found at:
www.righthouse.com/david-archer

ROGUE THRILLERS
Gates of Hell (Book 1)
Hell's Fury (Book 2)
Ice Burn (Book 3)
Judgement by Fire (Book 4)

BEN CARTER LEGAL THRILLERS
Dead Man's Jury (Book 1)
Trial by Murder (Book 2)
The Hitman's Lawyer (Book 3)
Final Defense (Book 4)

JACOB HUNTER THRILLERS
The Kyiv File (Book 1)
The Bogota File (Book 2)
The Havana File (Book 3)
The Amsterdam File (Book 4)

PETER BLACK THRILLERS
Burden of the Assassin (Book 1)
The Man Without A Face (Book 2)
Unpunished Deeds (Book 3)
Hunter Killer (Book 4)
Silent Shadows (Book 5)

The Last Run (Book 6)
Dark Corners (Book 7)
Ghost Operative (Book 8)
A Fire Burning (Book 9)
Dawnlight (Book 10)
Dead Ice (Book 11)

ALEX MASON THRILLERS
Odin (Book 1)
Ice Cold Spy (Book 2)
Mason's Law (Book 3)
Assets and Liabilities (Book 4)
Russian Roulette (Book 5)
Executive Order (Book 6)
Dead Man Talking (Book 7)
All The King's Men (Book 8)
Flashpoint (Book 9)
Brotherhood of the Goat (Book 10)
Dead Hot (Book 11)
Blood on Megiddo (Book 12)
Son of Hell (Book 13)
Merchant of Death (Book 14)
Extinction C-14 (Book 15)

NOAH WOLF THRILLERS
Code Name Camelot (Book 1)
Lone Wolf (Book 2)
In Sheep's Clothing (Book 3)
Hit for Hire (Book 4)
The Wolf's Bite (Book 5)
Black Sheep (Book 6)
Balance of Power (Book 7)

Time to Hunt (Book 8)
Red Square (Book 9)
Highest Order (Book 10)
Edge of Anarchy (Book 11)
Unknown Evil (Book 12)
Black Harvest (Book 13)
World Order (Book 14)
Caged Animal (Book 15)
Deep Allegiance (Book 16)
Pack Leader (Book 17)
High Treason (Book 18)
A Wolf Among Men (Book 19)
Rogue Intelligence (Book 20)
Alpha (Book 21)
Rogue Wolf (Book 22)
Shadows of Allegiance (Book 23)
In the Grip of Darkness (Book 24)
Wolves in the Dark (Book 25)
Olympus Must Fall (Book 26)

SAM PRICHARD MYSTERIES
The Grave Man (Book 1)
Death Sung Softly (Book 2)
Love and War (Book 3)
Framed (Book 4)
The Kill List (Book 5)
Drifter: Part One (Book 6)
Drifter: Part Two (Book 7)
Drifter: Part Three (Book 8)
The Last Song (Book 9)
Ghost (Book 10)
Hidden Agenda (Book 11)

SAM AND INDIE MYSTERIES
Aces and Eights (Book 1)
Fact or Fiction (Book 2)
Close to Home (Book 3)
Brave New World (Book 4)
Innocent Conspiracy (Book 5)
Unfinished Business (Book 6)
Live Bait (Book 7)
Alter Ego (Book 8)
More Than It Seems (Book 9)
Moving On (Book 10)
Worst Nightmare (Book 11)
Chasing Ghosts (Book 12)
Serial Superstition (Book 13)

CHANCE REDDICK THRILLERS
Innocent Injustice (Book 1)
Angel of Justice (Book 2)
High Stakes Hunting (Book 3)
Personal Asset (Book 4)

CASSIE MCGRAW MYSTERIES
What Lies Beneath (Book 1)
Can't Fight Fate (Book 2)
One Last Game (Book 3)
Never Really Gone (Book 4)

ABOUT US

Right House is an independent publisher created by authors for readers. We specialize in Action, Thriller, Mystery, and Crime novels.

If you enjoyed this novel, then there is a good chance you will like what else we have to offer! Please stay up to date by using any of the links below.

Join our mailing lists to stay up to date -->
righthouse.com/email
Visit our website --> righthouse.com
Contact us --> contact@righthouse.com

 facebook.com/righthousebooks
 x.com/righthousebooks
 instagram.com/righthousebooks

EXCLUSIVE SNEAK PEEK OF...

FINAL DEFENSE

CHAPTER ONE

ON THE MORNING OF JUNE 16, 2022, AT PRECISELY 10:34, a well-dressed man carrying a leather shoulder satchel walked into the Chase Bank located at 301 Grant Street in Pittsburgh and deposited a check for the value of nine hundred and forty-two thousand dollars into the account of William Carlson. Nobody batted an eyelid as the transaction took place, the man thanking the teller with a pleasant good morning before calmly walking out of the branch, where he hailed a nearby cab and directed the driver to take him to the airport.

That might have been the end of the story were it not for a murder that had taken place several hours earlier, and the suspected killer identified by a passerby who called police. Officers put out an APB for the suspect, and when the man tried to check in for his flight to Switzerland, his very short stint as a wanted fugitive came to an end.

The reason I know all of these details is that the man in question became my client just a few hours after being taken into custody and transported to the Zone 1 Police Station. What he didn't know is that I tried my absolute hardest not to take the case for one very good reason. Brian Watson happened to be the father of my deceased wife, a man with whom I hadn't spoken in more than five years. Were it not for a very persuasive boss, who knows who would have ended up with the case, but after a long and bitter argument, I gave in and agreed, thus becoming the man's lawyer.

I'd very nearly spoken to him just the previous day, even before the events I described above. In fact, I had every intention of doing so at the time, but things quickly changed when I saw two specific men walk into his place of business while my investigator and I sat parked in front of his building. Those two men opened my eyes to a reality that immediately shook me to the core, a reality I still struggle to comprehend fully. In short, they shouldn't have been there, and yet seeing them confirmed my suspicions in ways I could have never predicted.

When Riccardo Costa first sent me a card containing a cryptic message pertaining to my late wife, I was so sure of finally uncovering some dark secret that I willingly risked another case to find it. Despite the advice from my friends and colleagues, I couldn't believe that Costa would use me for his own amusement, and yet that's exactly how the subsequent meeting with him went.

Costa played me like a fiddle, more so face to face, when he smirked his way through a meeting that ended with me being dragged from the room and later having to eat humble pie for ignoring the advice of my friends. And yet everything I had believed before that confrontation came flooding back the second I saw those two men walk into Brian Watson's building.

The thing is, Linda and I had been in good spirits up until that moment. The previous twenty-four hours had been quite eventful, given the final confrontation with Corinne Lucas and her hired hitman. Linda even managed to find some information on Morris, who turned out to be a less-than-exemplary hitman after all. His real name was Angus Shaw, and if I had to use a single word to describe him, bumbling might come to mind.

Don't get me wrong; The hitman managed to slice Dale Rich up like a Christmas ham, but let's face it. He'd surprised the guy from behind, rendered him helpless within a couple of seconds, and finished his victim off while he lay bleeding on the ground. What he didn't know was that his employer had set up a video camera to film the attack and then blackmailed him into doing her bidding.

In a way, the recording she had orchestrated to blackmail the hitman out of his payment turned out to be a blessing. I don't think she ever expected to get arrested for the crime herself, and she used Morris to hire me, something he covered up well during our meetings. While Lucas played Morris, Morris played me, and I was the clueless schmuck at the end of the line lapping it all up.

Getting back to Linda and me sitting out front of Watson's business, seeing those two men walk in felt like a sledgehammer to the gut for me. All the volatile emotions I experienced during those brief days after finding Costa's card returned in an instant, the realization that it might not have all been complete bullshit after all. One look at Linda after that initial shock, and I could see the same thoughts running through her head, no doubt wondering whether her advice to me at the time had missed the mark.

Let me tell you what emotions like that feel like. In a weird kind of way, reality takes a sudden sidestep as a new existence takes its place. The temperature in the car immediately skyrocketed as raging heat seemed to rise up out from my collar. Beads of sweat formed on my brow in an instant, while the former slow and steady beating in my chest changed gears. Even my eyes reacted, the vision no longer clear and precise but somehow tinged red from the blood rushing to my face. My fingers shook from what I thought was fear, but I think they trembled from the body trying to use up an overload of energy caused by the sudden adrenaline dump.

"Ben, wait," Linda snapped when she saw me grab the door handle.

"Why the hell are they going to see him?" I could barely articulate the words, thanks to the adrenaline also numbing my lips. "I have to find out what—"

"No, not yet," she said, cutting me off with a tone surprisingly calm. I think she knew that if I heard or felt any sort of excitement or panic from her, it would have triggered my own. "There'll be plenty of time."

"Lin, I have to go *in* there," I said, but she only shook her head.

"I gave you bad advice the last time you came to me for help, and I am not going to fail you a second time, Ben Carter."

I think her second-naming me somehow conveyed the seriousness behind her words. She reached over and touched my arm as if needing a connection to convince me.

"What if Costa did know something about Naomi's accident? What if..." I paused to look through the windshield toward the car the two men had arrived in. "What if he had something to do with it?"

"Then we are going to find the connection and deal with it accordingly," Linda said.

All I could do was sit there and stare at the entrance to the building. My brain barely functioned, too stunned to think about anything but the numerous possibilities it now played out, each scene laid out end to end with the next. I barely noticed the silence in the car or Linda looking at me cautiously while no doubt wondering just how quickly I'd lose control if I did climb out.

We stayed long enough to watch the two men walk out again, just twenty minutes later. I noticed one of them rubbing the knuckles of his right hand incessantly during the walk from the entrance to their car and had a strange suspicion as to why. Linda also noticed, but the look exchanged between us didn't need words. The SUV remained sitting curbside with its engine idling for another few minutes before it finally drove off. I got a good look at the occupants when they passed us by and thought I recognized one as being the driver from the day Costa first met me in the parking lot of the prison, but I couldn't be sure.

When Linda started the car for us to also leave, I asked her to hold off and considered going in to see Brian anyway. He wouldn't have known about me seeing his most recent visitors, and I could have ascertained his condition at the same time. If the knuckle-rubbing had been due to dishing out a beating, then I could make sure he wasn't severely injured. I did, after all, still need answers.

This time, Linda didn't intervene the way I expected her to. Instead, she sat there silently gripping the steering wheel with one hand while resting the other on the gear shifter. I just sat there staring through the windshield, unsure of which decision would be the right one. If we left and Watson really was severely injured, then whatever happened next would be on me. If, however, he wasn't, and my highly emotional state persisted, then I could possibly blow my one chance to get the answers I so desperately needed.

"Catch 22," I whispered, more to myself, but Linda answered anyway.

"Better to have a choice than none at all" was what she said.

"Let's get out of here," I said once I knew I wouldn't be able to trust myself.

I had to face the harsh truth of knowing how unpredictable my own emotions would become if the situation didn't go as planned. Given my wrathful sense of urgency, I couldn't even imagine my reaction if Watson had greeted me with disrespect and refused to talk, especially with me now aware of his connections to a man who claimed to have knowledge about Naomi's accident.

Linda drove in silence, and for the next twenty minutes or so, it felt like each of us sat in our own bubble. She dropped me off in front of my building, where I thanked her for the ride before quietly making my way up to the apartment. Sleep didn't come easily, and when the alarm I'd set for early the next morning began jingling near my ear, I almost launched the cell-phone across the room in disgust.

It took me quite a long time to manage keeping my eyes open, thanks to the fatigue refusing to let go, but it wasn't entirely wasted. Memories of Naomi and me resurfaced, mainly conversations I'd had with her, recalling how a lot of the animosity she'd had for her father came about. It's funny how life sometimes plays out. I never in my wildest dreams thought that I'd ever need to recall those conversations for something as important as investigating her death, and yet there I lay with that exact thought running through my head.

The fatigue only truly faded away completely when I greeted both Grace and Linda in my office at around nine that morning. The latter had brought in a bag of donuts, and I think the sugar helped wake me up properly, it and the double-shot espresso I'd sipped on the way in.

"I can't believe I'm sitting here talking to you guys about

investigating Naomi's father," I said once I put away the last of the chocolate iced donut I'd been manhandling.

"I've already done a bit of poking around," Linda said, "and I might have found something interesting." She pointed to my laptop, and when I waved her forward, she spun it around and began typing. After a few seconds, she turned it far enough for both me and Grace to see what she'd brought up. I immediately recognized the website.

"Derby's?"

The transportation company operated dozens of trucks across the Eastern Seaboard, including both long- and short-distance routes. It offered varying distribution networks to all manner of clients, from small corner stores needing their wares transported from the local markets to huge factories needing raw materials. It wasn't exactly a secret that criminal gangs used transportation hubs to move drugs, money, stolen goods, and whatever else they needed shipped discreetly between locations. Derby's Transport would not have been my first guess at what Linda was about to share.

A man named Peter Derby owned the business with his brother, Jaxon, the pair inheriting the company from their father, who had passed away almost a decade earlier. Being the older brother, Peter not only made all the business decisions but was also the face of the company, quite literally. It was his grin that made up the company logo and stared out at the nation's traffic from practically all sides of each vehicle.

"Watson has been handling the accounts of Derby's for years, but what isn't so well known is that Derby's has also been under constant investigation by the IRS. They've audited the company twice in the last four years. Your old father-in-law has two full-time employees working just on this account, one of whom only started a few months ago because the previous guy got arrested for money laundering." Linda opened her cell phone screen and checked her information. "Lance Baker, sentenced to four years for laundering close to a quarter of a million dollars over six months."

"Laundering Derby's cash?"

"That we don't know," Linda said. "Baker owned a Go-Kart joint in Lawrenceville, which he'd purchased nine months before his arrest. He worked for Watson during the day and ran his own business at night with his wife. They somehow got themselves caught cooking the books and laundering a lot of cash through the business."

"I don't understand what this has to do with Derby's," I said.

"Authorities charged Jaxon Derby with possession of counterfeit notes last year," Linda said. "He was eventually acquitted of all charges, but some of those same notes just happened to be found at the Go-Kart track of Lance Baker."

"It was Jaxon Derby's money that Baker could have been laundering?"

Linda shrugged her shoulders. "Money had to come from somewhere, right? But that's not all. The lawyer representing Jaxon Derby?" She paused, waiting for me to answer, and when I didn't, she finally revealed the connection. "Winthrop Curtis."

Hearing the name immediately stirred something inside me, having seen the man on several prior occasions. I'd never met him personally or professionally, but I'd come close on one occasion. Originally from somewhere inside the United Kingdom, he spoke with this obnoxiously arrogant British accent that I called English snobbery. I should also probably mention that Winthrop Curtis only had a single client...the Costa crime family.

"Curtis represented Jaxon Derby?" I couldn't quite believe my ears. I might not have met the man myself, but I knew him by reputation alone, and that was enough to understand the significance of such a revelation.

"I thought that might prick your ears," Linda said. "Tell me there isn't a connection between the Derbys and the Costas."

"And given that we already know the Derbys to be a client of Brian, it's a link between him and the Costas," I finished. I pondered the idea for a few seconds, the vision of the two men walking into his building coming back to me. "But just how deep does that connection run?"

"That's what we have to find out," Grace said. "Let me get everything I can on this Jaxon Derby case for you. Must be something in there we can use."

"Am I interrupting?" We all turned to see Dwight peering around the corner.

"Not at all," I said as the rest of Dwight's body appeared. "Just going through our plan for investigating Brian Watson."

"Perfect," he said, walked into the room, and effectively changed the course of my day.

CHAPTER TWO

"Sorry to spoil the moment, but I gotta run," Linda said as she got up and gestured for Dwight to take her place, and then to me said, "But I'll deep-dive into Derby a little more to see just what they have going on behind closed doors."

"Thanks, Linda," I said.

Nobody spoke again until Linda disappeared through the door, and for some reason, I felt the air in the room suddenly grow uncomfortable with tension. Grace sat quietly watching, also unaware of what Dwight had in store. I think he was ready for a fight when he eventually broke the silence.

"Listen, Ben, I know you've got your blinkers on with Brian Watson and getting answers to some pretty traumatic questions. Plus, you've only just finished with this whole Corinne Lucas fiasco, but I need you to jump back into the saddle."

"Jump into the saddle with a new client?"

"I know it's not exactly an easy time, and normally I wouldn't even bother you with this. God knows I understand what you're going through, but this one requested you specifically."

I hated people beating around the bush, and Dwight normally wasn't one to do it, which is why it surprised me. The second I heard him say that the client had asked for me, an uneasiness washed over me, evoking a feeling of déjà vu, reminiscent of Walter Morris.

"Who?" I asked. Dwight exchanged a look with Grace, but not being clued in either, she stared back at him questioningly.

"Brian Watson."

The name hung between us for what felt like an eternity. I'd heard it clear as a bell but wasn't sure my brain had deciphered it properly. A part of me wondered whether my subconscious had somehow inserted it by mistake.

"Who?" I repeated.

"It's true, Ben. Brian Watson has been charged with murder and is currently sitting down at Zone 1 waiting for you."

"Murder?"

I honestly felt like English was no longer my first language, the words tangling themselves around invisible roadblocks between my ears and brain. Even Grace shook her head in disbelief and asked her husband to confirm it.

"Are you sure it's the same Brian Watson?"

"Yes, my love, it's him," Dwight said as he turned his attention back to me.

"I'm...I..."

Stuttering didn't help me confirm the reality any more by slowing the words, but it did give me enough time to understand the gravity of the situation.

"No," I finally managed, the word short, sharp, and fully intentional. Dwight didn't understand its meaning at first.

"Yes, Ben, it's true. He's down there. I confirmed it myself."

"No, I won't represent him," I said, clarifying it for him, for the first time since Naomi's death feeling like I owed it to her to avoid her father. Dwight, however, wasn't taking no for an answer. He looked at Grace and subtly nodded his head toward the door.

"Would you give us a minute, dear?"

Not one to argue or get in the middle of anything between her husband and me, she did as asked. She quietly closed the door behind herself, and once we were alone, Dwight tried to make his case.

"He insisted on you, and only you," he began. "Said he would refuse anybody else we sent down there to represent him."

"I don't care," I said. "Not only would it be a direct conflict of interest with what I'm already doing, but the emotions alone would impair my judgment." I shook my head as if needing a visual aid to amplify my answer. "No."

Dwight had never been one to force a client on to one of his lawyers, even ones with specific requests, which is why he surprised me. I could tell from his body language alone that he wasn't going to accept my answer.

"This is actually what you need, Ben."

"Oh yeah? How so?" I felt my temper rising, the heat intensifying with each passing second.

"You're already planning to investigate him. This is the perfect opportunity for you to get inside his head, his business, his entire life." Dwight leaned forward enough to drop his arms on top of the desk. "Think about it. You can ask any questions you have directly of the man himself. There is no need to waste valuable time and manpower, and you can send Linda to investigate other matters."

"No," I said, barely able to register his words. Looking back now, he made a valid argument. I just wish I had seen it earlier.

"Damn it, kid, see the logic in this."

"Stop calling me kid like I'm some junior around here," I snapped, my temper getting the upper hand. "This is about family, and I have the right to refuse."

I expected Dwight to fire back, his own temper ready to retaliate, but unlike me, he managed to control whatever emotion the argument stirred inside him.

"Brian Watson is a suspect in a murder investigation and needs representation. He's also somehow involved with a person who claimed to have knowledge about your wife's accident."

He spoke with an unbelievably empathic tone, the words holding just enough volume for me to hear them.

"Take away the fact he just happens to be Naomi's father, and you would jump at this case."

"That's a pretty big aspect to ignore," I said, still refusing to admit that he was right. All I could see was Watson's expression the last time he and I had stood face to face. "Get someone else to represent him and let me run this investigation from the sidelines."

"He's not accepting anybody else," Dwight said. "You don't go down there, and he'll end up represented by another firm. He did mention that Winthrop Curtis had already tried to represent him, but for some reason, Watson refused."

Hearing the lawyer's name for a second time inside an hour pricked my ears the way it had the first time.

"He said Curtis wanted to represent him?"

"He did," Dwight said. "And we both know who that man already represents."

While I tried to picture the pompous snob walking into Zone 1, Dwight leaned back in his chair and just stared at me. I think he could sense my defensive walls begin to crumble just a bit and tried to figure out a way of smashing them completely.

"You know, I had a similar dilemma myself a few years ago." He chuckled. "Actually, a *lot* of years ago. I had to defend my father after he knocked a cyclist off his bike and almost killed him."

"You defended your father?"

"Look, it was nothing like this situation, of course, but I think the emotions feel somewhat similar. I didn't want to defend him, no, sir."

"Why not?"

"My father wasn't known for being the most sober man around. He enjoyed his drink a little too much and often wouldn't make it much past eleven in the morning before cracking a bottle."

Dwight shook his head and looked up at the ceiling as I felt myself ease back into the chair.

"I hated hugging him, the stink of alcohol on his breath a permanent reminder of what I saw as his illness. Most days, he'd either remain home and drink himself into oblivion, or he'd walk down to the bar on the corner and then stumble home whenever the money ran out. But not that day."

"What happened?"

"That day, he hit the golf course with a couple of friends and then drove home around eight that night. He apparently didn't take losing too well and drank a lot more than usual. He also almost never ate, which meant he had nothing but alcohol in his gut. Well, he rounded the bend a little too wide, hit the cyclist, and pushed the unfortunate rider into the path of an oncoming car. Dad swerved about a second too late, smashed into the back of a cab, and ended up in the hospital for a few hours."

"Was he hurt?"

"Who, my dad?" Dwight sighed. "Only his pride. Concussion and a broken pinky finger. The rider, however, ended up in a wheelchair thanks to a broken spine." He shook his head and snapped his fingers as he must have imagined the scene. "Just like that, life changed in an instant."

"What happened?"

"What happened is that I got the call. Dad ended up with several charges and needed a lawyer to defend him."

"And I'm guessing you didn't put your hand up?"

"Not at first, no. I was disgusted. The man had nearly killed an innocent road user, a new father. The poor guy had only become a dad for the first time like a week earlier, and my father had robbed him of his legs."

"Did you end up defending him, though?"

Dwight didn't answer at first. Instead, he pushed himself out of the chair and walked to the window, where he stood with his back to me.

"I remember seeing the man's photo in the newspaper and feeling so much shame." He turned back to face me. "My father had become the type of man people would openly crucify for being so reckless, and here I was being told that it was my duty to defend him."

"Can't have been an easy decision."

"It wasn't," Dwight said as he slowly walked back to the chair, stood behind it, and leaned down enough to grab the backrest. "But sometimes, it's not really our decision to make. Sometimes, fate has a plan all of its own, and we just end up grabbing hold and seeing where it takes us. I ended up defending him, and because of that case, I opened up this business. I wanted to be the one to decide which cases I worked."

"Did you win?"

Dwight looked at me and grinned. "I think you're missing the point. See, it wasn't about winning but about the case taking me somewhere I never predicted."

"I understand that part, but did you win?"

"No, I didn't," Dwight said with a shake of the head. "It wasn't a case for me to win. My father pleaded guilty, and I negotiated with the prosecutor."

"What did he end up getting?"

"My father had an unblemished record up until that moment. He ended up picking litter off the side of the road for a couple of hundred hours and paid a fine." Dwight retook his seat and again leaned over the desk to get his point across. "But this isn't some drunken mistake. This is about so much more than that, Ben. You could really get some answers out of this if you play your cards right. Imagine getting up close and personal with a man possibly linked to someone who already stated knowing something about Naomi's accident. How often does this kind of opportunity come up, huh?"

I finally heard his words in a vastly different light from the one I'd had at the beginning of the conversation. They made so much more sense to me, and it was at that moment when I finally realized what my decision should be. With his eyes locked on me for my answer, I leaned forward and gave him the only one he wanted to hear.

"Fine, I'll do it," I said and effectively took on a fresh murder suspect just two days after my previous.

———

CHAPTER THREE

I CAN COUNT ON ONE HAND THE SPECIFIC TRIPS IN MY life that felt like defining moments set to shape my existence in some way. The most obvious to you, of course, would be the drive to the hospital after Naomi's accident. Those precious minutes spent in the car on my way to the ER felt like hours...*endless* hours, each passing second an individual moment in itself.

I can still recall the individual thoughts that ran through my head during that drive, a drive I insisted on taking myself, despite offers from others to drive me. I remember thinking that I couldn't trust anybody else to get me there, with me being the only one capable of reaching the hospital. The fear of not reaching Naomi in her time of need kept common sense out of reach, and I stubbornly drove myself.

Another drive I vividly remember is the one in the backseat of a car while sitting next to my aunt while driving to the church for my parents' funeral. I can still feel the smooth fabric of the black dress against my fingers as Aunt Shirley held my hand in her lap while dabbing at her eyes. While a five-year-old may not fully comprehend the finality of a plane crash, there's something to be said about seeing a grown-up crying in such close proximity.

There are two other drives I could explain to you, but they don't matter much to this story, and I doubt you'd find them interesting anyway, not the way you might find the latest addition to the list. When I walked out of the office shortly after finishing my talk with Dwight, I swear a boat anchor had somehow found its way into the pit of my stomach and made itself right at home.

The drive to Zone 1, where the police were currently holding my latest client, felt all too familiar, the dread of a meeting I'd put off for half a decade about to come full circle. Brian Watson never had much time for me to begin with, a trait that didn't really surprise me at the time of our first meeting. What father welcomes his daughter's husband with open arms the first time anyway? Perhaps someone who had organized an arranged marriage and been involved in choosing the proposed partner, but certainly not someone like my eventual father-in-law.

Given the strained relationship between father and daughter, I didn't hold out much hope for ours to fare any better, and so I had simply opted for a backseat when it came to deciding family events. Naomi took charge of that side of our life, and in a way, each of us understood our role. With no mother around to add some maternal influence, it was left to Naomi to shape those connections.

What might surprise you to know is that during all the years since Naomi's death, and all the countless times I had gone to visit her grave, I never crossed paths with her father. Not once. There was one time when I did see his vehicle parked in the cemetery parking lot, but I simply drove past the entrance and continued on down the street as if nothing had happened. I don't know whether he had actually gone to his daughter's grave or remained sitting in his car; I never found out. I didn't really care.

When I say I cut the man from my life, that is exactly what I mean. Our paths never crossed, his face never entered my mind, and each of us simply got on with our lives. I did my mourning on my side of the world, and he mourned on his side. I continued to visit Naomi's grave on the anniversaries of both her birthday and our wedding day and on random days when I just needed to be close to her. And in all the years, not once did Brian Watson and I cross paths.

The boat anchor shifted position when I turned the Mustang into the Zone 1 Police Station parking lot, the drive finally coming to the pivotal conclusion. I didn't climb out immediately. It felt surreal to be sitting there knowing that the man I'd avoided for all those years was literally sitting a few dozen yards from my position and awaiting my arrival. I mean, he was actually *waiting* for me to walk into whatever interview room they were holding him in and start defending him. The speed with which the direction of one's life can change truly is mesmerizing.

When the anticipation became too much for me, I shut off the engine, grabbed my briefcase, and climbed out. A heavy scent of diesel exhaust hung in the air courtesy of a recently departed bus pulling away from the stop in front of the station. I could still hear its engine but shut it out almost immediately as I turned for the precinct's front door. The time for me to put on my game face had arrived.

The turmoil in the building's foyer was exactly how you might expect to find the entrance to a popular police station. A number of people lined the main counter, the group standing three deep as a single officer tried to deal with them. I could see the frustration on his face, especially when one of the women, asking about her boyfriend or husband, called him completely useless.

"That is what they told me, ma'am," he said with forced calmness, "and if you don't wish to wait until then, you're more than welcome to return after three."

She didn't bother responding and was muttering something under her breath when she passed me on her way to the door. Thankfully, the cop recognized me from my multiple previous visits to the place.

"Straight up the stairs," he called to me. "Detective Perkins is the second door on the left."

"Thanks, Merv," I called back with an accompanying wave. A couple of the others waiting in line glared at me for jumping ahead of them, without me ever intending to, but I didn't stick around long enough to apologize for it.

I found Perkins sitting in his office, just as Mervin had told me. Introductions weren't needed, of course, due to my previous interactions with the detective. Normally, he was a friendly kind of guy, so it did take me back some when Perkins ignored my greeting completely.

"I'm surprised you agreed to take this one on, Carter," he instead said.

"Why is that?" The question caught me off guard, considering our relationship up until that moment had always been purely professional. In fact, the question annoyed me.

"You haven't heard what this son of a bitch did?"

"Whatever he did, he still deserves representation, does he not?"

Perkins shook his head in disgust and didn't bother trying to hide his contempt. "You lawyers are all the same," he said with overcompensated arrogance as he walked past me and out into the hallway. I wanted to respond but decided to bite my tongue instead.

When Perkins opened the door to the interview room where Watson was being held, he made some remark about it appearing as if his lawyer had finally arrived to save him. He did give me another up-and-down glance on his way back out of the room and closed the door. That was when the silence amplified the already tense emotion hanging in the air.

At first, I avoided looking at the man sitting at the table. I walked around to the other side, set my briefcase beside my chair, and took a seat. I could feel his eyes boring into the top of my head as I sat, still unable to look at him. Aside from the intense thumping in my chest, it was the smell hanging in the air that stirred memories for me. The cologne was something of a signature smell for him, Creed Aventus, the fragrance first bought for him by Naomi for a birthday. She told me that he became almost obsessed by it and bought several bottles shortly after that day in case they stopped making it.

That's the thing about Brian Watson. If he had been born several decades later, he might have found himself diagnosed with various conditions often described by a bunch of letters, namely ADHD and OCD. Throw in arrogance, pride, and a guy who laughs at his own jokes, and you might have an idea of the man I was dealing with.

"Wasn't sure you'd answer my call for help," Watson finally said when the silence became too much for him to sit through. His words were enough to draw my attention to him, and I finally laid eyes on the man I had sworn to cut from my life.

"I'm not here because I want to be," I said. "So don't think I've come answering the call for help."

"But you are here, and that means you are going to give me legal representation, are you not?"

I wish I could have said no, every fiber in my body telling me to get up and walk from the room, but I knew I couldn't.

"Yes, I'm here to provide you with legal representation," I said, the words feeling like woodchips in my mouth.

Watson grinned, his lips stretching wide enough to show teeth. He leaned back in his chair, and I half-expected him to fold his arms across his chest, but he didn't. I also expected him to start gloating about me folding first on whatever differences we had between us, but he again surprised me by changing course.

"Look, Ben, I know this isn't easy for you." He sighed and almost...*almost* sounded sincere. "It isn't for me either, but here we are, so maybe we can set aside our differences for the time being and focus on proving my innocence."

"So you're saying you didn't murder your neighbor?"

"I certainly did not," he snapped before lowering his defensive walls again. "I happened to like Libby. She always had a kind word to say."

"How long had you known her?"

"About a year. She moved into Donna Herrod's place after the old stick finally dropped off her perch."

"Mrs. Herrod died?"

It actually hurt me to hear of the old woman's passing. It was Naomi who introduced me to her during the first few months of our relationship, and while she did have a stern exterior that took some getting used to, she also baked the most delicious macarons in existence. The only person she couldn't tolerate also happened to be her neighbor, Brian Watson.

"She did, yes. I heard that it was a peaceful transition." He tried to sound sincere, but it came across as more arrogance.

"Well, let's hope she doesn't come back to haunt you," I said.

"Highly unlikely," Watson said. "Anyway, Libby and her husband moved in about three months after Donna's passing."

"And now you've been identified by a passer-by as leaving your neighbor's home just minutes before she was found dead inside."

"Libby was fine when I left her."

"What were you doing inside?"

He didn't answer immediately. Instead, I watched him shift in his seat, and it took me a second to realize the uncomfortable way he looked down at his hands. A blind man would have felt the guilt emanating from him, and so I went directly to the next most obvious question.

"Did the husband know?" It seemed like the least intrusive of the numerous questions I had.

"I suspected that he knew to a certain extent, but I couldn't be sure. In any case, I guess he really knows now," Watson said.

"How long have you been sleeping with his wife?"

"Look, it wasn't like that." When he saw that I wasn't buying his story, he tried to change tactics. "Her husband cheated on her himself. They had a kind of understanding. I wasn't Libby's first either."

"They had an open relationship?"

"I don't know if it was official or anything, but yes, that's how Libby described it."

"So tell me what happened?"

"We had our usual get-together on Wednesday night, which should have ended with us parting company at around nine with a kiss and a hug."

"Where would you meet?"

"Mostly my place, although there was a time or two when

she wanted to spice things up and asked me over to her house. Sometimes, we even visited a hotel. That night we met at her house against my better judgment, although it wasn't as intimate as it normally would have been."

"The parting with a kiss and a hug didn't happen?"

"No, it did not," Watson said. "She had seemed distracted more than usual for the entire evening, and it was only when we finished our...our..."

"I get it," I said when he couldn't bring himself to say the actual word. "Special cuddles?"

"When we finished our intimacy," Watson corrected, trying to keep his ego in check. "It was only then that she brought up the matter about her husband, said she was tired of all the cheating and needed to concentrate on her marriage."

"So she was calling it quits on her extra-marital affair, namely the relationship with you," I said, still feeling a need to come down on him as much as possible. I just couldn't make it easy on the guy, not when he had made Naomi's life such a misery and still appeared to spread the same type of torment to the present day.

"That's what she told me."

"And how did you take the news?"

"We got into an argument."

"You didn't agree with her decision?"

"It wasn't that I didn't agree with it," Watson said. "It's just that I know how much of an ass her husband is, and given the fact that we'd been discussing the possibility of her leaving him and moving in with me, her sudden change of heart just caught me by surprise."

"The police report states that a neighbor heard the two of you arguing," I said, holding the report in one hand while taking quick glances at it. "A Mrs. Herrington."

"Hillary Herrington is what you might call the neighborhood gossip. The woman constantly sticks her nose in where it doesn't belong."

"I see she also reported you leaving the Young house the next morning."

"Yes, I went back over to see whether Libby had cooled off during the night."

"And yet you had already booked your ticket out of the country and were just a few hours from boarding your flight," I said, skipping to the part of the story that really intrigued me.

That was when Watson looked down again, his expression losing all emotion as he turned on his poker face. I waited a few seconds for him to gather his thoughts before continuing with my questions.

"Tell me about the bank deposit."

"The deposit," Watson said, not asking but rather stating a fact. He closed his eyes and rubbed his forehead as if truly contemplating life.

"Nine hundred grand isn't exactly small potatoes," I said to bring him back into the room. "The thing is, the police aren't exactly sure why, considering the account is held by a man currently living in a Philly medical facility." When Watson still didn't answer me, I continued probing. "How long is it going to take them to find out who this money was really intended for?"

"They'll never find out," Watson said from under his hand before he lowered it to the table again and gazed over at me. "They'll never find out," he repeated with a more direct tone.

"Then tell me who," I said. When he slowly shook his head, I pushed harder. "Look, Brian, I am your attorney, bought and paid for. That gives you lawyer-client privilege. Anything you say to me is held in the—"

"Yeah, yeah, I know all that, but it won't be enough to protect you from...from them."

"From who?"

He didn't answer for a long time, but his eyes continued staring at me just the same. I could feel him weighing up the consequences of sharing whatever secret he felt he needed to hang on to.

"Brian, tell me who."

"You still don't get it, do you?" he snapped when his frustration became too much. "They won't stop with just me. They never do. If they find out that you know, then they'll kill you just as surely as they will me."

"Nobody is listening to us right now."

"No, but they will already be watching us. I guarantee it."

He was scared, not just for me or himself but scared of something more. I could feel the fear more than see it, radiating off him while he tried to cover it as best he could with little effect.

"Me being your lawyer isn't much of a secret, so if they know I'm in here talking to you, they're going to assume you told me anyway," I said. "So you might as well tell me now and save me needing to ask the same question multiple times."

"If they kill you, don't come back blaming me," he said with a hint of humor that didn't quite hit its mark. "Have you ever heard of a man named Alex Kent?" I scanned my memory banks for the name, but nothing came to mind. "I doubt you would have. Costa made sure to keep his kid separated as far as possible from himself."

"Costa? As in Riccardo Costa?" I felt myself sit a little taller hearing the name.

"The one and only. Only a few people knew of his existence, including me, for obvious reasons. Can't work the books without knowing all the payees."

"Wait, Costa has a son named Alex Kent?"

"That's him, yes, although Costa changed his surname after the kid's mother died. Used to be Gonzales. Anyway, that check went into his account, and it will be the kid who spends it."

"But it's in the name of William Carlson," I said, needing to clarify the information my brain continued to try to file.

"And so it will remain until whoever takes over from me decides to move it elsewhere."

"I don't understand," I said, and I really didn't.

"Carlson still owns a viable business, a construction company he set up forty years ago. It still operates just as it has for years, with one minor detail changed."

"What detail?"

"While the company is officially Carlson's, it's actually controlled by a conglomerate working for Costa, which the kid is now the head of."

"Money laundering?"

"It's amazing how much money can be moved through a business like that," Watson confirmed. "Carlson's daughter runs the office and works the phones, but she's well looked after by the silent partner." He leaned a little closer. "And this isn't even the only one. There are at least half a dozen other such setups operating right now. All with the same scenario. The owner is no longer able to look after the business; they take it over and run it as needed."

"This Alex Kent. How old is he? He can't be much—"

"Turned twenty-one earlier this year. Costa got his girl pregnant when he was sixteen. The family initially tried to hide it for the sake of their reputation, but that ended up becoming more permanent when Riccardo became more involved in the dark side of his business."

"OK, so they run an extensive money laundering operation," I said once I understood the basics. "But surely there are more sophisticated ways of transferring money between accounts. Why the check?"

"Because that money didn't come from any of their businesses." He sighed, looked at his fingers, and made a couple of fists. "That was *my* money."

"Yours?"

"I owed them for a personal debt," he said with barely enough volume for the words to reach me. "Let's just say I screwed up and needed to pay my way out of it. I promised to drop a check into the account, after which I planned to leave the country."

"Did they know you were planning to leave?"

He shook his head. "I wanted to buy myself some time with the check. They initially wanted cash, but I convinced them to funnel the money through the Carlson account."

"You could have transferred the money directly from your account into theirs," I said. "Why the theatrics?"

"Like I said, I needed time to make sure I could escape. I did the check so I could get to the bank and see if anybody was following me. I expected them to."

"I'm guessing when you saw nobody following, you high-tailed it to the airport?" He nodded. "And as it turned out, your plan failed to take into account the murder of your neighbor."

"Not something I could have foreseen," he said and looked over at me. "So I'm guessing bond is out?" I expected him to laugh at his own joke, but it appeared to be the day for continued change. Watson didn't even crack a smile.

"Yes, bond is out," I said. "I'll try and get you a bail hearing at the very earliest possibility, but I wouldn't be holding my breath on that one either." I leaned closer and lowered my voice. "These guys know about your connections, and I highly doubt they're going to risk letting you out and using them to facilitate your escape." That's when he did laugh, albeit a shallow one.

"I ain't jumping ship, Ben," he said. "Only a guilty man would be that stupid."

Scan the QR code below to purchase FINAL DEFENSE.
Or go to: righthouse.com/final-defense

Printed in Dunstable, United Kingdom

65807525R00170